Burn It Down:
Simply Priceless 4
By: Lee T. Lunsford

<u>Campaign Election Year</u>

Greensboro, North Carolina: on The Road to The Presidency…

Senator Belkin and his family were in their suite at a very fancy hotel establishment. The Senator was sitting on the couch at two thirty am rubbing his temples.

Kuwait Midnight Eastern Standard Time

"The threat has been confirmed. There will be a hit out on Senator Belkin and Senator Gonzales today." Special Operative CIA Agent John Feral announced.

Everyone went on high alert and began to guard the Democrat Arizona State Senator who was running for President of the United States. If the Arizona State Senator was to win the presidency Senator Gonzales would become the first Hispanic to take office of President of the United States. On the other hand, Senator Belkin would be the first African American to take office of President of the United States. These circumstances made for a-very-unique campaign year!

The secret service hit the Arizona senator's hotel room at the same time they made their arrived outside Senator Belkin's hotel room. Senator Gonzales's wife got her husband awake and out of bed.

Both senators were being briefed inside their hotel rooms. The secret service told both senators they would be by their side, and they had nothing to worry about. It was believed that both senators' lives were in danger because of their ethnicity.

There were two independents running for president. Charles Backston was one of those independents. Charles was a white Governor from North Carolina and Ahmed

Elraei. Ahmed Elraei was a Senator from Tennessee. Ahmed was in close ties with the Speaker of the House Alborz Al-Mughassil. Elraei won the election by a narrow margin, but he was very popular. No threats had been made on his life at that present time.

John Feral called the head of the CIA and made another startling announcement the North Carolina Governor's life was in danger. Governor Backston was alone at his hotel. Secret Service members went to his room. The elevator ride seemed longer than usual. The secret service got to his room and knocked on the door.

"Governor!" The leader of the unit said as he knocked once again. It had been a good couple of minutes no reply. They had the key card to the room. "Open it," The leader instructed. A secret service agent stuck the card in the door just as the governor was walking toward the door. When the card was brought out of the electronic key lock what sounded like a ring tone played briefly. Then BOOM! A giant explosion took place. The blast killed the majority of the secret service agents with a blast so powerful the blast knocked the governor across the room, out the glass doors to the balcony, over the guard rail, and down into the pool; dead.

The secret service for security reasons tightened security around Senator Elraei. Even though there was still no threat made against that senator's life. It was certain they were dealing with Middle Eastern terrorist.

Several events were still scheduled to take place for the presidential election, and none of the presidential candidates had any plans of changing their plans. It was too close to the election to drop what they had planned. The current president was a lame duck. It was time to elect a new President of The United States.

The President was awoken that night and brought into a conference room at the White House. He didn't have but two minutes to get dressed. The President put on dress pants, and just a dress shirt open over his t-shirt he slept in. Then he didn't even bother wearing shoes. He rushed into the conference room. He was faced with what just happened to the North Carolina Governor. He ordered that CTU begin their investigation. He called the leader of the Counter Terrorism Unit and gave a direct command for them to send in their best man.

"Hello?" Jasper answered his cell half asleep.

"Jasper, get your ass out of bed and be at CTU immediately." One of the higher ups of CTU ordered.

Jasper didn't ask what was going on. He didn't even say bye. He just got out of bed and got completely dressed. He figured it was another bullshit meeting. Jasper certainly didn't believe it was some act of terror which was heard in chatter that would on average never take place. Jasper Martin is about six foot tall, and physically fit. He is in his early thirties and moved up the ladder at CTU quick. He kissed his mid-twenties wife and told her he would be right back. She didn't hear him. She was sound asleep. She was his second wife in five years. Jasper cheated on his first wife with Gina only because his wife was an alcoholic and made his life and their daughter's life a living hell. Jasper left his bedroom then peered into his seventeen-year-old daughter Brittany's bedroom. She wasn't in bed.

Jasper looked at his clock on his oven in the kitchen. It was four am on a school night. He began to get mad. Brittany became a wild child after her mother died, and she came to live with Jasper. Brittany is tall like her father. She has his black hair. She is very tan with sparkling blue eyes. Men of all ages get lost in her eyes. She had a sugar daddy which Jasper didn't know about. The man was older than her father. He bought her whatever she wanted. She didn't even have to have sex with him. All she had to do, well that is not important! What is important was she had a sugar daddy and was entering the front door as Jasper was fixing to go out of it.

"Where the hell were you?" Jasper yelled trying not to wake up Brittany's stepmom.

"That's none of your god damn business father." Brittany sarcastically spoke shutting the door. Then she tried to walk pass her father. He grabbed her arm and stopped her. Jasper wasn't rough. "Keys, cell phone, now!"

"Yeah right." Brittany said trying to break loose from her father's grip.

"Now young lady. Don't make this harder than it must be."

"Fine." Brittany reached into her purse and pulled out her keys, and cell phone. She threw her keys and cell phone on to the kitchen table. Jasper let go of his daughter and order for her to stay in her room. She rolled her eyes. He rounded up Brittany's cell phone and keys then exited the house. Jasper got into his average family style sedan he threw his daughter's keys and cell phone in the glove compartment then drove straight into CTU.

Brittany went back to her bedroom and stripped down to her bra and panties. She proceeded to turn on some country music and begin to paint her toenails alternating between black and white. Nothing mattered to her especially her father coming down on her. Afterall Britt knew she still had her secret computer to contact John on.

John Omar Stevens was her sugar daddy. She met him on the internet. They talked on the internet for the longest before she went to his house one night. He is in his early fifties. John is overweight to a certain extent with dark eyes, and curly black hair. He is a CEO of a computer software company that is dedicated to flooring software. He had been married four times and has two children which live with his next to last ex-wife. He has nothing to do with his children. He might send a small check on occasion when he feels like it but not like he spoils Brittany.

John has had numerous girls he used to spoil. He likes to be used for his money by the right dominant girl or dominant couple. The site he met Brittany on was titled "Rape Your Wallet." It was a BDSM Personals website. Brittany's friend Amanda used the site to make money. Guys actually paid the women on "Rape Your Wallet" to dominate them or in some rare occasions just to talk to them on a girlfriend experience basis. For the payments to begin the dominant receiving payments off the website had to come on webcam to verify their identity first or even block their phone number, and call doing voice verification of the dominant proving they are the person that belongs to the "Rape Your Wallet" dominant profile.

Amanda and Brittany had their friend Luke work fake dominant profile accounts on financial domination website that are less strict on verification to make the girls money. He did good at it. He acted like a Catfish Dominatrix behind online chats and text messaging through free texting cell phone apps. Brittany referred to these website as "Bitches R Us."

John was putty in her hands. He got rid of all his other girls for Brittany. Brittany had him spoil Amanda and others from her life as well. Even though Amanda mostly had Luke she took the spare spoiling from John. Amanda and Luke were an on again and off again couple. Amanda used Luke bad and lied to him every chance she got. Luke knew it was wrong how Amanda treated him but couldn't help himself but do for her. He had given her his own money too. Till one day her only payment account pay buddy got froze because somebody rejected a payment, the slave made to her off "Rape Your Wallet."

Amanda was doing a Ranger Rick session with the slave. Ranger Rick is a computer program which gives other people access to your computer via remote access.

Ranger Rick allows maintenance of computers along with other devices. Ranger Rick was first released in the year 2005, and since then Ranger Rick's functionality has expanded step by step. Ranger Rick is proprietary software and does not require registration. Ranger Rick is a free download one hundred percent free of charge for non-commercial use.

The slave Amanda was conducting the Ranger Rick session with that night began the session willingly and without being forced. He gave Amanda his Ranger Rick password so Amanda could log into his computer from her location with her Ranger Rick program. The man was on the floor on his hands and knees in front of his laptop as he watched Goddess Amanda change all the settings on his laptop. Goddess Amanda fooled around in the slave's laptop for over an hour when the slave asked permission to go use the bathroom.

Goddess Amanda agreed to let him go pee, and once the slave was out of sight Goddess Amanda went into the slave's internet browser and checked out the pay buddy website. The slave had his pay buddy website password stored in the browser, so Goddess Amanda let herself in, and then during the time the slave was gone to the bathroom Goddess Amanda took it upon herself to send herself pay buddy payment after pay buddy payment until there was no longer any ability to send another payment from any of the cards both debit and credit that were linked to the pay buddy account.

Goddess Amanda took a photo of her flipping off the camera and then transferred that photo to the slave's computer and opened the photo up to cover the full screen. Goddess Amanda typed a memo and had that memo notepad opened on the laptop screen so the slave could see both the photo and the notepad note when he got back to the computer. Then Goddess Amanda exited her Ranger Rick program and did a speed withdraw of over a couple of thousand dollars from her pay buddy account to her bank account at the time.

The slave didn't find out how royally screwed over he was financially until the next morning when he woke up in his bed, and then went to get his laptop out of the living room and saw Goddess Amanda's message. He had fraud alerts via text messages from his main bank and multiple credit cards. He had so many regular monthly payments bouncing left and right and was thrown into a major debt ditch.

He was forced to call pay buddy and make up some lie about being unwillingly hacked. The slave told a major tall tale to get his money back and get his finances fixed. He was stressed as all get out and didn't know what he was going to do? He thought why did I lay down for a few moments after I pissed? He thought I should have known I would wind up falling asleep. Then he thought why did I agree to a Ranger Rick session in general? The slave really was stressing. He trusted Goddess Amanda and all his financial institutions told him it could take seven to ten days for a decision to be made of whether the investigations rule in the slave's favor and then another three to five days if they rule in the slave's favor for the refund to be placed back into the slave's various accounts.

Amanda meanwhile had her pay buddy account frozen, and it showed on her pay buddy account that she had a negative balance for the thousands of dollars she removed from the slave's account. Amanda was screwed! In the meantime, the slave bothered and harassed his financial institutions for several days attempting to get his money back earlier than the financial institutions were willing to refund the money.

That wasn't the first time Goddess Amanda stole from somebody with Ranger Rick, but it was the last. It also was the first time somebody made up a story of how they got robbed from to make the attempt to gain the financial amount taken from them back!

Amanda just opened a new bank account and gave Luke the account number. He made deposits directly into that new bank account. Luke would use his own pay buddy account to get money sent to him. Then he would withdraw the funds from his pay buddy account to his bank account. Only to then go to the bank he uses which is the bank Amanda uses, and then Luke would use his debit card to withdraw the funds, and then right afterward deposit all those funds into Amanda's account. Amanda was very pleased with Luke. He made her hundreds a week in online shopping gift cards on top of pay buddy payments posing as a catfish dominatrix.

Luke wasn't allowed to date. Amanda gave him affection when she chose. She was single too and wasn't planning to change her status. All he did was work Rape Your Wallet and work his job managing a discount movie theater. He was waiting the decision whether the movie theater would bring him on as the General Manager at the main movie theater which would mean a higher pay grade. Amanda hoped for the best. In fact, that night she was sleeping at his house. She was asleep in his bed while he slept locked in a dog kennel in the closet. Luke mistakenly made Amanda mad that night. As punishment she locked him in the dog cage, she had him buy because Luke didn't even own a dog. He had no way out. It was pad locked shut. He got used to the cramped space however, but he slept better in his bed.

Brittany got five hundred dollars from John that night. She has never had a giving whale slave as John can be refereed to. John was her dream slave. She was a great but strict financial dominatrix. She was fair though! She just wouldn't give someone the time of day if they couldn't pay. Brittany's must spoil me attitude was only fair with the perverts she dealt with on that site who sent her pictures of themselves in panties, diapers, maid uniforms, eating dog food, and various other kinky activities including men sucking other men off. Speaking of the later there are some straight men that want forced bisexuality which Brittany never got. However, she has seen it in person. Brittany finished her toes curled up and went to sleep.

While her father made it to CTU. He was brought up to date on the situation at hand. He knew it was going to be a long day. Jasper road to the Governors hotel room turned crime scene to begin his investigation because he was ready to get started on the adventure from hell. He was used to it, however. Only not on that extreme of a level! Threats on the United States happen daily! Some were just talk but this one was the real deal! Jasper was thinking who could have done this? When he was done investigating, he was brought back to CTU to begin to go over some files. This part was a very dull part of his job! It sucked but somebody had to do it!

<u>New Threat</u>

"Everybody down" a group of armed gunmen yelled running into a bar!

Men and women bar patron's coward in fear. If men were from Mars and women from Venus both planets suddenly joined and became one because all their responses were the same, pure fear.

"Give me the money!" The lead villain yelled.

A young eighteen-year-old bartender began to unload the money into a black garbage bag as other evil doers began to collect the tips and other moneys from the staff and stole anything they could from the bar's patrons.

"Ok guys almost done. Two more minutes!" The lead bad guy yelled.

"Come on guys we have to get out of here before she shows up." A fraidy cat villain spoke softly.

"Shut up idiot! We don't mention her." The lead bad guy commanded.

About that time "Why am I not invited to the party?" Simply Priceless asked.

All the bad guys simultaneously began firing rounds at her. The bullets ricocheted off Simply Priceless and only further irritated her as the bullets made her feel like she was being poked. Simply Priceless pushed her arms forward like she was doing a standing push up which caused the bullets to move back at the petty thieves knocking them to the ground wounded. None of their wounds were life threatening. Immediately following SWAT entered the bar and took the bad guys into custody.

"Thank you Simply Priceless." The leader of the SWAT team spoke.

"You're welcome, you can take it from here." Simply Priceless spoke then vanished as quickly as she arrived on scene.

Billy was experiencing a little action himself. Him and a tactical team were about to hit a major drug house. Inside this house was a Juan Mendez. Juan was a co gang leader over a newly formed gang in Atlanta. The La Nigeros! This new gang is a Mexican gang mixed up with a patsy African American gang. Nether gang could hold a candle to either black or Mexican gangs. These gang members were either kicked out or never selected for their counterpart gangs. The group of misfits joined together and began La Nigeros which has become a steady gang conducting their own crime waves.

Juan killed an officer Danny Sane who arrested Juan's brother-in-law Pedro on drug charges, and Juan in turn slain Danny along with his wife, and twin daughters. Billy was placed on the case because Danny was a good friend of Billy's.

Billy had his tact team ready. "Alright guys this place is heavily guarded, and we are majorly out manned. We need to hit them and hit them hard. On three SWAT will hit the front and back simultaneously. Immediately following the rest of us will strike. They will never know what hit them."

Billy counted to three into a walkie talkie. Two SWAT vans appeared like a thief in the night, and SWAT members rushed the front and back of the house. Billy then yelled into the radio "Go! Go! Go!"

Billy and the rest of his team rushed the house. Gang members were shooting down cops left and right.

Billy approached the side of the house. A man walked past a window. Billy fired him down and the man fell out of the window. Billy entered the house through the broken window. All he heard were Mexicans cussing in Spanish. Billy shot two more down in the living room. He slowly made his way into a kitchen area. Billy slowly approached a man from behind. He placed the man in a headlock and pressed his gun against the man's temple.

"Where is Juan?" Billy asked sternly.

"He is in the basement." The man squealed.

At that time Billy took a bullet to the right bicep. He fell to the ground and fired three bullets into the guy who shot him. Billy was full of rage, but he couldn't concentrate on his own emotions because he was kicked in the face by the guy who told him where Juan was at. Billy's nose shattered and blood poured out of it. The guy began to repeatedly punch Billy in his bloody face. Billy was saved by another tactical team member shooting the man assaulting Billy three times in the back.

Billy returned to his feet with a crimson mask. "He is in the basement." Billy said.

Suddenly a grenade was tossed through the kitchen window. Billy jumped into the other room as the grenade exploded killing two tactical members. Bodies were lying all around. A silhouette appeared on the outside door. It was another gang member. Billy reached behind him and grabbed a pump shotgun that was on the ground. He pumped it then fired a shot through the door, and into the villain's chest.

He then got up and proceeded toward the basement. Once Billy made it into the basement, he was taking fire.

He stood in the stairwell till the gunfire stopped then he jumped into the room firing rounds. He killed the gunman shooting at him. Billy reloaded his 9mm then stood up, He stared at Juan who had a naked young seventeen-year-old girl in a headlock with a gun firmly pressed against her temple.

"You even look at me the wrong way pig, and I will splatter this bitch's brains all over this floor." Juan commanded.

"Help me! Please help me!" The girl begged.

"Shut up bitch." Juan demanded.

"Shoot him. Shoot him!" The girl continued to plead.

Billy took aim. "Come on Juan what does that girl mean to me. I don't know her besides she is your only bargaining chip out of this dump! So, you're not going to kill her!" He explained.

Juan thought for a minute. He knew Billy was right. Billy had his aim on Juan's forehead. "Why don't you just give up Juan? Your men are dead!" Billy yelled.

"Please help me!" The girl yelled in a pleading tone.

"Shut up bitch. This nice officer is right you don't mean nothing to him or me either one." Juan said as he placed pressure on the trigger.

Billy quickly squeezed his trigger sailing a bullet through the air, and into Juan's skull. Blood and brain fragments exploded out the back of Juan's head onto the back wall as Juan fell to the ground dead, and the girl broke loose from Juan's grip and ran over to Billy saying "Thank you" repeatedly.

Other crime scene units arrived on the scene, and Billy and the young girl were taken to the hospital. They removed the bullet from Billy's arm, and said it was just a flesh wound that it would heal up very nicely. As Billy was walking out of the hospital, and into the parking lot Simply Priceless landed behind him.

"Where do you think you are going baby?" She asked.

Billy turned around his arm in a sling and walked up to his wife then kissed her. "What was that for?" Ashley asked.

"Just thankful you arrived so you can fly me home. That is all. Save on cab fare." Billy said in a joking manner.

"So, you're just using me." Ashley said faking a pouty face.

"I love you baby." Billy said then kissed Ashley "Simply Priceless" Hatch-Coatman. She quickly grabbed a hold of his waist and flew them back to their home. Ashley already brought Billy's Civic home. Ashley went to the station and picked it up. They went inside, and relieved Carmella from watching the kids. Ashley changed out of her costume, and prepared dinner as Billy and the kids watched TV.

Meanwhile in an underground fortress in Iraq there was a video conference between Iraq, Iran, Syria, Afghanistan, Pakistan, and Palestine. There were several men in each conference room. They all were speaking various Middle Eastern languages.

Finally, one man took charge of this little get together. The man stood seven foot tall, weighed over three hundred pounds with a muscular body. He was an Iraqi and was wearing a black suit with a white dress shirt, black dress shoes, and a black tie which had the image of blood running down it. His hair was black and was spiked up.

"My name is Ockmed Hussein. I have called these four terrorist groups together for one purpose! We are going to rage war against the beast known as the United States. We will begin with Atlanta, and then scatter our teams throughout the belly of the beast. I have come to your groups for help because my country Iraq has been smothered by foreign troops for way too long. All other countries have pulled out of this war except the snake known as the United States. Us four will drive the United States out of Iraq, after we stomp a mud hole in their own country for all the pain and suffering, they have caused so many innocent men and women and children of this country. I have supplied everyone with a good financial backing so if you want to back out back out now because our first set of troops deploy tonight. I have furnished each group with helicopters to fly some their most elite men to Kuwait where my men will be waiting to take the flight to a private airport in North Georgia which more of my men are overseeing. My men there will provide the men sent with Hummers to storm into Atlanta and conjure at our secret location to plan our next phase in the war to bring back terror."

Ockmed Hussein is the richest person in Iraq. He was born in Baghdad but grew up in New York City with his uncle and aunt3 who were very well off. They sent him to the most prominent schools, and he graduated top of his class. He has a degree in law. He made some wise investments when the stock market was up. Then pulled out when he was tipped things were fixing to fall. He is wanted on the counts of embezzling along with money laundering, and fraud. He has stolen and sold numerous people's identities. When his aunt and uncle died, they left him with a pretty penny of a fortune which topped him out at over a billion dollars net worth. He travels around to various hiding places he has in every country from the orient to the Middle East and everything in between.

The meeting lasted over two and a half hours. While the meeting was taking place Ashley and Billy were watching TV. They had it on WNN the World News Now station. Both kids were in their parent's bedroom playing a board game. A news report came on the air that a United States Navy Ship had been taken over out in the Pacific by a group of Somalia pirates. There was a bomb on the ship that the pirates threatened to blow if the Navy got anywhere close to their fallen brothers. The Navy was in negotiation with the terrorist on the ships.

Ashley tuned into this news program and was able to hear the negotiations in her head.

"They are going to invade the ship. I must do something." As soon as that last sentence came out of her mouth Billy saw a flash of light, and his wife was gone.

Simply Priceless flew faster than she ever flown before. She landed stealth like on the ship. She walked around a corner and saw an AK-47 sticking out in front of her. Simply Priceless grabbed the front of the gun and slung the guy who was holding it into the depths of the ocean. The guy was immediately eaten by a Great White Shark. The shark devoured the man in one bite. Let's just call the shark Jaws. Jaws bit the Somalian pirate in half throwing the pirate's upper body up in the air, then jumping up in the air and catching the upper part of the body and swallowing it.

Priceless walked down a set of steps. She started getting fired upon by two terrorists. Priceless pushed her hands forward and the bullet fired into those pirates killing them. Two pirates tried to attack her from behind. She did a sidekick to one of the men's chests. Priceless jumped in the air spun around and kicked the other men in the head. Both men were knocked out.

Billy suddenly saw his wife Ashley "Simply Priceless" Hatch-Coatman on TV taking out the Somalian pirates one by one. Billy sat up on the couch and watched intensely. He had all his attention focused on the boob tube like it was a championship sports match or in Billy's case Wrestler's Heaven pay per view the super bowl of wrestling pay per views.

Simply Priceless found a hatch and entered the vessel. She was fired upon immediately. She began firing lasers out of her eyes and blowing people at full force.

"Who the hell is this bitch?" The terrorist spoke in their own language. Simply Priceless clapped her hands real loud and the bad guys went sailing through the walls. Before Simply Priceless knew it she was the only one standing. She found the ship's crew in a storage part of the ship. She freed them. By that time the seal team moved in, and it was discovered no bomb existed on the ship. Simply Priceless took all their thanks and congratulations then flew even quicker back to Atlanta.

Billy already had the kids in bed and was lying in bed waiting on his wife's return. She walked in not disturbing the kids. She had taken her boots off in the living room and left them sitting beside the couch. This was something she never allowed the kids or Billy to do. She was breaking her own cardinal rule by leaving shoes in the living room. Shoes were always supposed to be brought back to your bedroom and placed in your closet. She would preach to everybody about this all the time, and she recognized she had to get her boots out of the living room and bring them back to hers and Billy's master bedroom before Billy or the kids woke up.

She walked into the bedroom. Billy was sitting up with his back pressed against the headboard falling in and out of sleep holding a wrestling magazine in his hand. Simply Priceless changed for bed. Then she slowly removed the magazine from her husband's hands and slid him down on his back. He rolled on his right side as she began to turn off the lights. He parted his eyes looking down at Ashley's purple painted with pink Simply Priceless logo toes. She didn't even realize he was awake till "You left your boots in the living room again didn't you" he spoke halfway asleep.

"Don't tell the kids I promise I will put them up before they wake up. Trust me I will make it worth your wild." Ashley spoke then kissed Billy's lips as she turned off the lights.

<u>Night Out</u>

Brittany was out like a light when she heard her bedroom window creek open. A guy a little over six foot one, with a baby face, brown eyes, and a clean short haircut came into her room. He wore a Simply Priceless t-shirt, jeans, and tennis shoes.

In one clean swoop he pulled Brittany's cover off her. He then began to tickle her feet. Brittany died laughing. "Luke, stop it!"

Brittany took a moment to wake up then asked, "What are you doing here?"

"Amanda is giving me to you. I mean after all you two have shared me off and on."

Brittany giggled. She always had a thing for Luke, and it was true, her friend Amanda and her shared Luke. He was basically both girls bitch boy. It was kind of pathetic, but Brittany found him cute, and very handsome. She liked him. In fact, Luke made her kind of giddy.

"What are you talking about?" Brittany asked.

"Check your email. You also have a text and voicemail. She called you while I was on my knees beside her after she let me out of the dog kennel prison inside the closet."

"She still ate at your house Luke?"

"Yes. She is moving in, but I hope since I have served you both to get you to move in too."

"I think you are just horny, and happy to be out of that cramped dog kennel."

"You know me all too well Britt."

Brittany checked her phone. Luke wasn't lying. Amanda was giving full ownership of Luke to Brittany after Luke's screw up earlier in the night. Brittany had a little tingle in her special place. She was thrilled. She wanted full ownership over Luke, but she was too afraid to ask her friend for it. Since Amanda used to confess how she truly liked Luke deep down. She said he kissed so soft and passionate.

Amanda was upset with Luke however, and deep down was ready for a real relationship. She just didn't know if Luke was the perfect fit for her life. Amanda liked all sorts of guys but mostly the meat heads. Muscle bound it is hard for them to wipe their own ass meat heads. Muscle up steroid taken geeks who don't know as much or have half the intelligence as Luke.

That didn't matter to Brittany, however. She knew how good it felt for Luke to suck on her toes and kiss her soft soles. He's all mine she thought. She was very happy. She didn't even want to talk to him about what happened between him and Amanda. She knew Amanda was serious this time about getting rid of Luke. Amanda explained a few weeks back that she was debating giving Luke to her. Brittany knew even though Luke and Amanda went back and forth that this time was the real deal, and finally Luke had a real dominant girlfriend in Brittany. Besides Luke was so much better looking than John. Brittany was creeped out by John's age because John was old enough to be her father, and because of this reason John never had a chance to be more than a paying bitch for Brittany. Luke was older but he was in his twenties only about ten years older which turned Brittany on having an older guy to be at her beck and call. That was so hot to her because she knew she would treat him right. Considering the fact, she always treated him better than Amanda ever treated Luke.

Brittany wasn't worried about Amanda still living with Luke because she knew she would be over their full time too soon enough, and the thought of a 24-hour 7 day a week 365 sometimes 366 days a year slave suited her very well.

"Come on baby get up we got a party to go to."

"What time is it?" Brittany asked.

Luke told her the time then added "Does it really matter."

She got up out of bed and dressed for the party. Brittany finished her cute outfit off when she placed her feet in a pair of black flip flops. Brittany and Luke then exited out the window Luke came through. Brittany left that window open every night for her man. She loved Luke and they developed a close bond once Luke began being submissive towards her. She became really attached to him and didn't want him doing for anybody else but her even though she shared Luke with Amanda she didn't like to. Luke didn't complain as much about serving Brittany compared to the amount of complaints, he had in regards to serving Amanda. Luke absolutely worshipped the ground Brittany stood upon.

They walked through the front yard and got into Luke's Silver Civic. He of course opened Britt's door. Then he got in and drove off. Luke always referred to Brittany as Princess Britt. She loved that title too. He was the only person allowed to call her Britt. She got pissed off when anybody else would try to call her that. She cussed plenty of guys out for calling her Britt. She would not only cuss out, but she would severely punish male slaves who tried to call Brittany Britt.

There was this slave named Garrett Hale. She met him on one of the BDSM Personal Sites. He contacted her to pay her. He paid her twenty-five dollars on pay buddy on a Friday by Sunday he disputed the charge. Her account got froze and was unable to send or receive payments for almost two weeks. She was pissed. She posted a bulletin blackmail post on all BDSM Personal Websites with Garrett's personal information for slaves and dominants to contact Garrett. She had his home address and telephone number from the pay buddy memo.

Pay buddy sends a memo when people send somebody money if somebody purchases something. Since Garrett sent his payment like he was purchasing something Princess Brittany got emailed his personal information to ship whatever uncategorized item to. She also posted all his email, instant messenger, and social networking information. As well as tell slaves that messaged her to prove themselves first before Brittany would own them by messaging and harassing Garrett, and telling Garrett what a loser he was, and how wrong it was to cheat a Princess like he did.

She had many takers which included nonpayers take up the task of harassing Garrett. Garrett was sending numerous messages to Princess Brittany begging for the harassment to stop! Garrett attempted just to call Brittany by not only Britt but by Brittany even though he was set straight each time for not addressing Princess Brittany properly. He begged her for the situation to stop. Pleading his case that somebody else filed that claim. Brittany knew

Garrett was a lying sack of shit so even when Pay Buddy ruled in her favor and unfroze her account. Princess Brittany didn't allow the harassment to stop because of Garrett's stupidity to try to screw over a Princess. Princess Brittany carried on and blackmailed Garrett telling him she will post his pictures and personal information on gay BDSM personal pages for gay Masters. Along with standard gay personal pages which she did just as she threatened even though Garrett bought her electronic gift cards since she would no longer accept Pay Buddy from him in fear he would pull the same bullshit, and she would get locked out of pay buddy for good the next time.

The car was set into motion, and Luke began to take them toward downtown.

"Where are we going baby?" Brittany asked. She was turned sideways in her seat with her seatbelt unbuckled. She rubbed the inside of Luke's thigh. Britt could feel her man getting very aroused. This placed a smile upon her face. She loved the fact she could gain such excitement out of him. It didn't take much to do so. She knew exactly where to touch. She was aware of exactly how to tone her voice. She was more in tune to his sexual needs than any other boyfriend. She loved him more too. The two flirted back and forth till they arrived at their final destination. Their destination was a vacant warehouse outside the skirts of downtown.

He parked the car around back and they got out to go inside. Luke let Brittany out of his car. Brittany helped herself to a Camel Light cigarette from Luke's pack which she took out of his right jean's pocket. She pulled his lighter out of the bottom of his right jean pocket and handed it to him.

"Light it, bitch." She smirked.

He smiled casually as he lit Brittany's cigarette. He always loved it when Britt called him bitch. That was his pet name in a sense. They walked up to the door to the warehouse. There were two giant muscular men outside. Luke placed forty dollars in an antique cigar box and then they were allowed to go inside the illegal rave.

The warehouse was pitch black, and people were shoulder to shoulder. On a stage a rock band was playing. Luke grabbed him and Brittany two beers from a bucket full of ice, and Britt led them to an empty corner.

They locked lips. Luke pressed Brittany against the wall. Then he began to suck on Brittany's neck. She loved having her neck sucked on. It was a major erogenous zone for her. She began to moan lightly. The moans were like music to Luke's ears. He knew he was going to get lucky that night.

He thought to himself. I was on good sub behavior. I was on good boyfriend behavior. He heard the way his girl was moaning. He knew it was a sealed deal, and he had the condoms in the glove compartment just to help in the deed.

They hung out at the club for about forty-five minutes. The entire time they were making out. While other people around them were focused on drugs the only drug Luke and Brittany were zoned in on was pure eroticism.

"Take me to get a suite you know where." Brittany purred out.

Luke smiled.

"You know I am not a cheap lay. I am not a motel hoe. I am styling and profiling, jet flying, limousine riding, spoiled bratty Princess bitch."

"Yes ma'am." Luke said.

They exited the rave and walked out toward Luke's Civic. One of the bouncers of sorts relieved himself at the corner of the building. The other was asleep inside a pickup truck. They made it to the back of the Civic when a black work van with a dragon painted down the side of it pulled up behind them and slammed on the breaks. The door flung open, and four men jumped out with ski masks and combat clothing. They were fully armed.

They were speaking a Middle Eastern tongue to one another. Brittany screamed as one of the men grabbed a fist full of her long hair jerking her back. Luke went to attack one of the guys when he was hit in the back of the head by the butt of a M-16. He fell to the ground knocked out. The group loaded Brittany and Luke up in the back of the van. They bound them before they tossed them inside, jumped back in themselves, and sped off.

<u>National Security</u>

The time was 3:45am. Billy's cell phone ringtone went off and his phone vibrated loudly against the wooden nightstand. Ashley jumped up off her husband chest which woke Billy up and they both wrestled to answer the phone. Ashley fell into the floor as Billy spoke "Yes captain" into his Carolina Blue Samsung Galaxy S22 Ultra.

"Billy, I hate to bother you, this late but get dressed and come into the prescient. Now! Billy right now!"

"Give me about five and a half hours" Billy smarted off not sensing the urgency on what was a pretty routine night!

"What's going on?" Ashley asked knowing the urgency using her super powers.

Ashley Hatch-Coatman seemed irritated sitting on the floor. She hates being woke up especially when she is sleeping good, Ashley's eyes glowed a dim red unaware of what was going on.

Another familiar voice took over the conversation "Billy it's Sean. I need you to come here to the station now. This is not a middle of the night prank! This openly and honesty is a matter of National Security. Jim is here and we need you here now. Don't bother taking a shower just get dressed and come now." FBI Special Agent Sean Black was very stern. Billy knew things had to be serious for Sean and Jim to be there.

"Ok, I am on my way." Billy said hanging up before anybody had a chance to say another word. Nobody even had the chance to think the word bye.

"What is going on Billy?" Ashley asked sitting back down on the bed.

"I don't know, Sean and Jim are there, and Sean said it was a matter of National Security. So, I must go." Billy kissed his wife and got up. He walked over to the closet and put on a pair of jeans, a Simply Priceless t-shirt, a casual red dress shirt on, open over the Simply Priceless t-shirt. Then he put on a pair of white gold toe socks and his tennis shoes. He grabbed his car keys. All while this was going on Ashley sat there trying to figure out what was going on.

"I'm going with you." Ashley spoke in a Simply Priceless tone.

"Ashley the kids are asleep we can't leave them alone."

"I can call Carmella."

"Ashley Carmella is at her mothers in North Carolina."

"Then I can call my sister." Ashley rebutted

"Baby Cali is sick remember. Robbie is taking care of her besides it is four am."

"Fine" Ashley Hatch-Coatman pouted.

"I always told you I am the real hero." Billy laughed.

"No, you didn't! No, you didn't just say that. Today is Friday you are not sleeping in this bed again till Monday night whenever I go to sleep, and you are not touching any part of me. Not my feet. Not even a hug! I don't even want you to touch my clothes." A dominant Ashley Hatch-Coatman fussed.

Billy knew he was in trouble, and he thought why did I just say that Billy thought to himself?

"Baby I'm sorry. Please don't say that. You don't mean that. I love you." Billy walked up to his wife, but she blew a mild wind forcing him back.

"I do mean that too, so go!"

Billy appeared to have misty eyes. He hated to upset his wife. He never wants to be in trouble with her. She knows just how to take her anger out on him. Ashley knows she always had the upper hand. She was his Princess, and he would do her bidding. He loved and worshiped his wife, and Ashley loved the control she has! Ashley does use all her control to her advantage most times. What Billy said really did hurt her because she hates sitting on the sidelines. She is a lead player. She is a team captain. She knew her husband was a team captain too. They were co-captains. What he just said was uncalled for.

"Goddess Priceless please….

"Billy, calm down we will talk about it later. You better go before you get in trouble it is 4:08am."

Billy started out of the room. He had his head slightly hung.

"Billy." Ashley spoke softly.

Billy turned and looked with a few tears that escaped his eyes.

"I love you too." Ashley spoke with a smile.

Billy smiled then left. He exited the house and ran down the outside steps and hopped in his Civic. He fired up the blue dash lights and floored it to the prescient. He ran inside and was ushered back to a conference room. There were several people in suits sitting around an oval table with a project slide on the wall. "Billy glad you could make it." Captain Beckham smarted off.

"What's going on capt? Ashley is pissed because she got woke up."

"Well Billy there is a major terror attack fixing to take place in the United States that will top nine eleven. All the chatter we are getting states either a nuclear, biological, cyber, president assignation, chemical, suicide bombers, or all." Sean explained.

"And you needed a male superhero this time?" Billy joked.

"Funny Billy." Jim said.

"Well, I am Atlanta's number one crime fighter." Billy spoke cockily.

"Why don't you tell Simply Priceless that Coatman?" Sean and Jim both spoke at the same time.

"Maybe I will."

"Right." Once again Sean and Jim spoke in unison

"Ok, guys we have a job at hand! I am sure Simply Priceless will be on top of this as soon as she can." Captain Beckham announced.

"I'm sure." Sean laughed.

"Ok enough with the jokes!" Billy yelled.

"We are on heightened alert. These attacks will begin any minute." Jim said.

"What do you want me to do?" asked Billy.

"You're the top guy in this department. Hopefully Priceless will be here sometime soon, and there are a few mosques I would like you to hit. There are known former terror organization members who attend these mosques that are supposed to have been rehabilitated. You are going to stay here the rest of the night and listen to some of the chatter. You will work closely with Sean and Jim as we wait on Simply Priceless. We must figure out what the hell is going on. This can either be a foul ball or could blow up like Hiroshima." Captain Beckham explained in grave detail.

"Yes captain, can I at least step outside, and call Ashley before we begin." Billy asked

"Make it quick."

Captain Beckham left the room through a backroom entrance. Billy stood up to leave the room but before Billy walked out the door Sean said "I'll be upstairs in room PB going over audio and video footage. I'll have all the evidence in there."

Billy nodded and walked outside. He called Ashley on her cell phone.

"What's going on?" She answered after one ring.

"There is a terrorist attack planned on Atlanta possibly!" Billy didn't sound too confident.

"Possibly?" Ashley interjected as Simply Priceless.

"There is just a lot of chatter. It is probably nothing. Just take care of the kids and tell Simply Priceless to come down here and help me." Billy said flashing his teeth.

"You don't have to worry about anyone telling her. She will be there no questions asked. It is not up for debate."

"Baby it wasn't my call. If there was someone to watch the kids, of course I would have you beside me here." Billy explained.

"I'm know! I am sorry I got upset. Forget what I said about this weekend."

"Thank you. You would be bored anyway. All we are going to do is listen to some audio recordings, watch some movies, look at a few files, boring stuff really." Billy tried to calm his wife down,

"Billy I am already calm. There is no need to trying to sugarcoat things." Ashley laughed.

"Come on Billy it is after five am." Jim shouted from the doorway.

"I guess you better go."

"Yeah." Billy replied.

"I'll see you in a few hours. After I get the kids to school." Ashley said.

"Ok. Get some sleep. Ok."

"I'll try but I can't promise. I'll be fine trust me. I love you."

"I know baby. I love you too." Billy replied.

"Billy!" Jim yelled.

"You better go. See you in a couple of hours. Love you. Bye." Ashley Hatch-Coatman didn't give Billy a chance to say bye. She does that when she knows all he will do is keep talking when he should be doing something important. Billy was very distracted by his wife when it came to work. He had major attention problems. All he thought was their romantic life, and what he should be doing for her and please her. Ashley Hatch-Coatman loved being spoiled the way Billy spoiled her. He did treat her like a true Goddess. She loved her husband even more every second. He was so good to her. There are not words to describe how good. Cali was always jealous but since Robbie and her have been engaged she has had just as good of a man as her sister had in Billy Coatman.

Billy mouthed "bye" then placed his cell phone back into his leather cell phone holder on his belt. Billy walked into the little area under the stairs which had soda and snack machines. He bought himself a chocolate covered peanut caramel bar and a soft drink.

"Come on Billy!" Sean yelled from the top of the stairs.

"Damn it man I'm coming! Shit!" Billy smarted off.

"Watch the attitude this is serious." Jim spoke very annoyed.

Billy was upstairs and went into the evidence room. Anyone could tell he was in a mood.

"Billy this isn't your average case. Think death count of Python's nuclear bomb times a million. This is a whole grander scale Coatman. The only thing more deadly than this would be if the monsters took over but other than that these aren't super villains! They are human terrorist, and they don't have a fear of dying. They are ready to go to heaven to meet their hundred virgins or whatever? "Sean explained.

"I'm sorry, ok! There I said it, ok, I made a mistake. I am just upset but regular humans I also like. Either arrest them or kill them."

"Billy who have you arrested." Sean laughed.

"I've arrested a few." Billy replied.

Jim counted to ten out loud moving his fingers. "I'm out Billy. I'm out. I'm pretty sure Sean can count too, and we will still be out. You could count too….

"Jim can we just get to work on this evidence? We have a major threat." Billy ordered in a sarcastic tone.

"Oh, now he wants to work." Sean joked.

"Yes, now please where do we start." Billy seemed irritated as he bit into his candy bar.

"Ok thanks now look at this folder. Here are some of the major people of interest complete with the FBI's ten most wanted list." Jim said sliding a folder to Billy.

The three men began to review all the information, as a formation was taking place.

Formation

Midway from Kuwait to Dalton, GA was flight containing 50 terrorists ranging in physical size. These terrorists were between ages 18 and 40. The underbelly of the plane was full of all types of military type weaponry. Most the men were sleeping while others were reading, and one was even playing a portable video game system. Islamic music was blaring.

There was a man sitting in a seat which had a table mounted in front of it. That man had a very dark complexion with a thick black beard. He was wearing a suit with a red head wrap on his head. There was a giant jagged knife beside a bunch of pictures of Atlanta tourist sites. He had pictures of the GA Dome, Phillips Arena, Turner Field, CNN Center, and more. The man was conducting business making several phone calls to sleeper cells already inside Georgia

The terror would begin at noon today. The plane landed several hours later. The men went inside a small building where fifteen of them suited up in tactical gear. The other 35 were still dressed in regular clothes, and each loaded up into several regular cars, and drove to Atlanta while the other men began sorting weapons and began to go over the plan of attacking downtown Atlanta.

A Slur to End Any Political Campaign

"This is Kimberly McPherson with WKAB. In the news today it has been confirmed that Arizona Governor and Democratic Presidential Candidate Alberto Gonzolaus said the N word. We have confirmed via video and audio. We will play those tapes after this commercial break."

Senator Gonzolaus flipped off the TV. He began to go into a rage. The Arizona Senator was a top runner in the Presidential Race. He was leading above Senator Belkin by five percent. When the news came back on another reporter was interviewing people, and another reporter interviewed other government officials on this top news story. All the government officials that were interviewed called for the Arizona Senator to step down from his place in the election. The entire WKAB Broadcast was dedicated to the Presidential Race.

The Arizona Senator yelled out the f bomb and then dropped the n word before he paused momentarily and said the n word three times in a row, and he followed that up by yelling "Fucking black turds!" He went on to say they are all a bunch of n words, and they are watermelon stealing monkeys. He finished his racist rant by using the Lord's name in vain saying God damn followed by using the n words two more times in a row!

An African American Secret Service Agent walked into the room. "Sir what is your problem?"

The Arizona Senator told the Secret Service Agent to get out of the room followed by calling the Secret Service Agent a smelly n word."

"Excuse me sir that is uncalled for!" The Secret Service Agent Yelled.

The Arizona Senator dropped the n bomb three more times in a row, and then yelled at the Secret Service Agent "You are blacker than my shit! My shit looks better than your black ass you fucking!" The Arizona Senator took a breath before dropping the n word again. Then the Arizona Senator yelled to the Secret Service Agent for him to die followed by using n word!

The Secret Service Agent left the room fuming.

WKAB began to play the video proof of the Arizona Senator saying the N word. The Senator was in a country club standing with two Secret Service Agents looking at a set of golf clubs. A PGA Tournament was playing on the television.

The video's content played showing the Arizona Senator speaking with one of his secret service agents inside a country club. In the video the secret service was speaking to Senator Gonzolus about gambling on the PGA golf tournament that was on TV. Then the Arizona Senator went on to answer the Senator's question after saying he wasn't allowed to get caught gambling being in the government by saying he for sure wouldn't bet on that PGA n word in reference to the famous African American playing inside the golf tournament."

The news footage ended, and the Senator went to bar and fixed himself a drink. Then he lit a cigarette. He hadn't smoked in months. In fact, it was his last pack of cigarette to the last carton he had. He kept the last pack unopened just as a trophy to quitting. He kept to himself the remainder of the morning. He knew he would have to do a press briefing sometime soon to apologize for his crude remarks.

He knew him dropping out of the presidential race would be the best option in his political career. He had the money to just back out and lay low. He could live in peace. No more having his actions criticized by the American people. The Senator refused to drop out though. He had his plan for a major whopper to why he used the n word inside that video from the country club. He was going to say the tape was doctored. Proving the tape wasn't doctored would take a while. By then he would already be President of The United States the Arizona Senator believed. He was going to blame it on him being Hispanic. That was his main idea to reverse the race card and play the race card himself.

<u>Counter Terrorism Unit</u>

Director Bundy of CTU passed out the follow sheet to all agents, aids, and various other government officials in the room. Jasper stared at his sheet knowing today was going to be the longest day of his life.

1. Eng Ahmed Ahmed Refaat
2. Ali Jamal Awad
3. Av Yaseen
4. Ismail Alzwawi
5. Abdullah Alamami
6. Ahmed Bashir
7. Aiman Salem
8. Awheda Bendardaf
9. Hamid Werfalli
10. Ibrahim Jamal Awad
11. Hebatullah Elzwawi
12. Mohamed Ben Jmia
13. Mohammad Alazzam
14. Kald Mohmad Mhirey
15. Khamess Mohammad
16. Mohaned F Elmajbre
17. Mohi Babo
18. Seraj Alzwawi
19. Vedat Efe
20. Safsaf Zwawi
21. Ahmed Ebeid
22. Riham Kamal Elraei
23. Ahmed Elraei
24. Hala Elraei

25. Davut Ozkan

26. Khalid Sheikh Mohammed,

27. Adnan Shukrijumah

28. Isaiah Mustafa

29. Ahmed Refaat-Mohamed Refaat

30. Hatem Abou Ghareeb

31. Ahmed Hatem Ahmed

32. Mazen Mohammad

Director Bundy was deciding on his words. He knew he had to explain this situation with precise excellence. Everybody had to understand their role in the major dilemma to the United States. He swallowed hard then looked down at his own copy of the thirty-two listed names he passed out. Then he began.

"Ladies, gentleman the list I passed are thirty-two confirm terrorist in the United States. We have our suspicions that all these men are nearby on the east coast. They are planning a major scale attack with hundreds of others which will rock this nation. We need our technical teams running names in the terror data bank. We need last known locations, and our field agents will go search this out. We are answering straight from the White House. All government agencies are involved and for more specific instructions check your email."

Jasper started to exit the conference room, but Director Bundy stopped him.

"Jasper, we believe to have moles in the agency. You are the only one I can trust. I want you right on top of this, and you answer to only me."

"Yes sir." Jasper replied.

"I want you to go to this address and check it out. There should be information on what is going on with the presidential candidates along with the terror that lies ahead." Director Bundy slipped a small folded up piece of paper into Jasper's pocket. Then gave him a firm pat on the back and exited the office.

Jasper walked out into the main CTU work area. There were computers everywhere. A bunch of chatter was going on. A young woman stopped Jasper.

"What did Director Bundy want?" She asked.

"Nothing Tara get to work."

"Scotty is working on some stuff he wants you to see." Tara replied.

Jasper walked over to Scotty's station. He was sitting there eating a jelly doughnut with one hand and typing with the other. He was a very overweight bald guy. He resembled what most would think was a child molester with his thick black glasses, and massive obese weight. There was a stack of comic books beside his monitor. One of which was open.

"What Scotty?" Jasper asked.

"I found something. One of the terrorist leaders on that list and three others shared a loft apartment here in town. Their lease is still current, but no activity has been seen at the place in several days." Scotty went to pick up his comic book. Jasper knocked the comic book out of Scotty's hand. Then Jasper knocked the rest of the comics off Scotty's desk and reprimanded Scotty. Then he turned around walked outside to his car. Once he got inside, he looked at the paper Director Bundy placed into his pocket, and it was the same address as the terrorist loft apartment.

Jasper investigated his glove compartment, and when he made sure he had his weapon off Jasper went on his handpicked adventure.

<u>Real World</u>

Jasper arrived at the apartment building. He removed his gun from the glove compartment and exited the car. He walked inside and took the elevator up to the fifth floor. The apartment building was vacant. The lights were dim. Jasper pulled back the slide on his weapon.

Once he was on the floor Jasper began to take gun fire. He ran and busted open a locked door into an empty room. His shoulder popped out of place when he rammed the door. Jasper quickly slammed his shoulder against the wall knocking it back into place.

He stuck his gun around the corner and fired three shots. He heard a scream and a thud. He looked and saw he struck the guy firing at him in the stomach and shoulder. He walked up and kicked the man's gun away.

"Who are you?" Jasper asked with clear aim at the center of the Middle Eastern man's forehead.

"Kill me."

Jasper fired a shot into the man's leg. Then kicked him in the face.

"Wait! Wait!" The man yelled.

"Tell me what I need to know." Jasper ordered.

"Armageddon is going to take place inside the United States. There are a series of terrorist in the United States. We are talking hundreds if not thousands who have created our own army to bring down the evil snake of America." The Middle Eastern man explained.

"Who is involved." Jasper asked as the man began to cough up blood.

The man didn't answer. He just made a quick movement revealing another gun, and Jasper filled the terrorist full of holes. Jasper went down to the apartment he was sent to investigate on that floor. He kicked the door in. Jasper began to clear the apartment. He searched room by room. Nobody was there.

Jasper began to go through desk drawers. He found all sorts of paperwork on missions. They were written in code however so he couldn't make heads or tails out of it. Suddenly a rocket sailed through the front window and exploded against the wall. Gunfire erupted through the wall. Jasper was surrounded. He had nowhere to go. He was wading in the wading pool of death.

He got himself cornered in a back room. Like a rat in a maze Jasper had nowhere to run. He pulled out his cell phone and called Director Bundy.

"Director! It's Jasper! I need help! I need a team of agents sent here to bail my ass out.'

Director Bundy could hear the gunfire. He told Jasper he was sending in a special team. Jasper hung up. He shot down two people coming his direction. Every time he killed someone Jasper disarmed them of their weapon. The bullets were getting closer and closer. The walls looked like Swiss cheese. Jasper had nothing he could do but shoot in defense and wait.

The seconds felt like minutes. The minutes felt like hours. Several more rockets were fired into the apartment. The place was blazing with flames. Smoke filled the hallway as the place began to burn. Jasper knew he had to get out of there before he died of smoke inhalation. Jasper took off down the hallway. He was coughing even though he tried to hold his breath. He killed three more terrorists. He heard massive gunfire in the hallway.

He looked outside and saw a CTU Special Team out there like gorillas in the mist killing the terrorist outside. Two CTU Special Agents arrived inside the apartment building and located Jasper. Those agents led Jasper outside, just as fire fighters arrived to extinguish the fire. As fire fighters were doing their job fighting the blaze a giant explosion took place, and the building crumbled to the ground in front of Jasper and the CTU Special Team's eyes.

<u>High Noon</u>

Helicopters full of terrorist were on their way to downtown Atlanta. Simply Priceless made it to the police station at 8:15am and got caught up to date on the Armageddon scenario.

"Do you think this is real?" Billy asked Simply Priceless as they stood alone.

"I don't know Billy; we have faced stranger threats. Middle Eastern terrorist don't sound that bad for opposition."

All of a sudden, the police station was in a commotion. Everybody was running around and grabbing weapons. Billy walked out into the hallway.

"They're attacking downtown Atlanta come on Billy!" Sean yelled.

Billy ran downstairs with Sean and Jim. They loaded up in a black SUV as Simply Priceless jumped out the open window in the room Billy and her were in and took off flying. She got there first, and there were helicopters swarming around the giant buildings of downtown Atlanta firing rockets into them. Men were on the ground with automatic weapons shooting anybody in their sight. It was like a scene out of a video game only this was real. Simply Priceless flew toward one of the helicopters.

"What the fuck is that?" One of the men spoke to the pilot in Arabic.

"I don't know, kill it." The pilot yelled.

The man with the rocket launcher fired a rocket towards Simply Priceless. She didn't react quick enough, and the rocket struck her in her chest exploding. A giant fire ball filled the air as she was bounced backward. She wound up falling into one of the glass buildings through the window. Simply Priceless crashed through a desk, and she laid stunned. She never been shot with a rocket launcher before. First time for everything she thought. Her costume had a bunch of holes in it, and she was black from the smoke. Simply Priceless pulled herself back up to her feet then like a mad woman at lightning speed sped toward the chopper.

"I got it whatever it was." The man said laughing hysterically.

"What's so funny?" Simply Priceless asked the man.

The man that fired the rocket launcher screamed as another man who was in the back of the chopper fired an AK-47 at Simply Priceless. "I wouldn't do that." Simply Priceless said as she flew down, and grabbed the railing of the helicopter, then like a fast softball pitcher she tossed the helicopter into the other helicopter causing a major explosion.

Men were planting bombs at Phillips Arena as Billy and Sean arrived on scene. Billy pulled his 9mm and pulled back the slid. "Let's rock and roll" Billy said as he jumped out of the car while it was still moving

"Billy!" Sean and Jim yelled.

Sean parked the SUV. Then Sean and Jim got out and pulled out some machine guns. Then they put on bulletproof vest. Jim grabbed a third bulletproof vest for Billy, but he hated wearing them. He made it behind one of the cars which was abandoned as people ran in mass panic.

He closed his eyes then popped up firing two shots into two separate guys. All four shots entered the men's faces.

Sean and Jim finally made it up to Billy but not before they killed some men themselves. The three men sat with their back up against the car.

"Put this on!" Sean ordered.

"I'll be fine without it!"

"Put it on Billy." Jim insisted.

"No!" Billy yelled about that time Simply Priceless landed.

"You're going to put that on Billy!" Simply Priceless ordered.

Billy knew he had to listen to his wife. The last thing he needed was for her to be mad at him in the middle of a warzone. This warzone topped the one in DC years back with Psychotica's men at the State of The Union Address.

Billy slid the jacket over his clothing. Then he saw one of the men reloading. Within a blink of an eye Billy jumped over the hood of the car that was shielding his team and dove onto the man who was reloading. Billy began to beat the holy hell out of the guy smashing his head against the concrete. Sean and Jim were covering Billy. The man pulled a knife and was able to cut Billy's arm before Billy broke the terrorist's arm. The young ballsy detective picked the man up and led him over to the car Sean, Jim, and Simply Priceless were behind. Billy had the terrorist in a headlock when in one quick motion he threw the terrorist over the hood of the car. Jim punched the terrorist in the face knocking him out. Sean removed all the terrorist's weapons.

A S.W.A.T. team member that was on scene came up and put a plastic zip tie around the man's wrist. Then drug him to the back of a patrol car which hadn't been shot to hell. He hogtied the guy and placed him in the back of the paddy wagon. The man was driven back to the prescient and was led in by several officers. They then tossed him in lockup.

"Good you didn't kill him." Simply Priceless spoke aggravated.

"Funny." Billy said.

Billy went to the sidewalk and began to push forward. He was taking heavy fire, so he had to dive through a window to a sports card shop which sells various sport memorabilia. He lay on the ground as a terrorist entered the shop Billy tried to fire at the men, but he was out of bullets. He began to fear for his life. Billy did a single leg take down then knocked the man's weapon out of his hand.

The two men began to go round and round. Finally, they both made it to their feet. Billy got in a martial arts stance. The man laughed as Billy quickly did a front kick to the man's face breaking the terrorist's nose. Blood poured down the guy's chin. The terrorist countered with a sidekick connecting with Billy's right-side ribs breaking them. The man approached Billy, but Billy quickly did a judo throw tossing the man to the ground. Once the terrorist was on the ground the skilled lawman broke the man's right arm then jerked it out of the socket.

The man attempted to pull a gun, but Billy kicked it out of his hand. Billy's gun was mere inches away. Suddenly the gunfire began again. Billy dove for his gun, and quickly released the clips and reloaded. He saw the guy shooting outside the broken window. He quickly sailed a bullet into the man's skull, and blood exploded through the air.

The guy Billy beat down tried to get up, but Billy gave him the same treatment. Billy walked out of the store but was ambushed when he was kicked in the left kneecap. The man that kicked him picked Billy up slamming him down. Billy hit his knee again. He screamed in pain as the man went to work on that leg. Suddenly Billy heard a gunshot, and blood and brain matter was all over his face. The guy hurting Billy fell on him and Sean was standing a few feet back.

Billy picked up his gun and tried to stand but he fell. His leg was severely hurt. Simply Priceless came and helped her husband up as the street began to clear from the terrorist. Some of the terrorist got away which most were wounded or injured. They made it over a few blocks where helicopters picked them up. The damage had been done. Buildings were on fire, and there was a mass supply of dead bodies. Simply Priceless flew her husband to the hospital.

Once at the hospital they stitched up his arm and did some X-Rays. His knee was pretty banged up. They told him that he needed surgery, but he refused explaining that he was a cop, and due to the circumstances of today he couldn't be out. Ashley "Simply Priceless: Hatch-Coatman was conflicted by the medical news because she knew he was right, but she didn't want to see her husband hurt. Billy ribs were confirmed to be broken.

The nurse wrapped his ribs, and the doctor got Billy a metal knee brace. They cleaned him up from all his cuts. He needed a couple of stitches in his right ear from jumping through that window. Other than that, it was cuts and scrapes. He got dressed and was released. He wore the knee brace limping out of the hospital.

Once they got to the parking lot Simply Priceless spoke in an Ashley Hatch-Coatman tone "You really are stupid Billy."

"Why is that hun?" Billy smiled.

"Don't give me that look you know I can't resist that look but right now I am going to try. You have gotten your butt kicked on the first day. We are not even halfway through with stopping this threat and look how banged up you are." Ashley Hatch-Coatman spoke very dramatic moving her arms all around really reading her husband his rights.

Billy could sense his wife's tension. He knew she was mad.

"You could have stayed with Jim and Sean and had backup, but you always choose to do things by yourself. They're terrorist Billy these aren't some low lives Python or Finisher or even Loveman hired that doesn't know what they are doing! They are terrorist. They are trained to kill Billy. They do this daily like we do our personal hygiene on a daily basis….

Billy kissed his wife's lips. She pushed him back. He about fell so she had to catch him.

"I'm sorry Ashley. Please forgive me. I get carried away sometimes. All that matters to me are you and the kids. I'll straighten up. I promise." Billy kissed his wife again.

"That is what you always say." Ashley Hatch-Coatman said with tears in her eyes.

"Baby don't cry. I can't afford for you to get depressed and get sick. I seriously will do better. Please believe me."

Billy hugged his wife. She rested her head casually on his right shoulder. She jerked her head up quickly which once again about made her husband fall. She caught him once more.

"You promise?" Ashley asked.

"Yes, I promise."

"Pinky swear on it then." Ashley Hatch-Coatman said holding up her left pinky.

Billy took his pinky of his right hand and curled it around his wife's left pinky. "Ashley "Simply Priceless" Hatch-Coatman I pinky swear that I will be more careful. Especially in major dangerous situations for you and the kids along with myself because I don't want to feel any worse than what I do now."

"Now kiss me." Ashley demanded with a smile as she took both Billy's hands into hers.

Billy kissed his wife with a lot of love. Then she flew him home where she changed into another Simply Priceless suit.

"I might be able to fix that." Simply Priceless said speaking of the suit that got ruined.

"I doubt it." Billy said as he got on the bed to lay down.

"I work miracles Billy. Remember I am Simply Priceless."

"I know who you are." Billy laughed.

"Well, you should you worship the ground I walk on." Ashley laughed.

"Don't laugh. It is true! I do!" Billy confirmed.

"Ok you stay here and rest a little while I will come get you when Sean is ready to interrogate our Middle Eastern Nightmare."

"Ok." Billy said leaning back on the pillow and closing his eyes. Ashley gave Billy a soft kiss on the lips. When Billy opened his eyes, his wife was gone. "I hate when she does that."

I Smell A Rat

Hours earlier at CTU's main office in Atlanta at the exact same time that Jasper left on his drive to the loft apartment...

Scotty excused himself to the bathroom. When he got inside, he reached under the bathroom sink, and pulled a taped cellular phone out from underneath the sink. He walked into the back stall and closed the door. Scotty pressed nine then send, and it dialed an unlisted number.

"Hello." A Middle Eastern man answered.

"He's on his way." Scotty replied.

"Excellent." The Middle Eastern man hung up the phone. Scotty retaped the phone under the sink, and back to his desk he went.

<u>Interrogation</u>

Billy limped into the interrogation room. The terrorist that was caught hours earlier was shackled, handcuffed, and chained to a metal chair. He had a spit mask on his head to keep him from spitting on people. The spit mask is like a fencing mask, but it is closed in at the bottom to block salvia. There were several officers in the room including Jim and Sean who were sitting, at the table.

"Has the jackass said anything?" Billy asked.

"No. Just a bunch of Middle Eastern language gibberish." Sean answered.

"I bet if I put a bullet in his leg, he would say something."

Billy turned the guy around to face him. Captain Beckham came into the room. There was a giant book on a table behind Billy. He picked it up. This book was thicker than a phonebook, and bigger than a dictionary.

"What is your group's plan?" Billy yelled.

"Fuck you." The man uttered.

"Fuck me. Fuck me. Sounds like this rag head speaks English very well."

Billy picked up that book.

"It is funny how pretty much anybody speaking a new language learns cuss words first. Fuck me? No fuck you!" Billy yelled hitting the man in the face with the book. He hit both sides of the terrorist's face then cracked him on top of the head. The brazen detective kicked the man in the chest knocking him over. Then he picked up a chair and sat it across the man's body. Billy leaned down having the bottom of the chair choke the terrorist.

"Billy, you're killing him!" Simply Priceless yelled coming into the room.

Billy leaned up. "No, he will beg for death before I kill this bastard."

"Billy, watch your mouth." Simply Priceless corrected.

He ignored his wife and leaned back down. The man began to speak. Billy eased the pressure off the man's throat.

"Are you saying something?"

"Ockmed Hussein the richest man in Iraq gathered together terror groups from all Middle Eastern countries. We are talking Iraq, Iran, Syria, Pakistan, Afghanistan, everywhere! It is a group known as Allah's Jihad Destroyers of Destruction. Our leader that is here on American soil is Abu Bomback. They're planning all sorts of terror attacks, but I don't know specifics on everyone. The only thing I know is right now there is a woman who injected herself with a deadly strain of flu where every flu known to us on planet earth was combined into one deadly strain. It was a mistake that the center for disease control screwed up on. She is on a flight from Kuwait to here in Atlanta. She should land in about 17 hours. The whole plane is probably infected right now. It only takes an hour after coming across to be infected and another six hours to begin to show mild systems like a stomachache. Another ten hours after that you are in full blown flu mode, and you will die within the next three hours after that." The terrorist explained.

"What's the flight number?" Captain Beckham asked.

"I don't know but there are only five flights out of Kuwait a day to the United States."

"Give us a name." Simply Priceless commanded.

"All I heard was it is a British last name like Sears."

Billy got up and moved the chair. Several police officer led the terrorist back to a holding cell. Billy and Simply Priceless were walking outside when they heard Captain Beckham yell "There all down!"

"What?" Billy yelled running to the best of his ability towards the captain.

"There has been a cyber-attack Billy all our computers are down."

"What!" Billy yelled again.

"We have to stop this! Now!" Simply Priceless yelled.

Simply Priceless began to worry about her kids. She couldn't have anything happen to where they got hurt. She didn't want to see Billy hurt either but both Billy and Ashley would rather have something happen to them than anything happen to their children.

"We will." Billy said turning around and walking into Sophisticated Intimidation who was now standing directly behind Billy completely decked out in superhero attire.

"Sorry Intimidation."

Robbie walked up. "Just thought the varsity would come help the b team out."

"Now is not the time for jokes Robbie." Simply Priceless corrected.

"She's right." Sophisticated Intimidation replied in a Cali tone to her fiancée.

Robbie apologized, and the gang told him it was alright. Then he asked what was their next plan of action?

<u>Tickle Torture</u>

Brittany was tied up stripped down to her bra and panties. She was in a giant room with a television playing, and a few chairs. Brittany's boyfriend was stuffed bound and gagged in the closet down the hall. There was one man in the room with Brittany. He was unarmed. He sat on the floor in front of the footstool that Brittany's feet rested upon. The man was playing with her feet as she sat there and cried.

The man began licking Brittany's feet. He ran his tongue slowly up and down her foot, and between her toes. He worshiped her feet as she cried. Brittany usually enjoyed having her feet worshipped but this was disgusting her. The man had been up to this action for over an hour. When he wasn't playing with her feet. He was tickling her feet.

It was terrible. Brittany hated being tickled. It got on her damn nerves. She was biting hard into her gag trying not to continue laughing. She was laughing so hard she peed herself. The man went and got a large feather. He began to tickle her feet with the feather running it up and down her soles. He also ran the feather between her toes.

It was almost like this terrorist was a real-life Don Turtelli from the 1987 Teenage Mutant Ninja Turtles cartoon series. Of course, everyone remembers Don Turtelli was the mafia boss and grandson of The Tickler Tony Turtelli. Don Turtelli is best known for tickling the Teenage Mutant Ninja Turtle character April's feet in an episode of the 1987 Teenage Mutant Ninja Turtle cartoon.

Brittany was very fidgety. All she wanted was her dad. She knew her dad would kill every one of these people involved in her kidnapping. What she didn't know was soon enough her father was going to be notified. These men were part of a very elaborate plan.

"You are very pretty." The man said in a creepy tone.

Brittany closed her eyes and cried harder.

"You love me?"

The man kissed Brittany's forehead then groped her breast. Then started tickling her again. Brittany laughed and jerked.

"You are going to learn to like this one day."

Brittany began acting flirty. The flirtiest she could act being gagged.

"Want to say something?"

Brittany nodded.

The man removed the gag and leaned down close to her face. She leaned in like she was going to kiss him. The man closed his eyes with excitement but was quickly let down when Brittany locked onto his nose like a pit bull. She bit his nose off. He slapped her as hard as he could. The terrorist was getting ready to shoot Brittany when suddenly another terrorist fired a gunshot in the air.

"We need her alive jackass." The other terrorist commanded.

The man who got his nose bit off left the room. The other terrorist gagged Brittany once again and sent another man in the room to watch her. The new guard was told that if he touched her in anyway inappropriate that he would be killed on the spot.

<u>Next Plan of Action</u>

"We need an IT Team here now!" Captain Beckham yelled.

"They will be here as soon as they can every computer is out Capt. This is worse than Y2K ever predicted" another official spoke in a panic.

Billy, Robbie, and the sister super duo were plotting out their next plan of action.

"We need to find out how they have locked us out of our own system." Billy spoke the obvious.

"A worm. A big bad fucked up worm." Robbie answered.

"How do you know this" asked Billy.

"I heard some of the guys talking a bunch of spam mail seeped into the inbox of the Atlanta PD. A bunch of free membership porn and some penis enlargement free pill offer. The usual sexual scams. Some of the newer officers opened some of the porno offers up. It spoke of DVD deals and such. Had a few videos. One was French Foot Worship. This young blonde teen was dominating this guy rubbing her cleats on his face. Then she had him take off her cleats so she could rub her dirty sweat-soaked socks on his face. Only to make him take her sweaty dirty socks off and then she began to rub her feet on his face. She stuck her feet in his mouth and had him lick her feet and such. All while degrading him in French. I didn't understand a damn thing she said." Robbie explained with a chuckle.

"Robbie!" Cali sternly spoke.

"Yes."

"We're going to have a talk when this is over." Cali spoke sterner.

Robbie acted like he was going to say something, but Cali cut him off "Nope not right now."

"Enough with the romantic drama. What on earth do we do?" Billy asked.

"We have to trace down the worm. We must find its source. You know the original computer it was sent from." Robbie explained.

"You know this computer jargon?" Simply Priceless asked.

"I know a little bit."

"More than just French porn sites." Billy snickered.

"Now's not the time Billy." Cali said.

Billy threw both hands up in the air knowing he better be quiet.

"Then what are we going to do?" Simply Priceless said

"I need to tap into the main hub at district. From there I can see what I can do."

Jim ran into the room. "Come on guys there are loads of terrorist located at Hartsfield Jackson Airport causing a major ruckus. Billy are you up for this?"

"I'm fine Jimbo."

"Are you sure?" Simply Priceless asked in a concerned wife tone.

"Trust me."

"Billy now is not the time to be a bad ass." Robbie spoke clearly.

"When is?"

"Billy it's not funny." Simply Priceless sternly spoke.

Sean came into the room. "We don't have time for this either you all come on or sit on the sidelines. Your choice."

Billy stood up and walked toward the door. Sophisticated Intimidation explained she would fly Robbie to district then she would come to the airport. Simply Priceless told them that she would meet them there. She disappeared quick. Sophisticated Intimidation grabbed hold of Robbie and flew him to district. Billy loaded up with Sean and Jim and they sped as fast as they could to the airport.

Up! Up! And Away!

Sean parked the SUV in the parking deck. Everyone got out of the car and went to the back of the SUV to collect their weaponry. Sean and Jim pulled out machine guns from the back. Billy grabbed a pump shotgun. All the men were dressed for war. Billy made his way toward the airport's entrance. There wasn't any terrorist in sight. Sean and Jim were right behind Billy. Dead bodies were scattered about. It looked like a scene from The Walking Dead and law enforcement were just waiting for the zombie to spring out from nowhere!

A mass supply of officers were on scene. Billy leaned against the wall. He peered in through the automatic doors. He counted six terrorists right off the bat.

"What's your plan on this one?" Billy asked.

"The grand detective really going to plot things out. Not going in their Wild Wild West style." Jim joked.

"Funny. I promised Ashley I would be careful."

About that time the ceiling began to crumble and there were two holes in the roof. It was Simply Priceless and Sophisticated Intimidation. They began to go to war with the terrorist inside Hartfield Jackson Airport. Billy saw a terrorist trying to attack Simply Priceless. He took aim with the shotgun and blew a hole into that man's back. Billy entered the building and shot another terrorist that was still standing.

The terrorist in that sector were down. Sean and Jim were inside along with S.W.A.T. officers.

"We need to clear this airport!" Sean yelled.

GBI Agents came inside. Billy walked through the security checkpoint and made his way down the terminal.

Nobody noticed he was gone till finally Simply Priceless realized. She at super speed ran and found him. Billy got down by the tram that led people to the various terminals. There were four terrorists there who had Billy pinned down with gunfire.

"What are you doing?" Simply Priceless asked.

"Clearing the airport and you?" Billy spoke very sarcastic.

"Don't get that tone with me you promised me something."

"I'm sorry but you're here to back me up now." Billy smiled.

"Now's not the time to get cute." Billy's wife gave a halfway smile showing her bright white teeth.

"Let's just do this thing then we can argue later."

"Deal." Simply Priceless replied.

Billy came out of hiding and fired a shot into two of the men. The men standing began firing back, and Billy hid behind a giant square tile post. Simply Priceless blew the men into the wall knocking them out. Billy was out of rounds for the shotgun. He dropped it and pulled his 9mm.

A heard of terrorist showed up like a thief in the night and rushed Simply Priceless. Billy tried to shoot them down, but he was grabbed by three men and tossed into the tram. Billy fought the men off him as the tram began to move. The brash detective took a fighting stance as the first terrorist approached him. He had a knife pulled. The other two were being spectators. Billy kicked the man in the chest then grabbed the hand with the knife in it. He broke his arm then kicked him in the face. Billy quickly disarmed the man and threw the knife into the neck of the closest guy to him. Then he snapped the man who held the knife's neck.

"Come on Osama let's go."

The man rushed Billy spearing him back into the back window. The glass shattered. Billy hooked the man's head and began punching his side. Then Billy threw the man into one of the steel poles. Billy slammed the man's face into the pole. The guy kicked Billy in his broken ribs. Billy screamed in pain. The man punched Billy twice in his face which busted his lips, and then his nose. Billy fell to the ground. The man pulled a gun. Billy tripped the man up then kicked his firearm out of his hand. Billy began slamming the man's head in the floor. Both men battled to their feet. Billy grabbed the guy and spun around throwing the man through the cracked glass and out onto the tracks. The man began to fry. A sizzling and screaming sound was all that was heard.

The doors opened back at the platform Billy was at. Simply Priceless stood in the doorway. "Final stop heaven. Looking for this." She said getting into the tram handing Billy his gun.

Billy sat down when suddenly he heard Sean's voice. One of the dead bad guys had a walkie talkie. Billy removed the radio from the man's belt.

"Sean, it's Billy! I am going to concourse b. These terrorists have radios, and they are hearing everything we are saying."

"Great Billy I am sending men to all concourses, and we will take this place back over. Keep your nose clean."

"Too late it is already bloody." Billy said ending the chat.

Billy and Simply Priceless walked out on the concourse. Billy stuck the radio in his pants like he was John McClain from Die Hard 2: Die Harder. They were met with a familiar scene. There were dead bodies everywhere. Billy and Priceless came up to a restaurant. They looked inside, and there was a large group of terrorists inside eating. The restaurant staff were still alive.

"Do your thing." Billy told his wife.

"Only if you promise me, you are not going to get yourself killed."

"Have I yet." Billy smirked.

"There is a first time for everything." Simply Priceless replied in a concerned Ashley Hatch-Coatman tone.

"My game isn't over with yet baby. Now go kick some ass."

"Yes sir." Simply Priceless smiled then went into the restaurant.

Billy hid next to the restaurant.

"Table for one." Simply Priceless spoke with authority.

The men tried to pull their guns but Simply Priceless blew freezing the men's guns. Which also froze the men's hands they held their weapon in. Simply Priceless kicked the table knocking the piece of furniture into the men's hands which shattered them. Two more men came out of a bathroom area. She blew them straight through the wall.

Everybody was down. Two terrorists came down the other end of the airport near Billy. They spotted Billy and began firing. He dove into the bathroom. The young detective stuck his hand out from around the corner and began firing. He was able to strike one of them. The other one began firing a machine gun toward Billy. He ran deeper into the bathroom tripping over a dead body. He hid in one of the stalls. The man with the machine came into the bathroom and began firing rounds into every stall. When he got to Billy's stall Billy fired three rounds through the door, and into the man's chest.

Billy exited the bathroom and was met by S.W.A.T. Simply Priceless passed the live restaurant employees off to some of the S.W.A.T. officers who escorted them out safety.

Sean and Jim showed up.

"We are making one last sweep, but we believe all the terrorists seem to be dead." Jim said.

"Billy, clean yourself up! Then you need to meet up with Robbie. He called before the cell phones went down." Sean ordered.

"Cell phones are down?" Billy said.

"Yes, the satellites are down." Sean answered.

"When is this going to end?" Billy asked.

"Why not having fun?" Jim asked.

"Look at me don't you see the smile on my face?"

"No, I just see the blood running down into your mouth, and the rest dripping off your chin." Jim said.

"It shows the effort I am putting into this thing."

"Come on guys we have to keep going we don't have time for in-depth conversations." Sophisticated Intimidation said walking up behind Sean and Jim.

Robbie from district went in the backdoor of his jailbroken I-Phone and was able to use an illegal free texting application to get Sean and Jim a text about what landed flight the Sears woman was located on. Sean and Jim then began to planning stages for solving this issue.

Billy went back to the main lobby then outside. An ambulance cleaned Billy up. His nose was broken. He was taken to the hospital where his nose was set, and he was given a face mask. Simply Priceless met him at the hospital then flew him and dropped her husband off at district before she left and went to patrol with Sophisticated Intimidation as Sean and Jim put their plan in affect.

Germ-A-Phob

Priceless and Intimidation were patrolling the city as Sean and Jim came up with a way to extract those passengers from the plane without allowing the virus to hit the air. The Center for Disease Control sealed off the airport right after Robbie found out about this act of terrorism and found out the exact airline gate the plane was docked at. Inside was a giant tent with a tunnel that led back outside to where there was another tent. In that tent the passengers would be placed in their own suits but not before being given a new strain of flu shot created for worse case scenarios like this one. The CDC had a bunch of these shots created in fear something like this would happen. In fact, they were still creating them. They barely had enough to cover everyone but somehow, they pulled it off.

Sean and Jim were in blue bio suits looking at each other in the corridor waiting for agents to open the hatch to the plane. Jim was notified by Sean where their terrorist was sitting. The agents opened the door to the plane. Sean and Jim entered first followed by six tactical team members Some of the passengers were screaming at the top of their lungs. Others were vomiting. The virus was midway through its stages of death with some folks. The plane was evacuated in less than ten minutes.

Sean and Jim evacuated the terrorist row last. They got the two innocent passengers away from her then pulled their guns aiming on the woman.

The woman looked as green as Linda Blair from The Exorcist. "Is she alive?" Jim asked Sean looked at the woman in fear who appeared lifeless when out of nowhere Bah! Bah! The woman vomited at Sean's feet.

"You always have that effect on women." Jim laughed.

"Just jerk her ass up! And let's take her to the CDC." Sean ordered.

Jim holstered his weapon and as he was pulling the woman up, she suddenly grabbed Jim's 9mm and fired a round into Sean's chest. He stumbled back and tripped over the arm rest across the aisle and fell onto those seats. Jim kicked the deathly ill woman in the chest. She dropped his weapon. They began a short struggle in the small space till Agent Turner snapped the woman's neck. She fell to the ground dead. Jim didn't have time to turn around till he was hit in the back of the head.

"Nice one asshole!! What if she shot me in my head?" Sean asked reaching down picking up Jim's gun and handing it back to him.

They exited the plane and went and got decontaminated. The passengers were placed into bio suits and then placed in the back of vans after getting their injections and being segregated by men, women, and children. Then they were taken to the Center of Disease Control hospital.

Sean and Jim got a ride to the hospital where they met with Doctor Diane Richardson.

"Ok doc what are we looking at?" Sean asked.

"Things seem to be stable right now. We have had two fatalities a few are in critical condition, but we are treating everyone. Most should make a full recovery! They will be quarantined until we know there is no threat of virus remaining in them." The doctor explained.

The doctor left the room. "How are we going to handle things in the press?" Jim asked.

"Regular routine training exercise."

"Think people are going to buy that bullshit Black?" Jim laughed then slapped Sean on the back.

Sean ignored the question "We need to find out more where the terrorist got this virus."

"I got your answer to that. Three British scientist were abducted from their lab in London approximately eight months ago. They were working on a cure to a virus worse than this one that British Intelligence believes a Russian terrorist group is trying to plot out their own bio attack. British Intelligence believes a man named Emanuel Reed has something to do with it. I have traced all my back channels to find out information on Emanuel Reed, but it is my friend Agent Johnson who is working on this case from a CIA standpoint. He wouldn't tell me much! All he said was the CIA has it covered. All I know this is an extreme case for Agent Johnson to have come out of retirement." Jim explained out of left field.

"Charlie man we haven't seen him in forever. Between him and his ringer he sure did beat the hell out of anyone in golf."

"Man, I don't believe he is worried about 18 holes right now." Jim replied.

"I certainly doubt it. This is the same Charlies Johnson who dated Billy Coatman's mother for a while during her life?" Sean asked.

Billy's mom had seen Charlie off and on, and Charlie was the only male figure in Billy's life. He considered Billy his son. Even though he had his own kids, he took care of Billy like he was his own. Charlie was in and out of Billy and Billy's mother lives for long periods of time. Billy's mom told Billy Charlie was on business trips. Billy talked to a therapist once about not trusting guys in his life. The therapist didn't offer too much advice on that issue. She just knew it was because of his father screwing him over.

Growing up without a father really scared Billy, and then he had seen men abuse his mom growing up that she attempted to date before she met Charlie. Now it was here or there whether or not Charlie would stay in her life. He was always gone, and deep down that got old for her. She was fine with it at first, and then attachment issues set in for Billy's mom. Billy didn't understand why Charlie was gone for so long. Especially since Charlie was an "area rug" dealer. Supposedly working a territory of the east coast with sometimes having to attend expos in Vegas and California, and he supposedly went to Canada once or twice.

Charlie was gone for weeks sometimes, and he has even been gone months at a time. Billy began to check into Charles Johnson. If that was his real name? He told the same stories repeatedly. Military stories about being over in Vietnam, and it all just cracked him up. The stories never changed. No matter how many margaritas he drank at the Mexican Restaurant when all of them would go. Billy was amazed. He hacked his computer one night when Mr. Johnson spent the night. He slept on the couch out of respect for Billy's mom. Even though Billy was more than of age he didn't want him to think anything negative of his mother. You wouldn't think Charlie would care. He honestly loved Billy's mother. Why not sleep with her? They had been together for a long time. Charlie was past that point in his life, and so was Billy's mom.

Billy toyed around in Charlie's computer. He went through anything and everything he could get into. He finally got on a black screen. Billy didn't know what he clicked on for that screen to pop up. All he saw was normal stuff, and he made the wrong turn in Charlie's browser history and got to a spot that contained history behind the history.

"Ok. Here we go." Billy whispered under his breath, and then he clicked on the little skull in the corner in the lower right-hand corner of the laptop screen. The skull began to bleed from the eyes, and then bled from the mouth. Seven seconds passed and the skull exploded.

Then he was brought to pages containing various topics involving him working for....

Billy's left shoulder was slammed down on with a firm grip He looked up and saw Charlie gripping his left shoulder with his right hand. He stood there in his underwear gripping his smartphone which alerted him somebody was in those files.

"What am I supposed to do?" He asked.

Bill thought is this the end of me or am I going to have to kill my mom's boyfriend?

"Well? A Special Ops team is in route to this location right now. They know somebody other than me has accessed my files, seeing the fact this time of night is *considered a dead point for me, unless there is an emergency." Charlie calmly spoke but Billy didn't know how to reply.*

"So, you are CIA?" Billy said then attempted to sit up but was forcefully pushed back down in the chair.

"Look I'm tired, and I don't think you would enjoy being incarcerated in a Secret CIA Prison over in Syria. I don't know how I would explain that to your mom. I love her you know. Even though I want to bend her over my knees at times, spank that ass, and dump her on the floor for her decisions. However, she does have the prettiest feet in the world."

"I knew you were still Special Ops or in the military." Billy chimed in.

"I know we all have secrets. So how about I just call in the code because tactical teams are less than 30 seconds away."

Charlie smiled and typed in "Pretty Feet" into an opened password menu on his phone. The sound of a helicopter swooped very closely over making a loud noise. It was ready to diplo tact teams repealing down from the various helicopters that were in route. The tact teams were ready to do whatever was needed to do to remedy the situation. Charlie walked off, and Billy ran to bed.

Later the next day when they were off alone eating in the car from going through a drive-thru burger place. Charlie and Billy were having a nice conversation where Billy swore to not reveal Charlie's secret. Charlie explained a United State Government Secret about how there was a file on Simply Priceless, and that there are other superheroes across the United States that the United

States Government keep tabs on. Charlie forked over this information after Billy asked what the most secret stuff was the CIA into. Billy listened and soaked up all the knowledge he could from Charlie and the various people he had talked to in various fields of Law Enforcement. After this car lunch get together Billy and Charlie had a major bond from that point forward.

"Come on let's go back and check on Robbie to see what the next phase of action is." Sean said.

Jim and Sean walked outside to their vehicle. They got in and Jim pulled out a bottle of germ disinfectant out and began to apply that to his hands.

"Pass some of that over here I am a big germaphobe." Sean laughed.

<u>Wired</u>

Billy was standing beside Robbie looking over his shoulder. Simply Priceless, Sophisticated Intimidation, Sean, and Jim all walked in around the same time. Robbie was busy on the computer not paying attention to anyone else in the room.

"It's a fire sale." Robbie spoke breaking the silence.

"Like in Live Free or Die Hard?" Billy asked.

"Exactly like Live Free or Die Hard, Detective Coatman." Robbie replied.

"What is the next plan of action?" Billy asked.

"There is talk about a nuclear bomb being brought to Atlanta. It doesn't say where or when, but it does say it will be on the way." Robbie answered.

"What else?" Sophisticated Intimidation asked.

Sean and Jim were in the background calling in reinforcements from jailbroke illegal call applications. Sean finished his conversation with the Governor and announced that the Governor was sending in the National Guard. Along with the President was meeting with his defense secretary to plan a war attack once it is determined which country is responsible for this travesty.

"It also explains there is a plan to kill the President of the United States along with there are biohazard bombs planted all around the city which will be used with chemical terrorism."

"Anything else?" Billy asked dreading the worse.

"Nothing other than the violence has ended for the day." Robbie spoke.

"What's the next plan with this fire sale?" Jim asked.

"Well transportation and telecommunications are down for the most part. Unless you know how to run the jailbroke applications you are shit out of luck so the next is financial and utilities." Robbie answered.

"What are we going to do?" Sean asked.

"I'll keep monitoring these terrorist websites I got through the backdoor to, and I will let you all know something."

"You're so smart." Sophisticated Intimidation spoke in a Cali Cooper congratulations tone.

"I know." Robbie smiled.

Billy and Simply Priceless finished up the conversation. Sean handed Billy an encrypted radio and told him to be on standby. Simply Priceless flew Billy to get his Civic. She flew home, and he came in shortly behind his wife. Carmella was back in town and had brought the kids home from school. Schools let out due to the terror till further notice. Billy took a shower then laid in bed. Ashley was dressed in a pair of pink sweats and a blue tank top. She had pink flip flops on. Billy stripped down to his Star Wars boxers. She brought in ice packs. Billy began to ice his leg as he wrapped some heating pads around his ribs. Ashley then brought him a few pain pills.

He laid there resting as she tended to the kids.

"Is dad, ok?" Wesley asked.

"He'll be fine babe."

"What is going on mom?" Ashley Kelly asked.

The kids were no longer kids. They were now preteens.

"Your dad is a little banged up that is all." Ashley answered trying not to scare her children.

"What's new." Ashley Kelly smarted off.

"Now's not time for that attitude young lady."

"Hey, don't give your mother any trouble you really don't want me to get up from here!" Billy yelled from the bedroom

"Sorry." Ashley Kelly walked to her bedroom and laid down.

Wesley followed going into his room.

Ashley Hatch-Coatman came back to the bedroom. She closed the door and climbed onto the bed. She didn't want to touch her husband because she knew he was hurt. He was bruised all over, and his lip had a crusty spot to where it was scabbing over. His nose was several different colors.

"Think we are in over our heads?" Billy asked.

"I think we can handle it."

"How do you know Ash?"

"Billy, we have stopped monsters so we can stop pretty much anything." Ashley replied.

"That's true we have stopped a nuclear bomb before, and a gas that puts the end to love." Billy responded.

"We'll do this if you can hold yourself together. You are kind of like humpty dumpty you are falling apart." Ashley smiled.

"Hey it's not funny."

"I know. I still love you. Where's the radio?" Ashley asked.

"It is in my pants." Billy answered.

Ashley got up and pulled the radio Sean gave Billy out of his pants. She turned the volume up to full blast and sat it on the nightstand.

"I'm going to fix dinner. Rest I will bring you something to eat when dinner is done."

"Ok." Billy said with a smile. He loved when his wife babied him.

"I love you." Ashley said.

"I love you too."

Ashley leaned down, and kissed Billy lips. He quenched in pain because she touched his nose by accident. Ashley apologized and Billy told her it was ok. She left the room to fix dinner. "Baby!" Billy yelled.

"Yes!" Ashley yelled back.

"Can you get my cell phone out of my pants and sit it on the nightstand?" Billy asked.

Simply Priceless used her mind powers to do what her husband requested.

"Thank you!" Billy said with a smile.

"You're welcome. Now get some sleep."

"Yes Princess." Billy said.

Billy closed his eyes and drifted off to sleep. He knew his computer was down, but he wanted to get online, and get wired catching up on the latest terrorist news. He was a bit jealous that Robbie was able to handle things so well because as anyone knows Billy is a big egomaniac. He is a narcissist. Everything must go his way, and he must lead the way. He was proud of Robbie though. Billy drifted off to sleep as his wife fixed some barbeque chicken. About an hour and half passed and Ashley brought Billy a plate with a piece of barbeque chicken, corn, and broccoli on it.

She brought him a glass of tea. She ate in the kitchen with the kids. Then she helped them with their homework. After that she came and got Billy's plate. She did the dishes then the kids went to sleep. Ashley came back to the bedroom. She laid down and tried to get some sleep, but she had a restless night.

<u>Reunite</u>

The terrorist was planning their next phase in their devastation plan for destruction. Several innocent lives had been slain, and even though they have had fallen comrades, things overall were going 98.9% right. They didn't expect to have such trouble in the form of two female superheroes and one bad ass renegade detective. There was a group sitting around a table at an undisclosed location making their preparations for their next plan of action. Some of the men were speaking Middles Eastern languages. While others spoke English to broken English. Most of the men speaking broken English sounded like those customer service reps everyone winds up talking to over in the Middle East since America outsources their work. These customer service agents always have white male or female names, and they never understand the customer that is calling into customer service, and the customer calling in never understands these agents but to the men at the table these broken English speaking men were speaking proper English.

The two men were Makin Al-Yacoub and Abdul-Aliyy AlRashid. Both men were average build. Abdul had a scar underneath his right eye and spoke with a lisp. He was a distant cousin to Ockmed.

"Get the suicide bombers ready?" Makin asked.

"They are ready to fly." Abdul replied.

"Fly?" Makin laughed. He leaned back with his hands behind his head with his fingers interlaced.

"I'm talking boom." The man made an explosion gesture with his hands.

"Perfect." Makin replied moving his fingers touching them together.

A purple limousine pulled up, and a very muscular man got out of the backseat. He was dressed in a white suit with a gray turtleneck. He wore very expensive sunglass, and had two sets of earrings in each ear

He walked up to two double doors. Two men inside saw him and slid the doors open. He walked inside and removed his sunglasses.

"Makin." The man said.

"Mr. Bomback." Abdul was in shock.

"Did I address you?" Bomback asked sternly.

Abdul began to stutter.

"No" Abu Bomback answered in a hateful tone.

Abdul acted like he was fixing to apologize but Bomback told him not to speak in a meaner tone.

"The Four Noutes are in Atlanta at the new federal prison Gallop Pri Corrections where they hold the worse of the worse, and we are going to spring them. They are supposed to be brought on trial in the upcoming weeks for their involvement in terrorist activities." Bomback explained.

"The Four Gods are here?" Abdul spoke.

"Yes Abdul, they are here, and we are going to get them out of jail. Tomorrow! Gather your best men because it is going to be a blood bath." Bomback explained then walked out the way he came in.

"These are the worse of the worse." Makin said to Abdul.

"I know and with them we will be unstoppable."

<u>Overseas</u>

Overseas in the Middle East at a prison camp run by Emanuel Reed in Iraq there were teenagers and young adults bound at the wrist, around the neck, and underneath the arms by wire. The wire was attached to a vine that was bolted in the dirt ground in various stations fenced off like a farm. The group of prisoners were surrounded by a giant wire fence. There was a river which appeared to be a way out. Half-dressed attractive girls were bathing the prisoners. The girls there were not bound and can free others if they chose even through, they are prisoners themselves. A seventeen-year-old was trying to convince this very attractive girl who was washing his bare back to let him go. She explains she is a prisoner, and they would kill her. The male explains he would bring her with him and would protect her.

It started getting dark and the female prisoner tells the guy that they bury the new prisoners their first night and dig them up the next morning and the teen was one of the new detainees.

"Where does that river go" asked the teen.

"It leads to Emanuel Reed's place and then goes further but nobody had made it passed Reed's place."

"It's worth a shot my name is Mel by the way."

Mel convivences the girl to let him go. She undoes Mel's binds. "Tell the others I will be back for them."

"What about me? The name is Jenna."

"Come with me let's make our escape." Mel spoke with confidence and authority.

Jenna passed the word through some of the other female prisoners to tell the other guys as Mel and Jenna took off running toward the river. Nobody noticed them getting away but the fellow prisoners. They held hands as they jumped into the deep murky river and began to be drifted down stream by the rapid current. Muddy water got in both of their mouths as they struggled to keep their heads above water. Mel held Jenna above water as he plans his next plan of action.

"Hey where's the….

"I don't….

Two of the guards spoke to one another. Mel and Jenna came upon a giant branch overlooking the water. They grabbed a hold of it and pulled themselves out.

They were outside a giant palace. Emanuel Reed is a very rich man. He made his money inside the criminal underworld as well as through oil.

"Come on we have to be as quiet as a mouse. We are talking ghost quiet." Mel explained.

"This is as far as anybody made it. How do you expect us to make it any further?" Jenna asked regretting what she got herself into.

"Look Jen. Can I call you Jen?". Mel tried to flirt. "I have played enough PlayBox video games to know how to be stealth. I beat The Cell in a record time. The Cell is an espionage game about being a spy going undercover."

"This is no game. These are real men, and they kill and torture people, like us. If we are going to escape get out of the game zone and let's go." Jenna ordered then kissed Mel's cheek.

About that time a siren sounded. German Shepherds and Rottweilers began to bark as search teams went in search for the escapees. Mel and Jenna stayed deep in the woods. They made it toward the front of the palace. There was a vacant military jeep in front. Nobody was around. The engine was running. Mel saw two guards in the distance smoking cigarettes horse playing around.

"Let's run for it." Mel commanded.

"On three." Jenna said.

"Three! Come on!" Mel said taking grasp over Jenna's wrist and taking off running toward their horse to freedom. They dove into the jeep and Mel sped off. He busted through an iron gate and went down a dirt road as bullets flew their direction, but they were too far ahead to get hit.

<u>!Explosive Day Ahead!</u>

The break was over and Simply Priceless was back on the case. It was one of the most important adventures of their life. One of Atlanta biggest threats was these Middle Eastern terrorists. Sure, the rock monsters, robots, and the monsters was a giant threat and did major damage to the city which the city was continuing to recover from. This current threat was a high death count and big destruction mess itself.

"We heard chatter that Bomback is stepping up the game today." Sean explained.

"What do you mean?" Simply Priceless asked.

"We don't really know they were speaking in some sort of code that we never heard before. They are getting smarter with their attacks."

"Well, I am tired of this shit already."

"Billy!" Simply Priceless firmly corrected in an Ashley Hatch-Coatman tone.

"Sorry."

Billy forgets to watch his language around his wife at times especially when he is mad. He has never cussed at her in a fight or anything like that but when he gets mad, he unleashes a line of cuss words worse than a sailor. Other times he has Ashley has been there keeping him straight. To his knowledge he had never cussed in front of the kids. In his mind he does good at not doing that. His wife has threatened to wash his mouth out with soap even going to the unopened bar she has saved for the occasion. He knows she would do it too, so he gets down on his knees and begs her not to. It is a funny sight to Ashley. She loves seeing him in fear sometimes. Now that is priceless, she thought.

The rough tough nothing will ever stop me, I will take on the biggest man in the room, one man army Detective Billy Coatman down on his knees wrapping his arms around his wife's legs holding on to them begging her not to sit him on the toilet with a bar of soap in his mouth for a time period of her choosing. It just amazed her. She knew she had the power, and she knew she still after all those years hadn't let Billy out of the deal where he had to do what she wanted for however long she wanted either. She always would use that to her advantage especially when there is something that needs to be done that she doesn't want to do. She would clear her throat and say "Remember?" He would stop whatever he was doing and say, "Yes ma'am" or if they were at home alone "Yes Goddess Priceless" and do whatever Ashley needed to have done. They would laugh about it later, but Ashley knew even if she did let her husband out of their arrangement, he would still do what she wanted because he worshiped the ground she walked on and had kissed her feet enough to prove it.

"Good boy." Simply Priceless patted Billy on top of his head.

While this conversation was taking place several suicide bombers walked into various venues of the city. Some walked into banks, a few walked into the museum, other jewelry stores and the post office just to name a few. Each bomber began to speak something in Arabic before setting off their bomb blowing themselves and who was around them into smithereens. News media were all over town trying to cover this story of the mass suicide attack as other members of A.J.D.O.D. were suiting up about to bust the Four Gods out of prison which would only make their unit stronger.

"Excuse me, Ladies gentleman." A female officer who worked as a receptionist said.

"Yes?" Sean replied.

"We have just had over fifty phone calls of suicide bombing across pretty much every part of town imaginable." She answered.

"What?" Billy said.

He looked to his side, and Simply Priceless was missing. She took off like an angel on a mission to help in the process of putting the fires out. As she was nearing the first location she was met in the air by Sophisticated Intimidation.

"Beat you to it sis." Sophisticated Intimidation spoke cocky with a smile.

"You already put the fires out?" Simply Priceless replied in shock.

"Yep." Sophisticated Intimidation smiled big.

"Ho…

"What can I say Simply Priceless I learned from the best but who's the sidekick now grasshopper?" Cali burst into laughter then took off toward the police station with Simply Priceless trailing her which turned into a race, and they both made it back at the same time.

A race between Simply Priceless and Sophisticated Intimidation would be on the level of a race between Superman and The Flash if Priceless and Intimidation were to ever-seriously-race. If Simply Priceless and her sister ever seriously race the victor would be hard to determine. Meanwhile on earth Superman cannot run faster than the speed of light, while The Flash is able to move faster than the speed of light when he enters speed force. The friction within the air also causes Superman to slow down, and The Flash doesn't have these types of problems because The Flash is frictionless due to the speed force. So, with all these factors in determining the outcome of a race between The Flash and Superman the winner of that race would be The Flash.

A group of Hummers pulled up in front of the Federal Prison in front of the prison gates. Four men got out of the Hummers with rocket launchers and fired them. Two fired them through the gates as the other two fired at the guard towers. Inmates began to riot in the yard as two Hummers sped through the burning gates.

Men began to exit the Hummers as two more rockets were fired into the remaining two guard towers. A helicopter hovered overhead as more Hummers pulled up. Terrorist began to exit these Hummers and began to enter the penitentiary. They slaughtered the guards like pigs along with any felon that stood in their way.

Bomback was there and he entered the main office, and found out which cell block the Four Gods were being held in.

More terrorist arrived on scene as the key cards of the deceased guards were being high jacked. It was a state of the arch operation. Terrorists from the main phantom compound had already hacked the alarm system where no calls will dial out, and the alarm would go off. Simply Priceless and Sophisticated Intimidation were deep concentrating in the conversation they were in with the guys especially with the news Robbie just brought them.

The news came over the police scanner that more places have been attacked by suicide bombers. The death toll was rising. Billy had to sit down. His knee was bothering him. Ashley could tell something was wrong. She placed her hand on his shoulder and began to sense the pain in his knee. She felt the same pain in her arm without saying anything. When she removed her hand, the pain went away in her arm.

"Billy, you need to go home." His wife ordered.

"I'm fine."

Cali understood what was going on because she felt the vibes through her sister. "Billy, go home. Just for now and rest." Cali agreed.

"I'm fine." The tough as nails detective raised his voice.

"Don't take that tone. I am not asking you! I am telling you, go home." Ashley got just as heated.

"Damn it Simply Priceless I'm fine!" Billy halfway yelled standing up.

"Billy!" Cali, Robbie, and Sean yelled.

Billy had a deer in headlights look.

Ashley was biting her lower lips. She was hurt with the way Billy just snapped at her. He hadn't snapped at her that hateful in that tone of voice since the street at the car lot when the Python ordeal was transpiring.

She appeared to be about to cry. Cali wrapped her arms around her sister. "Simply Priceless." Billy calmly spoke.

"Go home Billy." Cali ordered.

"Simply Priceless I'm sorry."

Tears began to roll down Simply Priceless's cheeks.

"Please Simply Priceless don't cry. I can't have you sick especially right now. Can all you please leave the room so I can talk to Simply Priceless."

Sean and Robbie looked at each other then left together. "I'm not leaving. You don't talk to my sister that way Billy. You shouldn't talk to any woman that way. Especially a woman that loves you the way my sister loves you! You are lucky I am holding Ashley right now because if I wasn't....

"Just go Cali let me talk to him. I believe he has got the point."

"But Ashley are you sure?"

"Yes Cal, I'll talk to you in a couple minutes. We'll be fine." Ashley got out of Cali's grasps, and Cali walked toward the door. She stopped "Billy you know I have super hearing like my sister so if you take any kind of tone but a positive one, I am coming back in here!" Cali just had to get the last word in. Cali shut the door behind her, and Billy approached his wife. He reached out to take her hands, but she jerked back. "Back up Billy, I don't want you near me or touching me." Ashley ordered.

"Mind if I sit down then?"

"Do what you want but get to the point, and quick, I am giving you twenty seconds starting now." Simply Priceless dominated.

"Ashley, I love you, and I can't do anything to take back what I said to you. You didn't deserve that, and I swear it will never happen again. If it did happen again which it never will, I will let you have the kids and I will go because I wouldn't deserve to have you in my life if you were to forgive me, and me make that same mistake again because you or no other woman deserves to be talked to like that. Cali is right. I'm sorry Ashley but I am sure my time is up so I am going home to mope because I know how you can be, but I know I deserve….

"Shut up Billy." Ashley said with dry eyes and a smile on her face. She walked up to her husband and took his hands. "It's ok."

"Ashley it is never ok to make you cry much less talk to you the way I did. That was completely utterly wrong, and I want to make up for it."

"Well, there is no way you can make up for it till this deal with terrorist is over but tell me why did you do it? That can be a start to making up for it by finding the root to why you did what you did, and then never doing it again." Ashley spoke very smart.

"You a psychology major or something." Billy laughed.

"I went to college and yes, I took psychology. Now tell me. We don't have time to fool around!"

"My knee is killing me. I can barely stand on it. I don't know if I am capable to finishing this one. It hurts so bad, and my ego is broken." He explained.

"Not used to getting your butt kicked this bad huh." Ashley replied, kissing Billy's left hand.

"No baby I'm not."

"Go home and rest some, and maybe later you can come back to help out. Even the best athletes have to spend some time on the bench." Ashley tried to give moral support to her husband.

"So, I'm the best athlete?" He smiled.

"Well, your second string when I'm on the team."
She laughed.

"You know it."

"Well at least you agree. Want me to fly you home?"

"That would be nice."

Ashley helped Billy up, and they walked over to the window. He opened the window then she picked him up and flew out. He had his eyes shut till they landed briefly. "You can open your eyes now." Simply Priceless said with Billy standing on the balcony. He opened his eyes and looked up at his wife.

"I promise that will never happen again. I hope you know…

"I know you didn't mean it Billy. I always knew you didn't mean it but that didn't change the fact that I still heard it. You can make it up to me soon but right now I am taking up more time than I need to currently on this issue. I must go. Stay here rest and think about what you've done until I get home tonight." Simply Priceless ordered floating up in the air.

"Yes, Goddess Priceless. I love you."

Simply Priceless floated higher with a red face embarrassed with what her husband just said as she tried to hold back laughter while thinking if she should respond.

"Bye baby." Ashley smiled then vanished so quick that the wind about knocked her husband over in the chair. He had no time to blink.

Finally, Billy stood up. He looked over the balcony and yelled "That's mean but I deserve it." He walked into the house and got into bed.

As this was going on Simply Priceless and Sophisticated Intimidation were gossiping briefly like a couple of hens clucking.

"You didn't tell him you loved him back? That was cruel sis." Cali said.

"Hey, you have done worse to Robbie."

"Done worse what?" Robbie asked.

"Robbie adults are talking why don't you go play with your computer or gizmos or something." Cali said shooing him away with her hand.

"But I didn't do anything."

"Robbie are you really going to make me repeat myself." Cali gave a stern look much sterner than her sister has ever given Billy.

"No ma'am." Robbie walked off.

"These boys are so whipped." Ashley laughed.

"If anything in our lives had ever made sense that statement just has." Cali replied.

The terrorist group found the Four Gods and removed them from their cells. Then quicker than Santa Claus traveling around the world at Christmas time they ushered the Four Gods out of the prison. They exited the way all of them came in. All the terrorist loaded up in their Hummers and left what appeared to be a battlefield full of dead bodies as Bomback and the Four Gods got in the chopper and took off. Everybody left like nothing happened and went back to the main hideout as Billy slept.

<u>DOUBLE 0 JOHNSON</u>

Senior CIA Agent Charlie Johnson walked into the director's Bartoo's office.

"Agent Johnson, I assume you know why I called you in here?" CIA Director Bartoo asked in a voice which he knew Agent Johnson already knew the answer to.

"I assume it is about Emanuel Reed. I have been busting my ass to get that information together."

Steven Bartoo nodded then stood up. He walked over to a massive filing cabinet and pulled out a large brown file folder. He passed the folder to Charlie. "We need you to go undercover. We are sending you to Emanuel Reed's ball where he is meeting with some higher ups which are involved in this massive terrorist attack on Atlanta. We are planning military action beginning with extracting Reed to get answers and gain leverage on these terrorists."

"Yes sir." Charlie replied taking the folder.

"Your flight leaves in three hours. Drivers will take you to your residence to pack then leave."

"Yes sir."

Charlie left the office and was led downstairs by Director Bartoo's secretary. He was led to a limousine. The limo drove Charlie's home. He packed a quick bag and left.

<u>Tagged In</u>

Billy woke up to a nibble on his right ear. He smiled and parted his eyes. He was looking into the crystal-clear blue eyes of his wife. He smiled then asked what time it was, and Ashley answered.

"Ready to be tagged back in?" Simply Priceless asked holding her left hand up.

Billy gave her five then replied, "Yes I am partner."

Sophisticated Intimidation walked into the bedroom "Come on peeps let's do this thing." Ashley and Billy began to stir as Sophisticated Intimidation went back to the living room as Billy and Ashley got ready.

Billy got up. His leg was feeling a little bit better. Sophisticated Intimidation flew off to the prescient as Ashley and Billy finished getting ready. Then after they were ready Simply Priceless flew Billy to the police headquarters that they were holding the investigation at.

"Welcome back hop along." Robbie poked fun

"Rob I still have a gun don't make me shoot you." Billy replied pulling his gun out of the back of his pants.

"Billy that's not funny." Sophisticated Intimidation replied taking the gun from Billy and sitting it on the counter.

"Who says I was joking?" Billy smirked.

Simply Priceless popped Billy on the back of the head. His head whipped forward then she grabbed a hold of him pulled him to her chest and apologized. She then quickly let him go realizing what she just did. Everyone was staring at her. "What!" She sternly said. Then everyone went back to work.

"Ok what's on the agenda?" Billy asked getting down to business.

"There is a warehouse in Buckhead where a lot of electric activity is taking place." Robbie explained.

"So?" Billy interjected.

"Let him finish!" Simply Priceless and Sophisticated Intimidation said at the same time already aware of what was going on.

"A man with the name Shahzad bought this commercial property approximately four months ago. We believe the cyber attack is being infiltrated from there." Robbie finished.

"Then let's go." Billy said picking up his gun.

"We'll meet you there." Sean said.

Sophisticated Intimidation, Simply Priceless, and their boy toys walked outside. Each superhero took hold of their loved one, and off they went.

<u>Techno Geeks</u>

"We need to get out of here!" One of the terrorists said to the leader of the group.

It was a massive warehouse. Inside looked like a massive overseas outsourced customer service building full of various cubicles with computers.

The leader cussed in Arabic. Then he whistled. Two men were quickly behind the guy whose mouth overshot his ass. They jerked him up and lead him out of the room screaming.

About that time a woman in a vale came into the room. She whispered something into the guy's ear then he snapped his fingers. All the men immediately left their stations. They ran outside and piled into the back of an eighteen-wheeler as the leader of the group typed in a secret code which transferred all the information, they were working on there to another worksite. He and his wife rushed out of the building as several armed terrorist entered awaiting their challengers.

The man and his wife got in the back of a limousine and were driven away. Shortly afterward Simply Priceless and the gang landed.

"Be careful Billy ok."

"Don't baby me right now Ash."

As they talked Sophisticated Intimidation and Robbie made entry into the warehouse and began to take extreme fire. Robbie dropped to the ground and crawled under a desk as two terrorist approached Sophisticated Intimidation. Sophisticated Intimidation kicked the man in front of her. Then she punched the other guy quickly grabbing both men by their heads and slamming their heads together.

Simply Priceless made it on to the scene. She made it into the building. She blew knocking the terrorists that were firing at her down. Billy started up the steps into the warehouse when something caught his eye out front. A black workers van that somebody just flipped a cigarette out the driver's side window.

The brash detective hid behind a dumpster as he examined the van. Billy reached down and picked up a brick then slung it through the air and into one of the back windows of the van. Two heavily armed terrorist came out that Billy killed with two swift bullets to the head. Blood and brain matter went everywhere. He approached the van as another terrorist came out the passenger side which met the same fate with multiple bullets to the chest. Billy was chop blocked from behind smashing his same bad leg on the pavement. Billy's gun slid across the pavement as rain began to fall from the sky.

The terrorist went to work on Billy's leg jerking on it and smashing it against the ground. Billy screamed in pain closing his eyes when a gust of wind blew him back hitting his back against a brick wall. When he opened his eyes, Billy saw his wife standing in front of him. She drove the terrorist through the brick wall of the next building. The terrorist lay dead in a pile of rubble.

Billy made it up to his feet as Simply Priceless handed him his gun. "Are you ok?"

"I'm fine." Billy answered.

Simply Priceless used her X-Ray vision and saw Billy's knee was badly injured.

"Billy, you need knee surgery. Go find a corner to hide in and then I am flying you home."

Robbie shot and killed three terrorists then made his way to the main computer. The screen was locked. He had no access to anything. Another program was hacked into the system from a separate server. A red light caught his eye from a backroom. He wandered into the room and found a bomb with less than three minutes left on the timer.

"Bomb!" Robbie yelled.

He ran out of the room and was kicked in the gut. A terrorist kicked Robbie's gun out of his hand. He then picked up Robbie's right arm and jerked it out of the socket. Robbie screamed in pain.

"Billy, we got to go there is a bomb inside! Now come on!"

"What about Robbie?" Billy asked as Simply Priceless grabbed him and took to the air.

Sophisticated Intimidation grabbed the terrorist jerked him back and violently snapped his neck. Then she picked Robbie up and placed his gun securely in his pants and took to the air. She punched a hole in the roof and flew Robbie to the hospital where Billy and Simply Priceless were waiting.

Meanwhile at another terrorist technological base camp location two of the nerds were talking to one another.

"They won't be able to trace this right? I don't want to feel the wrath of Atlanta's superheroes."

"Look you knew what you were doing when you signed up for this job."

"Nothing like this."

"Calm down they can't trace it! The pings are hitting all over the place everywhere from Calhoun to McDonough so they will have no clue we are in Buckhead."

"If you say so."

The terrorist worked out of an office building owned by Emanuel Reed.

<u>Odds Are He Wont See Tomorrow</u>

Charlie was picked up from the airport by CIA Operative Steve Cole. He drove Charlie to the hotel he would be residing in over the next couple of days.

Once in the room Steve combed the room for bugs. Once things were all clear Agent Cole and Agent Johnson began a conversation.

"You know I never liked you, Cole." Charlie hatefully spoke.

"You have no choice but to work with me though. You think this was my idea?"

"I guess you are right."

Agent Cole gave Agent Johnson the time of the ball, and explicit instructions on what needs to be done before he left. Agent Johnson went downstairs to the bar and ordered himself a frozen margarita. He took a seat at the bar and noticed a young what appeared to be an American girl probably late twenties early thirties sitting by herself in the corner of the room smoking a cigarette.

"Don't do it." Charlie said to himself.

The girl looked over her Sarah Palin glasses and gave Charlie a wink.

"I'm going to do it." Charlie spoke once again to himself before he walked over to the woman who looked up undressing Charlie with her eyes.

"May I take a seat?" Charlie said gesturing to the vacant seat beside of her.

"Shouldn't you ask something else?" The woman spoke in a British accent.

Charlie looked puzzled.

"Is this…. The woman's accent suddenly sounded a bit Russian.

"Yes, excuse me is this seat taken?" Charlie asked taking a sip of his drink.

"I guess it is now. Sit down."

Charlie took the seat and the woman asked him to introduce himself.

"Johnson. Charles Johnson." He smiled.

"I am a fan of those movies Mr. Johnson. Does that work with the ladies in America?" the girl asked.

"Not really and you are?" Charlie rebutted.

"Leeann."

"Does Leeann have a husband or boyfriend." Charlie asked before he realized what he said.

"You're awfully forward. Aren't you, and no" Leeann let out a sigh?

Charlie tried further to flirt "There overrated."

"I agree. I dated somebody four years only to find out he was screwing my twin sister Ursula three and half years of that four-year relationship. They are now married, and I have a niece and a nephew that I am not allowed to see. Probably because I bitch slapped the bastard at their wedding which I wasn't invited to and wound up getting arrested." Leeann giggled.

"Probably." Charlie sarcastically spoke rolling his eyes.

"What brings you to the Middle East Mister Johnson?"

"Please call me Charlie."

"Ok what brings you to the Middle East? Are you here to see The Beast from the Middle East put up his AWF wrestling world championship tonight at the new big arena that was constructed?" Leeann repeated her question.

"No. Just business."

"Personal business or business, business?" Leeann laughed.

"A little of both I guess." Charlie lied.

"What field are you in Mister Johnson excuse me, Charlie?" Leeann corrected herself.

"I am an entrepreneur. Looking for people to invest in an alternative fuel idea I have."

"You're in the wrong country for that. I doubt the Saudis would give up all their oil." Leeann flirted then touched Charlie's hand which made him jerk and knock his frozen drink to the floor.

Leeann fought back laughter as the busboy cleaned up the spill and a server brought Charlie another round.

"Jerkie are we? That's kinda cute."

"Well thanks. So, what are you doing tonight?"

"I am going to Emanuel Reed's party. I am his party coordinator. You know you should come. Since you are not going to The Beast from The Middle East's big championship wrestling match tonight." Leeann invited.

"I might just have to do that." The secret agent smirked.

"Ok great." Leeann pulled a pen out of her purse and wrote the address down on a beverage napkin. She then told Charlie where he could get a ride to the event. "Tell the bouncers you are Leeann Cox's guest of honor." Leeann kissed Charlie's cheek and then strolled off.

He finished his drink then walked out into the lobby of the hotel to use the bathroom because there wasn't a restroom inside the restaurant lounge part. He walked into the bathroom followed by a giant heavyset man. Charlie's hair on the back of his neck stood up. As he walked up to the urinal the man struck him from behind. Then tossed him onto the sink and into the mirror cracking his forehead open. The villain pulled a gun which Charlie was able to gain control of the man's right hand and snap the man's wrist causing him to drop the weapon. Charlie then did two rapid actions kicking the man in his man business then taking the palm of his right hand and ramming the man's nose bone into his skull. Charlie then hid the body deep inside a broom closet inside the bathroom.

He used the bathroom then exited into the lobby where he had a gun shoved into the back of his head and two other big guys walked up in front of him.

"Put your hands behind your back." The man with the gun spoke.

Charlie complied and got handcuffed. He looked around and saw no other guests in the hotel lobby, and all hotel employees were going about their regular business like this was an everyday occurrence. A black pillowcase was placed over Charlie's head which was secured by one of the men tying a rope around Charlie's neck to hold the pillowcase in place. They ushered him outside and placed him into the back of a minivan and took off.

They probably only drove for thirty minutes but to Agent Johnson it felt like several days. He was brought inside a giant room and was made to sit in a chair unbound.

<u>ER</u>

Billy sat in a private room on a hospital bed with his wife sitting beside him.

"Baby it will be ok." Ashley said.

"No, it won't. I want to stay involved in the action."

Ashley kissed her husband's cheek "It will be ok. Even the star athletes get sidelined for awhile. Just stay home get your knee better then you can come back in tip top shape."

"Ok." Billy replied sobbing a little before he kissed his wife.

About that time the doctor walked in with the X-Rays. "Detective Coatman as you have been told before you need knee surgery. I am just going to shoot straight from the hip. You are going to be very messed up if much more damage gets done to your knee. We don't have the staff to do the surgery today because we are overrun with so many tragic cases. So, continue to wear your knee brace until the orthopedic can get you scheduled. We can call you to schedule surgery once the havoc calms down. We will send you home with some more pain killers and we suggest you get plenty of rest. Alternate between cold and heat but we will send you home with a complete set of instructions of how to remedy your situation."

The doctor had his back turned toward Billy and Ashley the entire time. Ashley got down from the bed and walked over and leaned against the wall with her hands behind her back palms against the wall. Billy was facing down at her boots watching as she tapped her right foot.

"Do you understand Mr. Coatman?" The doctor asked turning around.

Billy just nodded About that time the nurse came in with a pair or crutches. The doctor dismissed Billy and hop along Coatman exited into the ER lobby.

The doctor's set Robbie's arm, and him and Cali came out into the lobby. He was told the same thing that he no longer should be a part of this adventure. He called Captain Beckham and Beckham had a desk assignment for him but not Billy. Sophisticated Intimidation and Simply Priceless talked outside. Then Sophisticated Intimidation flew Robbie to the prescient and Simply Priceless flew Billy home and sat him up in bed.

He was pouting like a two-year-old.

"There's no way you can kiss me and make me better or turn back time?" He asked.

"No Billy, you know my various powers only work when they want, and those powers won't work on you right now. I will come back if they kick in. Now get some rest. You're all set up. I put your six favorite superhero movies in our six-disc changing DVD player you have both remotes. I brought you a drink and some snack foods. Just relax and be careful making your way to the bathroom. I will zone in my hearing and my heart and mind to keep a close eye on you. Just rest, and don't go trying to do anything stupid because I took all keys to all vehicles. Now rest and remember you still must listen to me….

"I know, I know, now kiss me and get back to work." Billy smirked.

Priceless gave Billy a passionate kiss. Then she told her hubby "Bye" and was gone before he could blink his eyes.

"Man, I love that girl." He said to himself leaning back and going to sleep.

Bio-Chem

Terrorists dressed in technician's uniforms were at the Marta station. They were placing small bombs that appeared to look like security cameras in various spots that there weren't any. Inside those imposter cameras were mustard and chlorine gas which was about to be unleashed upon unsuspecting Marta users. The terrorist planted the cameras in other areas of town as well. Nobody was expecting what was going to happen next.

Once the cameras were finished at the Marta station one of the terrorists told the supervisor of the Marta station that his group would be back tomorrow to finish the wiring so they can view the sections of the station the cameras are located. The terrorist team leader explained to the Marta station supervisor, "With all this terrorism the guys forgot to pack the right wiring." Then he left speeding back to the main hideout!

<u>Four Noutes</u>

The Four Gods and Bomback were standing in a circle discussing their plan of action. It was apparent that Bomback would answer to and have no superiority over the Four Gods. The names of the Four Gods are Shahrzad Yousef, Saed Al-Shafai, Ahmad Abualsami, and Abu Moosaq.

"Where's the bomb?" Shahrzad spoke gruffly.

"It will be here today we are planting it in two days in the middle of downtown when we drive it to its location in the SWAT team van, we acquired." Mr. Bomback spoke.

Mr. Bomback seemed nervous. He stood there a bit shaky, and his teeth kind of chattered as he spoke.

"We are arranging more suicide attacks again tonight and we are sending men out with rocket launchers to begin a full-scale attack against all police prescients and fire houses."

"That's great Mr. Bomback but I hear you are having problems with some girl." Al-Shafai spoke coldly.

"We got that covered." Mr. Bomback lied his ass off about Simply Priceless.

"Did you not do your research all evil doers around the world know about Simply Priceless and Sophisticated Intimidation." Mr. Moosaq chimed in.

"We will take care of this little dilemma, trust me."

"You know Ockmed and Mr. Reed are going to be very upset if this mission fails. We have more troops coming in tonight to counter act the damage the super bitches have done already." Shahrzad added to the conversation.

"The cyber attack is still going good soon all communication will be down within the next forty-five minutes. They don't know about the nuclear bomb or any of the suitcase bombs which are being planted around the city as we speak, the viral attack will go as planned, and I didn't tell you this, but I arranged to fly another person here infected with a deadly virus in case the federal agents stopped my original germ monster at Hartsfield Airport. He will be here late tonight about the same time the chemical agents go off around town, and we have a man inside the White House to kill the President of the United States." Mr. Bomback boasted.

"A man inside the White House?" The Four Gods spoke at the same time.

"Yes, he is a Secret Service Agent to the President! He is going to kill him tonight on national television when the President is being interviewed during his press conference for all the World News Stations."

"It's not that we don't trust you, but I would like you to send two main leaders into the field to oversee this process. Got anybody in mind?" Mr. Moosaq asked in an authoritative voice

"Makin and Abdul."

"Great do you know when my son is coming?" Shahzad asked.

Shahzad's son was who purchased the property where the cyber attack was stationed previous.

"He should be here any minute." Bomback answered.

"Great, you're dismissed solider." Mr. Moosaq commanded.

The Four Gods went into a conference room and stretched out in chairs and couches. Makin and Abdul were notified of their mission by Bomback then Bomback went and smoked a cigarette.

"We still going to attack the GA Dome, CNN Center, Phillips Arena, and Turner Field tonight?" Abdul asked.

"Yes Makin, I organized our own men, I say it is time to go into business for ourselves."

Makin and Abdul shook hands.

I Am Your Father

Billy lay in bed drifting in and out of sleep. While at the base camp which was set up inside the Georgia Dome Jim was flipping out. "No! No! No! Why him? Why?" He was acting like someone just killed Sean or even Billy.

"Snap out of it and be professional." Sean ordered shaking his friend, best friend at that, and colleague.

"You don't understand I can't work around him. He will criticize every…

"There's my boy." A man walked into the room standing at five foot eleven inches weighing around two hundred pounds with a bald head wearing glasses and dressed in his General Army Military Uniform went up to his son.

"Hello again General." Agent Black politely spoke extending his hand.

"Why so serious Sean call me Jim. Everybody else around here can call me General. What son not going to speak to your old man?"

GBI Agent Turner stood there with a sour look on his face.

"Son is this still about Emma?"

Jim began to seriously have an OCD ponder back flashback from hell moment.

Future Georgia Bureau of Investigation Agent Jim lies in bed hearing his dad yell at him from down the stairs. "Little Jim get your ass down her!" General Jim Turner yelled.

Little Jim got up in his boxer shorts and proceeded to put the clothes back on his body that he wore that day on his date with Emma.

Emma and Jim had been going together for over a year, and they had the discussion that night of marriage. This was brought on by Emma hinting around at the Italian Restaurant that she may be pregnant. Little Jim didn't know what to think about this. He had a future to take care of. He loved Emma. He knew Emma would be the one he would marry one day but he wasn't ready to jump start a family life at that moment with his future in the GBI lying ahead.

Little Jim packed a bag and stormed out into the hallway. He looked over the wooden balcony and yelled "Get the fuck out of my way dad, I am done! I am done with your bullshit!"

"Damn it, son….

Jim went to the steps and walked up three steps and just stood.

"Look dad I hate to be disrespectful but if you come up here, I am probably going to knock your head clear off! So, move!"

"I am not going to fight you." The General walked back down to the floor. "If you want to fuck your life up, go right ahead."

"I love her dad. Ok, I love her. Unlike you I actually have feelings." Jim walked toward the top of the steps.

"I have feelings son. Just because I am hard as nails doesn't mean I have feelings so if you are going to go, go!" Jim yelled then opened the front door and walked back to his bedroom.

Little Jim thought for a split second then stomped down the stairs, stormed out the door not even shutting it

"I don't wish to talk about it, father. Now do your General duties. Since the United States Army is coming on scene to help or take over the effort to stop these rag heads, so which is it?" Jim asked with a smart mouth.

General Turner just walked off.

<u>Mayhem</u>

The other terrorist Mr. Bomback was speaking of arrived and Makin and Abdul got the troops together. They had over fifty men ready to go on the following mission. They talked to a fellow brother in the cause Liron Aaban. Liron was ready to rock and roll.

Billy turned off the superhero movie he was watching which didn't even play a fourth of the way through its run-time. The time Billy was able to watch was only about forty-five minutes. Ashley "Simply Priceless" Hatch-Coatman never came to check on him. He wondered constantly what they were doing. He had a heating pad on his leg and took some pain killers. He was feeling pretty good when Buffy jumped up on the bed beside him. This was actually; Buffy the second or Buffy the third. Buffy is a Golden Labrador. Buffy is a name Billy named all of his Golden Labs and is named after Buffy from Buffy the Vampire Slayer.

Buffy laid her big block head on Billy's stomach. Then she licked his neck and cheek. He kissed the top of her head then turned on the TV. President DiBIase was about to address the world behind him stood two secret service agents.

"Mr. President! Mr. President! The reporters chanted."

"I am taking no questions at this time so sit down and listen to what I got to say!" The President spoke very hateful.

The reports got the point and zipped their lips. Some noted how hateful President DiBIase was. He was always like that though. He said more than once whenever something bad happened that he wondered whom ass to kick. He would say this to news reporters, and it got mixed reviews from the American people! It must not have hurt the American people's feelings too much because this was President DiBIase's second term in office.

"I am just going to be straight up. I am going to wage war against the Middle East. Due to a captured terrorist, I know what countries are doing this, and those countries will be feeling the wrath of the United States in the near future. The War on Terror has officially rebegun. The damn thing shouldn't have ended anyway. We had a mission we didn't complete due to the pussy democrats in power but now that the republicans reign supreme the war is back on! It is time for the world to see that we will not fear our foes. That America will stand up in the face of danger, and we will bitch slap whoever is trying to harm us in anyway. We will not fear! We will not die!"

That was all the President got out because now standing behind him was the newest member of his Secret Service team. Since the other Secret Service Agent walked off to send a text message to his Mistress. Not a Dominatrix but the Mistress he was cheating on his beautiful young pregnant wife with. The secret service agent who just recently received the approval to work with the President of the United States removed his weapon and fired a bullet through the back of the President's skull. Blood and brain fragments splatter on top of a female cameraman in the front row. Several Secret Service Agents entered the area as the news media fled. The secret service agents pulled their guns on the guy. He threw down his gun without the Secret Service Agents who had laser sights on the murderer giving him an order to do so. The Middle Eastern Secret Service murderer said some sort of angry rage filled speech in Arabic then reached into his pocket pulled out a small game stick. He pressed the controller and blew himself up which killed most of the people in the room, and severely injured the rest.

The TV screen went black. Billy sat up in bed speechless. He couldn't believe what he just saw. He began flipping through the TV channels. On every channel it spoke of the President's demise. It was like nine eleven all over again because there wasn't a channel with regular scheduled programming. Every channel just had the biggest news story in the world playing on it. Billy laid back down closed his eyes and began to beat the bed.

Vice President Riley was brought to a secret hiding place which was more secure than Fort Knox and was sworn in as the new President of the United States. The first thing he ordered was for the bomber to hit the sites of interest in Iraq, Afghanistan, Iran, Palestine, and the other various spots the terrorist Billy captured mentioned to the authorities.

A limousine pulled up outside the terrorist location. A person exited the limo dressed in a black robe. His face was completely covered. It is unaware if the person was male or female. The person came up to the door. The door opened and Bomback stood there with his gun drawn pointed in the persons face.

"Show yourself." Bomback ordered.

"It is eight thirty shouldn't you get ready for prayer?" The masked person spoke in Arabic.

Bomback began to put pressure on the trigger and yelled in Arabic "Show yourself! You miserable fool or you will be seeing those virgins in our heaven."

"You will regret it if you pull that trigger! Now move so I can come inside." The person said as it began to rain."

"Bomback, holster your weapon. If you kill him death will be a paradise compared to what will happen to you." Ahmad Abualsami ordered.

Bomback backed off. The person walked in and flipped the hood off his head. It was the number one terrorist on the FBI most wanted list Yusuf Al-Qaradawi. He has been performing terror attacks all over the world. His last attack happened in Russia at a KGB secret headquarters which killed everyone in sight. His group kidnapped a secretary that worked for the KGB who ratted out the secret building before she was murdered. He has also hit the MI5 headquarters on Millbank in London along with Ireland at a G-2, Army Ranger Wing, and Au Garda Siochana. He has also hit the OECD Financial Action Task Force on Money Laundering and Interpol.

The other three of the Four Gods were downstairs by that point greeting Yusuf. Everybody knew business was about to pick up.

Numerous men were out just sitting suitcases down in parks and other public areas. While others went to various places and blew themselves up. The war picked up again. There was so much action Simply Priceless and Sophisticated Intimidation had no clue where to start. Explosion after explosion took place as jeeps drove to fire houses and police stations firing rockets into them

Meanwhile at three hotels in downtown twenty men took over the lobby and sealed the door. It was like something out of famous action movie. National Guard soldiers were shooting it out with terrorist in the middle of the street. Billy was watching the carnage unfold live on national television. He could even hear gunshots in the distance.

Billy got up and got his gun just in case he needed it because the gunshots sounded like they were creeping closer and closer. He sat at the foot of the bed holding his 9mm watching TV wondering what Simply Priceless was doing.

Simply Priceless and Sophisticated Intimidation split up. Simply Priceless landed outside of one of the hotels that were taken over. She began to do a quick hand battle with one terrorist. She wound up picking him up and hurling him through the air from several feet away from the hotel through the front glass door. She walked up a set of steps and began to get fired upon. The bullets exploded as they hit her body. It was like she was being electrocuted the sparks on her suit.

"You know I really hate that!" Simply Priceless yelled.

Simply Priceless clapped her hands as hard as she could and the terrorist in the lobby flew through the air and into the wall. Simply Priceless walked into the hotel. The shards of glass crunching beneath her feet. She picked up each man's gun that was knocked out in the lobby and heated up her hands with her mind turning her hands into a flame melting each one of the guns down.

Meanwhile basecamp had a visitor. Army soldiers were in a warzone outside as several terrorist units pulled up. The terrorist outnumbered the army soldiers! It was easy for them to takeover. They entered the Georgia Dome. A gun battle erupted but it was useless. It didn't take long at all for the terrorist to have the people inside who were standing above those good guys that were bound on the ground. Those good guys bound included Robbie, Sean, and Big and Little Jim. The terrorist planted bombs all over the Georgia Dome. There were enough explosives where the Georgia Dome wouldn't just need a paint job when the explosives exploded because the Georgia Dome was going to be brought down to rubble.

Billy didn't get left out of the action because the door entering the loft apartment was kicked in. Buffy jumped down off the bed and Billy stood up. A man was walking down the hallway. Buffy pounced him and was attacking him. The man was getting mauled by Buffy. Billy fixed that terrorist pain with a bullet going into the man's right eye and exiting the back of his skull.

"Buffy, come here!" Billy yelled.

Another man came into the Luxury Loft Apartment and Billy fired a round into the arm the man was holding his handgun in. The terrorist dropped his gun and Billy kicked it away. The terrorist was bleeding bad. Billy fired a round into each of the terrorist's kneecaps then began to question the terrorist as soon as the terrorist hit the floor.

"How many are you?" Billy asked very loudly. Buffy began to maul this terrorist too.

"Get your dog off me." The man spoke in English.

"Fuck you. How many of you are there?"

"Damn it, dude get your dog please." The terrorist begged.

"You're not an active listener rag head how many of you are there, and if you don't answer me, I am going to command my slayer here to bite your nuts off!" Billy yelled.

"Ok! Ok! There are five! Three are outside, but they will probably be coming up soon!"

"Good boy." Billy talked to the terrorist like he was a dog and patted his head. Then Billy ordered Buffy to attack the terrorist's man area. The terrorist jerked on the floor in pain as Billy kicked the terrorist's chest with his good leg even though Billy was in extreme pain as he used his bad leg to support him. The terrorist was bloodied and battered, and he was too broken physically and emotionally to move. Billy pulled a pump shotgun out of the closet before shutting Buffy up inside that same closet.

Billy walked down the short hallway between the living room, and the bedrooms of the Luxury Apartment. The defeated terrorist in the hallway was rolling around in pain. Billy put that terrorist out of his misery like he was Old Yeller. Billy motionless fired two shots into the terrorist's face.

The well-trained detective placed his 9mm in the back of his pants. The gun was loaded and ready to go. A terrorist was coming up the steps outside as Billy stood in the doorway of the entrance to the Luxury Apartment. Billy fired a quick round into the man's chest. He went backward and rolled down the steps. The terrorist's chest wound killed him but the terrorist breaking his neck by the time he reached the parking lot of Ashley "Simply Priceless"

Hatch-Coatman's Luxury Apartment was an added insult to injury. Before the other two terrorist on scene had time to react Billy fired a round into the gas tank of their jeep causing a huge explosion! The two terrorists remaining at Billy's family resident now were caught on fire by the jeep blast. They ran around like a couple of chickens with their head cut off! Their flesh slowly melted away from their body. Billy walked back into the house after he saw the terrorist who were on fire fall to the ground dead. The lethal weapon then got in the closet with Buffy hoping to see Simply Priceless very soon!

Simply Priceless used her X-Ray vision and looked up at the ceiling. She saw numerous terrorists on each floor. She knew she would be tired after all this was over with! Simply Priceless would be sure her hubby's hands won't be broken so he could give her a nice long foot massage that would include some sexy toe sucking. How she loves having her toes sucked. It just makes her tingle all over. Billy knows if he wants something and she says no he can just play with her feet, and she will give him what he wants on average.

Billy believes that playing with his wife's dominant feet is a way to get sex especially when she is not ready to give it up. Billy thinks he scored a lot of sex that was not originally wanted to put out sex by playing with his wife's feet but that certainly is not true. Ashley Hatch-Coatman just uses her husband worshiping and playing with his wife's feet as foreplay so in the end they both can have what they want. Especially since Billy isn't always into the foreplay side of a sexual experience, and Ashley Hatch-Coatman needs the foreplay experience when going all the way. This was in order to enjoy her sexual experience because foreplay makes Ashley Hatch-Coatman feel loved.

"Ali? Ali? Are you there Ali?"

Simply Priceless picked up the radio. "Ali can't come to the phone right now this is Simply Priceless how can I help you?"

The terrorist who radioed Ali didn't respond because he was too much in fear. The signs of seeing a horror movie scarier than The Exorcist read all over the terrorist's face that radioed for Ali. The fright night continued as Simply Priceless went into the stairwell and flew up to the next floor. When she walked out into the hallway from the room she crashed upward into. Simply Priceless was immediately stabbed in the side. The knife just bent. "Now! Now! Didn't your mother ever tell you not to play with knives?" Priceless said then did a sidekick to the terrorist in the stomach.

The man bent over with the air knocked out of him! Simply Priceless then hooked the terrorist's head and fell backward dropping him on top of his head. She learned this move watching wrestling with Billy. The move is called a DDT. She got up and began to walk down the hallway when she heard screaming in one of the rooms. She kicked the door down and saw a guy attempting to rape a younger girl a few years below the legal age to consent to sex if this was consensual sex. Simply Priceless blew hard. The force of the air knocked the terrorist who was attempting to rape the 16-year-old through the window shirtless with his pants around his ankles. The man fell from that top floor down onto the pool deck.

"Get in the closet and hide. Don't come out till one of the good guys gets you. Got it!" Simply Priceless ordered. The girl was in too much shock to respond. She just did as Simply Priceless ordered as Atlanta's superhero continued her mission to get these terrorists out of this hotel. She knew as she acted out her superhero actions that if the proper authorities on the city's payroll didn't step up their game and take back over the other hotels then she had two more to sweep.

"What do you do?" A terrorist asked Robbie.

"Go to hell."

"We are in hell! Can't you see that we are Satan's minions? Now watch your smart mouth or I will shut it by jabbing my gun in there, and making you suck it like a dick before blowing your head off."

Robbie spit on the guy. The guy picked up Robbie and carried him out just as Sophisticated Intimidation walked in. She was being attacked by four people at once. She spun around real fast which the air knocked them down. She kicked one of the men in the face which broke his nose and knocked all his front teeth out. A terrorist began shooting at her. She countered that by firing lasers at the guy catching him on fire. A terrorist tried to run up behind her. She caught him in the nose with a back elbow. Then swiftly like some ice skater Sophisticated Intimidation turned around and snapped his neck.

The terrorist began to flee the scene as Sophisticated Intimidation took care of the remaining terrorist. Sophisticated Intimidation began to break people from their bounds since she exterminated the terrorists that were at the Georgia Dome. She asked Little Jim where

Robbie was at as she was freeing the Original Gangster Simply Priceless team, and he explained the terrorist left with Robbie. Sophisticated Intimidation swallowed hard as she broke the OG Simply Priceless Team all from their bounds. Once people were free, they took off running out of there and were rushed to safety just in time as the GA Dome exploded into a pile of rubble!

Sophisticated Intimidation took to the air trying to find her man once all these innocents were brought to safety.

In downtown a group of terrorists led by Makin took over CNN Center where news anchor, producers, and writers just to name some of the news crew were heavy at work. Makin had a group of terrorist plant bombs there as a beginning task for his terror team to layout. Makin was sitting on top of a desk just watching and making sure his men did everything right. Makin demanded that everything be up to par and go as planned on this mission.

Bomback and the other terrorist just got up from their knees after praying to Allah. They watched on the TV what kind of hell was being unleashed on the city of Atlanta. The city would have never guessed so many terrorist Islamic Cells from the United States joined part in this massacre in Atlanta, and how many people were flown in to contribute to the rampage that was underway on the city of Atlanta which was a city that faced so much terror and destruction all ready as is covered inside the Simply Priceless timeline.

The guy with the virus landed on a runway controlled by the terrorist. He was met by medically educated terrorist in bio-suits and was ushered to a nice large private residence that terrorist took over. The man sat the kitchen table sicker than a dog for a total of three hours before being brought to a full restaurant of innocent people to spread the airborne virus to. The sick man was sealed inside the restaurant with innocent bystanders sick and coughing as the restaurant guests were ordered to continue normally with their dinners and they would not get harmed. The terrorists did not plan on killing anybody in that restaurant. The terrorists planned on releasing them back into the city to affect other people with this gain of function virus their human germ was infected with and was affecting the air as he was sick and coughing inside a restaurant that was perfectly sealed to conceal the germs inside the restaurant that everybody was passing back and forth among each other.

Sophisticated Intimidation flew all around the city. All Intimidation saw was burning buildings. She had no clue what to do. Her head wasn't clear at all. She was lost in her own mind thinking of her love machine Detective Robbie Brewer. Thinking how much she loved her love machine and thinking of how much she couldn't wait to marry her black knight and have beautiful babies with him. She knew Robbie could be just as good of a father as Billy if not better. She of course is bias as she feels Robbie is better than Billy! Even if she does see how Billy holds her sister up on a pedestal. Maybe she is a little bit bias? Maybe, shoot she is! Robbie is like a king in her eyes. He is royalty. She was his Goddess, however and Robbie lived to make his Goddess happy! Right now, however, she didn't even want to imagine what was being done to her lover.

Robbie was brought to the main terrorist hideout along with a CNN cameraman. They brought both restrained men were brought to the back of the main terrorist hideout where the terrorist had a television set up complete with a stage and proper decoration for professional on-air broadcasting. The terrorist running the camera got in position. The CNN cameraman and Robbie were placed into trunks. The live feed to CNN news that was taking place on television just showed the set of the Islamic Terrorist there at the main terrorist hideout.

Suddenly Bomback put on a ski mask and walked out in front of the camera.

Blood Money

Bomback was holding a book when he began a long drug out speech which he had to pause and take several breaths to finish "O ye who believe! The law of equality is prescribed to you in cases of murder; the free for the free, the slave for the slave, the woman for the woman. But if any remission is made by the brother of the slain, then grant any reasonable demand, and compensate him with handsome gratitude, this is a concession and a mercy from your Lord. After this whoever exceeds the limits shall be in grave penalty."

Bomback cleared his throat. "For the children of Israel, the punishment for the crime was Al-Qisas only and the payment of blood money was not permitted as an alternate. But Allah said to this nation O you who believe Qisas is prescribed for you in case of murder."

Bomback cleared his throat again. Bomback shifted his position feeling very full of himself. "Remission in this verse, means to accept the blood money in an intentional murder. Then the relatives should demand blood money in a reasonable manner means that the demand should be reasonable, and it is to be compensated with handsome gratitude."

Bomback was fixing to get to the point, and he was getting very excited about it. "The law of Qisas was prescribed for the children of Israel, but the Diya so Allah said to the nation. O you who believe! The law of Al-Qisas is prescribed for you in cases of murder: the free for the free, the slave for the slave, and the female for the female. But if the relatives of the killed forgive their brother, then the relatives should demand blood money in a reasonable manner and the killer must pay with handsome gratitude. This is an alleviation and a mercy from your Lord, so after this, whoever transgresses the limits shall have a painful torment."

A terrorist in a clown mask walked over and took the book. Bomback scolded the man on camera for wearing a clown mask and slapped him hard. Then he returned to his official business.

"What I just read clearly points out the Almighty Allah used to punish to those who commit intentional murders among the People of Israel. This law remains in effect in Islam, and killing the murderer is still a valid law in Islam, but there is however another alternative in these corrective measures, and that is accepting by choice the blood money. If the relatives of the slain person wish to have an open and forgiving heart such as myself, then they can forgive the murderer under the condition that he compensate them with money for the slain victim. The demand should be reasonable. If the relatives do not wish to forgive the murderer, then he is to get executed by the Islamic ruling authority."

Finally, Bomback got to the point. "Years after years you have invaded our countries, we are punishing you now under Islamic law with murder. You have held us back from nuclear technology. Atlanta is only the beginning. I can have hundreds more join our cause, and we will crush the United States. A nuclear bomb is going to go off in Atlanta in 48 hours so set your watch unless you are willing to pay the blood money for us to forgive you. I figure if the United States Government under your new President Mr. Riley comes together you can come up with 100 billion dollars. Consider it another bailout. We want a 100 billion dollars and immunity. We want to be sent back to our home countries with the same agreement John Fitzgerald Kennedy made with Cuba that you will not attack us. You don't bother us we won't bother you. One more thing no sanctions on us, and we are allowed to work on a nuclear program with the agreement we will not fire one at you. Cross my heart hope to die but I can't promise Israel will still be around." Bomback burst into laughter. Then the news feed cut off.

Let's Play Get Away

Charlie's vision was blurred when the hood was pulled from his head. Agent Johnson was securely chained to a chair. He found himself in a plain white walled room with an emerald-green tile floor. There were rows of florescent lights above head. A bathtub was behind Agent Johnson. Charlie could barely breath because every time he did Charlie was faced with the smell of decay. Blood was splattered all over the floor and the walls like an artist would splash paint on a canvas.

The blood on the walls and floor resembled a faulty timed artist trying to paint a portrait under a time restraint time limit. Those skilled artists usually have their professional looking portrait complete inside the time they allot themselves and their portraits turn out more like a professional tattoo artist placing a perfect resemblance of a celebrity or a common man on someone's body other than a crack head painting like Hunter Biden would make spitting paint through a straw!

There was one person in the room with Agent Johnson sitting on a stool in front of Charles holding a cattle prod. Two heavily armed men stood outside the door. Charlie was just now getting his awareness back when the questioning began to fly his direction.

"Who sent you."

"I'm sorry." Charlie replied playing dumb.

"Don't play dumb with me American! Who do you work for?" The guy questioned then fired up the cattle prod.

"I'm from America. That means I am unemployed."

The man shocked Charlie with the cattle prod. Agent Johnson jerked as the volts of electricity went through his body.

"I'm not playing games." The terrorist threatened.

Agent Johnson has been trained to endure a lot of pain, and not speak. They were going to have to kill him because they weren't going to get anything out of him.

"Don't make me cut out your tongue."

"You're really going to get me to talk that way dumb ass." Charlie said then spit in the terrorist's face.

The terrorist wiped off the spit then shocked Charlie some more. The terrorist then stood up and quickly kicked Charlie in his right knee. The terrorist quickly punched Charlie twice in the left then right side of Charlie's face.

The terrorist interrogating Charlie was average build. The terrorist was about Agent Johnson's size; no bigger.

The pain Charlie felt still hurt like hell that this terrorist was placing on Agent Charles Johnson.

"I'm not going to ask you again." The terrorist demanded.

Charlie's forehead was still bleeding. The man walked over to a counter and pulled out a box of salt. He sat it down on the stool.

"I'm sorry I don't understand the question." Charlie replied casually.

The terrorist pulled out a knife and evilly jabbed it into Charlie's knee. He pulled it out then poured salt in the open wound. Then he put salt into Charlie's forehead wound and threw it into Charlie's eyes.

The man began to repeatedly stab Charlie's leg with the small but very sharp knife. He poured salt in the wounds. Charlie bit his lower lip in pain so hard it was bleeding. Charlie didn't like the metallic taste of his own blood.

"Ok. Ok! You want to know? I'll tell you." Charlie yelled

"Who?" The man yelled back.

Charlie whispered softly. The terrorist couldn't understand Agent Johnson. Charlie just kept whispering until the terrorist got close enough for Charlie to headbutt him. Then Charlie kicked the terrorist between the legs. The terrorist fell to his knees Charlie wrapped his unbound legs around the terrorist neck and snapped it quickly. The spy tipped his chair over Charlie was able to reach into the terrorist's pocket and find the chain keys. Charlie was able to unlock himself. Then he pulled a gun out from the dead terrorist's pants.

Agent Johnson then retrieved the man's cell phone. It was a newer blackberry. Charlie walked up to the door. There was no way to open it from the inside. Charlie kicked the bottom of the door twice real hard. When the guard on the outside of it opened the door up, he fired two bullets into the man's chest. Then he fired a third round into the second guard's head. The CIA agent walked out into the hallway but not before dragging the two dead guards inside the interrogation room and shutting the door.

The salt and pepper colored hair man hid in a corridor trying to call out, but he didn't have a signal. Charlie pocketed the phone then quickly noticed the cameras. "I'm getting too old for this shit." Charlie said the classic Murtaugh quote from the Lethal Weapon movie and television franchise to himself!

He timed the motioned of the cameras then went under all the cameras. Charlie was outside a double door. The door was keypad locked with both a hand censor and a key passcode pad. Lucky a guy was coming through the door. Charlie kicked the men in the chest the grabbed him slinging him against the wall. He struck the guy face first into the wall shattering his nose and busting out his top row of teeth. Then Agent Johnson bent the man back where his back was arched, and he was facing the ceiling and jerked his own body weight snapping the man's neck. Then he entered through the door.

He found himself in a computer customer service setting. There were people on phones talking to other people. Charlie just walked through there like he owned the place, but he walked in a cautious manner. It was part of the outsourcing America had been doing over the years. The place Charlie found himself in was a debt collection agency.

He made his way to the other end of the room. A door swung open with an armed guard with a machine gun. Charlie fired a bullet into the man's skull then took his machine gun and draped it around his neck. He also took the man's radio. He walked up the set of steps as far as it went then opened the door. He appeared to be in a housing area. There were numerous armed guards in there sleeping of cots. There had to be at least fifteen or twenty.

"God damn it! I'm fucked!" Charlie said to himself as he found himself in a real-life version of that Bugs Bunny cartoon where Bugs Bunny must go through the lair of sleeping lions.

Then Charlie saw an air vent on the left-hand side wall between two cots where armed guards were sleeping. Charlie flipped the radio off. He didn't want anyone to talk and wake up the sleeping lions.

Charlie lowered himself on his belly and began a military crawl. He just closed his eyes and prayed to whoever was listening to get out of their alive.

He had somebody special on the other side of the world. It was someone he dated after the relationship with Billy's mother ended for good after Billy's mother's death. Miranda was the love of his life. Even though they rarely dated anymore he still loved her. The job got in the way as always. They came close to marriage once or twice, but it always fell through. She had enough. She told him when he was ready to give up playing spy then she would talk to him about marriage once again. She wound up dating Steve for a little while. It shouldn't be classified as a date. Agent Cole was there for her at various times of need in her life. She didn't care for him the way she did Charlie, however. She loved Charlie but Charlie was too bullheaded to see that about hers and Steve's relationship was just a friendship. It was a friendship that only developed because Charlie introduced them. Charlie and Steve used to be close prior to the point Charlie believed Agent Cole was making moves on his woman. Agent Johnson and Agent Cole played golf together all the time. Agent Johnson always beat Cole out of his money which was funny. Agent Johnson also kicked Cole's ass a few times when he believed he was getting too close to Miranda Both CIA Agents had jealousy toward the other only Charlie didn't catch onto Miranda's signals because Charlie had nothing to worry about.

Charlie thought about how much he loved Miranda, and he knew if he made it through this mission in the Middle East he would finally retire. In fact, he was going to call the CIA Director and retire as soon as he made it to the extraction point.

Agent Johnson made it between the cots. One of the terrorist's hands fell beside him and missed Charlie's shoulder. Charlie was sweating at this point. Finally, he was able to stick his head in the air vent. Then his body all the way down to his feet. He began to ascend the vent trying hard for the machine gun not to swing and hit the metal vent making any noise. He had bad footing and slid a little bit. It had been a while since he had been in this situation. Finally, he was able to pull himself up to level ground when the blackberry went off. It began to play the awfulness chicken squawking ringtone. Charlie pulled it out of his pocket and rejected the call.

The terrorist below him rose in bed and checked their cell phones. Then all began to yell at one another. After that they got up and began a battle royal fighting one another till a man came into the room and called them off one another. Charlie looked. He recognized that man. It was Hassan Mohammed Al-Badawi. He was number two of the FBI most wanted list. It was speculated that he died in a bombing in the Afghanistan mountains but obviously Charlie's eye determined that was just mere speculation.

Hassan Mohammed Al-Badawi was a mad man. He was probably worse than the Four Gods put together. He probably was cheated out of the number one spot on the FBI most wanted list. The guy could never be found. The CIA believed Pakistan's President was hiding him only there was no hard proof to prove fact to that accusation. President Kibler had thoughts of sending the army to invade Pakistan to find Al-Badawi, but she never did do it. That is women for you! A woman can never make up their minds. She feared the nuclear fallout from that decision.

President DiBIase didn't care about such fallouts. President DiBIase had no fear because Pakistan was one of the places the air force was going to strike once the new President of the United States gave the orders to strike back. President Riley planned to follow through with the late President DiBIase's military orders to light those Middle Eastern countries up like a Christmas tree and let all those rag heads say hello to Allah and have an orgy with all their virgins. The assassinated President orders weren't going to change as far as now President Riley was concerned. The bombs would sail. These terrorists waged war on America! Now we are going to stick bombs up their asses, and hopefully they will get the point.

Charlie began to think how he kept he was a CIA Agent from Miranda for the longest. He told her he was a golf pro. He kept his gun locked up in a lock box at the bank and left everyday dressed ready to manage a golf course, but he changed and got his gun and went into the pentagon.

Charlie was in his early sixties. He went through a

few CIA Directors. He had been offered the job of CIA Director, but he didn't want a desk job. He was too fidgety for that. Maybe he suffered from attention deficit hyperactivity disorder or ADHD. Who knows the truth? All he knew was he better get moving.

He crawled and worked his way around the vent like a mouse in a maze. He found an empty storage room. He pushed the grate off and crawled out. He placed the grate back on the vent. Then he saw a small desk. Charlie began to investigate this desk. He found a large hunting knife which he strapped to his leg. He also found plans. They were in some sort of code. Charlie didn't understand it at all although a blueprint nearby was a blueprint of the United Nations.

Charlie thought "what are they doing with this?" Charlie then found information about the President DiBIase execution and how this terrorist group would get someone on the inside to kill the President. The CIA Agent just swallowed. His mouth became dry, and he didn't know which way he was going to go. He looked at the blackberry and got the screen saver off. He had no signal.

"Go figure." Charlie said to himself.

He opened the door to the room he was in just a smidge and saw a large pain window straight ahead at the end of that hallway. There were about six cameras in the hallway that he would have to bypass. He stuck his arm out enough to get a signal on the cell phone. He texted Steve.

Trace this phone jackass and come pick my ass up. Your fat ass was supposed to have my back, but your lazy ass wasn't around when my dumb ass got taken on this stupid mission!

Steve woke up from a little nap when his phone went off. He knew it was Charlie because he was sleeping inside Charlie's hotel room. He called a CIA secret prison slash headquarters in Syria to trace the phone. In a matter of seconds, they gave Steve the location and the ballistics of the compound Charlie was at. Charlie got a text back.

Ok old man if your old wrinkly ass can make it to the roof, I can pick you via helicopter! I am on my way! Don't keep me waiting or I might just leave you there then I will have to be there for Miranda.

Charlie replied….

Fuck you! You, alcoholic golf pro wannabe. Remember who always kicks whose ass now get here and pray I don't kick your ass on the roof and leave you here.

Steve just laughed. He knew how to push Charlie's buttons and exactly which buttons to push. He knew Miranda didn't want him romantically. They never even shared a kiss. Not like Miranda and Charlie. They kissed so much it was sickening. It didn't matter if it was in public or private, they were always kissing.

Charlie put the blackberry back in his pocket when his location was given away. He couldn't time the camera now. Two armed guards saw the storage room door cracked and somebody standing in the doorway. They made commands in Arabic then acted like they were going to fire. Charlie fired quicker with his machine gun killing them both. He exited out into the hallway. Another guard came around the corner and that terrorist met the same demise.

Charlie collected ammo before he ran toward the window and slid the window open and stepped out on the ledge. He slid the window back closed and glued his body to the building that he slowly crept around. He knew he couldn't look down. He knew if he looked down that he would be screwed.

There were no other windows. Guards inside searched frantically for Agent Johnson. Hassan Mohammed Al-Badawi wanted Charlie's head. Finally, Charlie made it to an incline. The incline was steep, but it led directly to the roof. He began to crawl up it like a monkey. It took five minute to make it up the incline to the roof. The compound was that high. The compound was bigger than the Mall of Georgia. It was like three Mall of Georgia's high. Climbing this reminded him of when he walked up an incline at the hospital Miranda's parents were in with her middle son as a short cut. They got in trouble by hospital security but they both just laughed it off.

Before Charlie got onto the roof, he looked for cameras. There were none in sight. He rolled onto the roof and waited. Either Cole would be there, or terrorist would come out the only door leading up to the roof and kill him or capture him and torture him where he would wish he was dead. Either way it sucked but he didn't know what would be worse; riding in a helicopter along with Agent Cole or being tortured or killed by terrorist.

Charlie thought about Miranda. He couldn't call her yet, but he was going to call her when he got back to DC. If he got back to DC. Hours seemed to pass but it wasn't even twenty minutes. A military helicopter hovered overhead. Charlie looked up and saw Steve motioning for him to get up. Charlie jumped up as Cole lowered the chopper a little bit. Charlie grabbed the railing and pulled himself in the helicopter but not before dropping the blackberry to the ground and stomping it.

The number he texted Steve on didn't exist. It couldn't be traced. If they tried to trace that number, the trace would just bounce them around to several different numbers and never stop. Charlie sat in the back of the chopper speechless knowing that nightmare was over but the adventure with Reed and Hussein has just begun.

<u>**This Luxury Hotel Has Been Turned Into A Pay By The Week Extend-A-Stay Visit**</u>

Simply Priceless was up on the top floor of the first hotel that was taken over. The other two hotels still haven't been taken back over from the terrorist. She was sensing so many things she was tingling all over. Simply Priceless was anxious. Simply Priceless never, well, rarely, gets anxious. She's never been anxious like this though. She felt like she had no superpowers at all. She felt completely human but in a bad way. She was tingling all over, but she tried to fight her way through it. She started having visions. She envisioned Billy in the closet holding Buffy close. She saw Robbie being kidnapped but couldn't see where he was taken. She saw Cali frantic about ready to pull her hair out searching desperately to find her fiancé. She saw the National Guard and a limited amount of Army soldiers being defeated by the terrorists. She then saw a future of the United States in chaos. She saw the explosions of the bombs going off in the Middle East and saw that this would be the beginning of the end of mankind as we know it, and there would be nothing she could do about it.

Sophisticated Intimidation was in an absolute panic. She knew she had to find Robbie. She started having a vision herself. She saw Simply Priceless get hit in the back with a 2x4. Simply Priceless fell to the ground then began to get beat with kicks, punches, and being struck by foreign objects.

"Not so super now are you bitch?" A terrorist yelled looking at a lifeless Simply Priceless.

"Restrain her." Another terrorist spoke.

They handcuffed Simply Priceless hands behind her back then tied her down to a bed. Simply Priceless's eyes were shut, and she was tremoring. It was almost like she was having a seizure. Sophisticated Intimidation knew she had to save her sister, so she rocketed to the hotel and land on the balcony of the room her sister was tied up in. She didn't know what going on as she kicked the sliding glass door in. Bullets were quickly fired in her direction. The terrorist firing them quickly got the point that action of theirs did not work so they ran out of the room. As they ran, they yelled "There's two of them."

Sophisticated Intimidation checked on Simply Priceless. She scanned her body with her X-Ray vision. She found nothing wrong till she scanned her head. Ashley was having rapid manic thoughts. Almost on the level of somebody with bipolar but much worse. Sophisticated Intimidation heard the sirens and heard running footsteps and gunfire. She looked out into the lobby unnoticed and saw the Army and SWAT were there. She quickly jerked her sister out of her binds and flew her out of there, and to the only place she knew to go, Dr. Rod's.

Dr. Rod was at his farmhouse watching the news. Sophisticated Intimidation held her sister like a baby and walked up to the front door yelling for the doctor, "Open up."

Dr. Rod rushed to the door after looking out the window and seeing Simply Priceless in her sister's arms. He ran out onto the porch. "What's wrong?"

"She's having manic thoughts to very high extremes. I used my X-Ray vision and saw the chemicals in her brain moving more than they should."

"Bring her inside." Dr. Rod commanded.

They went inside and the doctor got his kit stethoscope, blood pressure cuff, reflex hammer, ear thermometer, and an otoscope. "God if you are listening give me the strength." Dr. Rod spoke softly.

He started off by getting Simply Priceless's pulse, blood pressure, and checking her heart. Simply Priceless's blood pressure was up, and her heartbeat was elevated but not enough to worry about. He then looked in her ears. They were normal. Dr. Rod had Cali open her sister's mouth and lift her up to look down her throat. That was normal too.

"Ok Cali, get in that bottom right-hand drawer and pull out two syringes. Cali used her telekinesis powers and got what the doctor requested while on her knees hold her sister's hand and stroking Ashley's hair with tears in her eyes. "Now I need the adrenaline and the Geodon and some alcoholic wipes out of the cabinet in the back broom closet that is my pharmacy of sorts."

Cali got those the same way. "Is her brain still acting the same way?"

Cali checked. "Yes doctor."

"Ok I need to get to her hip." Dr. Rod said not knowing how to undo the leather bodysuit.

Cali helped the doctor out. He put the adrenaline in one syringe and the Geodon in the other. "Those needles won't puncture her skin doctor." Cali spoke with concern.

"Just trust me who's the doctor here?" He said as he wiped off Ashley's hip and stuck her with the Geodon that was inside a special syringe that pierced Ashley's skin. He waited about thirty seconds then gave her the adrenalin out of another special syringe. "Carry her to the spare bedroom down the hall on the left. I need to monitor her! I don't know what exactly those drugs are going to do."

"She's not going to die, is she?" Cali shouted which rumbled the cabin the doctor lives in as she fixed Ashley's suit back.

"No, she's not going to die. Her superhero duties are done for one night though. She should be awake within the hour. I just don't know what a 320mg dose of Geodon will do. It could make her sleep longer or make her high, but it should just put her on an even kilter."

Cali thanked the doctor then brought her sister to the bedroom. She kissed the top of Ashley's head and looked once again with her X-Ray vision. The medicine seemed to be helping some. Cali flew to Ashley's apartment where she found Billy hiding in the closet.

"Ashley is sick. She is at Doctor Rod's. Would you like me to fly you there?" Cali asked.

"Yes!" Billy shouted.

Cali first flew Buffy and Ashley's and Billy's other animals to her apartment, and then came back and flew Billy to the doctor's. He laid in bed next to his wife with his head on her shoulder.

<u>Recruit-A-Mania</u>

Meanwhile at the county jail Bomback and his crew shot their way inside. Bomback's crew member began to ask inmates to join their cause. Those that accepted the task lived, and those that didn't; didn't have a fun experience. Other terrorist groups were doing the same thing at mental institutions and back at the federal prison with the inmates at the prison which were still alive. The terrorist army was growing.

Bomback made it to the traitor's cell. "Mr. Bomback, no, please….

"Shut the fuck up. You will have plenty of time for begging later." Bomback explained in a calm and collective manner as another terrorist opened that cell door. Bomback went inside and punched the traitor in the face. Then he rammed his head against his knee. After that two more terrorist came into the cell and shackled and cuffed the person who committed treason in Bomback's eyes.

Buses were drove at all the prison and mental institutions from where the terrorists stole the buses from the Atlanta school system to pick up the terrorist's new recruits from where the Islamic terrorists had Recruit-A-Mania. From the mental institutions they only kept the psychopaths that would be able to listen however they did keep a man they will call Prodigious because the guy was seven foot five over four hundred pounds with a muscular very physically fit body, long blue hair with red highlights, dark eyes, and tan skin. He was sent to the mental institution when he was declared mental insane, and unable to participate in his own trial of one hundred confirmed murders in a thirty-day time span. Billy didn't face off with him, but it took both Simply Priceless and Sophisticated Intimidation to bring him down to their level, and obviously it was time for round 2.

They drove the buses to a separate warehouse other than the main terrorist compound for their orders, and a change of clothes. Terrorist stormed malls and outlet malls to retrieve clothes in every size possible. Prodigious got his clothes he was arrested in from holding at the Federal Mental Hospital, and soon enough it was ready, set, match!

<u>The OG Original Gangsters of Team Priceless Regrouping 99.9% Complete</u>

Dr. Rod looked in the room. Billy kissed Ashley's cheek. Billy looked very concerned and inside he blamed himself for his wife's condition.

"She will be fine Billy. Where the kids?" Dr. Rod stuck his head into the room and spoke to Billy in a low serious reassuring tone.

"Carmella took them out of town to Myrtle Beach. They will be gone until we settle this. They left before everything fully erupted." Billy answered.

"Well, that is good at least you don't have to worry about them." Dr. Rod said.

"I just want to be alive when they comeback."

"You will be fine. Both of you will be." Dr. Rod shut the door and walked off.

Sophisticated Intimidation by this time had left the doctor's country home and flew to the second hotel. There were several dead National Guard, Army along with other military troops plus a lot of Atlanta's SWAT members outside the hotel. Sophisticated Intimidation stepped over dead body after dead body and entered the hotel. She saw a guy by the pool smoking a cigarette with an AK-47 hanging over his shoulder.

Sophisticated Intimidation ran at lighting speed and pushed the terrorist into the water. The man went all the way down to bottom and hit his head. Blood gushed out of his head. Water began to go down his throat and he drowned. Sophisticated Intimidation began to get shot at from behind. She spun around slapped her hands to the side. The bullets went back at the men. The wind from the slap knocked the two men down. Sophisticated Intimidation walked up and kicked one the men who was trying to get up in the side of the face which broke his jaw.

She picked the other one up. Sophisticated Intimidation held the man off the ground. "Where is he?"

The man began to speak Arabic. Sophisticated Intimidation threw him over the check in counter. She jumped the counter then picked the man up again and held him by his throat against the wall. "I am not going to ask you again. The cop taken from the Georgia Dome where is he?" Sophisticated Intimidation was on a one-woman suicide mission to find the love of her life Detective Robbie Brewer.

The man was choking as he tried to speak English. Sophisticated Intimidation turned around with him by the throat then leaned him over the counter pinned down by his shirt. "Let's start over. Where is the cop taken from the Georgia Dome?"

"I don't know?" The terrorist answered.

Sophisticated Intimidation punched the man in the face breaking the man's nose. Blood ran down the man's face into his mouth and down, dripping off his chin. Sophisticated Intimidation threw the man across the room into a glass aquarium wall. The man fell to the ground as water and fish fell on his body. Sophisticated Intimidation jumped the counter and walked over to the guy. She picked him up and leaned him inside the aquarium with his throat over the jagged half aquarium side glass.

"I have no problem cutting your throat. Now tell me who knows."

"Liron Aaban! Liron Aaban! Liron Aaban! Liron Aaban!"

"Where's he at?" Sophisticated Intimidation yelled.

Sophisticated Intimidation is much rougher than Simply Priceless. She will beat the living hell out of someone especially over Robbie. She is very protective of Rob as she refers to him as her little fan boy. There was plenty of times she rather smack-a-bitch than ponder on the consequences of her actions. Sophisticated Intimidation is a hot head, but her fiancé Detective Robbie Brewer could always calm her down. Just the way his eyes met hers with a smile of I love a woman who knows how to watch after what is theirs. Robbie always been turned on by psycho controlling women but not psycho to the point they will cut his dick off in the middle of the night.

"The last hotel that is still taken over. We got word that the authorities have taken back over the other hotel. It is only a matter of time before they get here." The terrorist pleaded. Sophisticated Intimidation didn't listen. She just picked him up by his throat and slammed him through a coffee table. She stepped on the man's throat and choked the life out of him.

She didn't give a damn anymore. She flew straight through the ceiling onto the next floor. She knew no matter how bad she wanted to go save her man that there are people in this hotel that need her help first. She found herself in a suite of the hotel. She walked up to the door and jerked it off its hinge then threw it out the sliding glass door.

Sophisticated Intimidation walked out into the hallway. She grabbed one of the terrorist AK-47 right off him then hit him in the face with the butt of the gun. The guy fell to the ground. Sophisticated Intimidation wasn't done there. She picked the guy up and rammed his head into the wall. Sophisticated Intimidation turned the corner and then another corner, and there were two terrorists. She let out a God-awful scream. The men fell to the ground bleeding from their ears.

That floor was done. She flew through the ceiling again. She wound up in a room with a bound family.

"Simply Priceless?" The mother asked.

"Wrong superhero. How many of them are they?"

"At least twenty." The father answered.

"Just the way I like it....

Sophisticated Intimidation heard sirens. "Sounds like backup is here. Hold onto me." Sophisticated Intimidation grabbed hold of the parents. Their kid climbed onto her back, and she flew them downstairs where two SWAT Team members escorted them to safety. Numerous authorities came into the lobby of the hotel. Intimidation looked up and used her X-Ray vision and saw there were more authorities.

"You got this, guys?" Sophisticated Intimidation stated then walked out.

The people that were in the restaurant that the terrorists group took over began to feel ill. The guy carrying the virus was already died.

"You will be released soon." One of the terrorists in the bio-suits spoke.

Billy moved down to the foot of the bed. He removed his wife's boots and socks. He just dropped them in the floor. He began to massage Ashley's feet. "Wake up Ash. Come on. Please!" Billy kissed the bottom of his wife's right foot. Then he just laid on his back. He closed his eyes tight. Eventually Billy heard the mattress creek, and something shift in the bed.

"Get up here." Ashley commanded. Billy's eyes popped open. "I said get up here, and that means now baby." Ashley repeated sitting up.

Billy got up as fast as he could with his bad knee and pushed Ashley down and climbed on top of her. He just began kissing her very forcefully. She pushed him off her which jarred his leg a little bit. He squinted in pain, but it was better when Ashley kissed him.

"I got to go Billy. I will see you in a little while."

Dr. Rod opened the door. "I heard you talking Ashley. You can't go anywhere tonight. I must monitor you."

"Do you know how the city is right now? I got to go!"

"Ashley you are staying here right beside me." Billy ordered.

"Billy, I don't have to listen to you. I didn't make the agreement to listen to someone for as long as they want! So quit telling me what to do!" Ashley sternly said glowing her eyes red.

"Fine Ashley I am moving out." Billy said.

"What?" Ashley replied.

"If you are going to risk your life when something happened that has never happened before when Cali

"Sophisticated Intimidation" Cooper is perfectly able to handle things and the military is involved then I don't want to be with you. I rather not be with you than have you die on me and us still be together." Billy explained.

"Billy that's not fair. That is just mean."

"Ashley I am serious. You are going to wait till you are cleared by the doctor. If I can't participate till my knee gets better, then till Dr. Rod clears you then you will be on the sideline with me." Billy explained.

Ashley had a pouty look on her face. She looked like she was about to have a temper tantrum. "Fine!" She spoke hateful.

"Don't get that attitude with me baby I love you, and I would kill myself if anything happened to you and we didn't have the kids."

"I know Billy. I love you too. So, what's wrong with me?" Ashley asked very concerned. Ashley had a little voice in the back of her head telling her what kind of medical questions to ask Dr. Rod so she could be taken off the bench, and she would know exactly how to handle whatever caused everything inside her to transpire.

<u>Higher Ups!</u>

President Riley had a DVD delivered to him. He began to play the DVD. The DVD was from Yusuf Al-Qaradawi. Yusuf started the video message introducing himself. Then when the camera panned a young teenage girl who was on her knees only in her bra and panties. President Riley recognized that young teenage girl his sixteen-year-old daughter. About a yard and half in front of the President's teenage daughter was the President's wife beheaded and nude. "Mr. President, I suggest you stop the bombers, or your daughter will meet a similar fate only I think with a body like this… This little bitch would look good on the human slave trade. Yusuf smiled then continued "You know what they say blondes have more fun. You have one hour to make your decision but the quicker you make it the sooner I will let what's left of your family go."

President Riley ran to the red phone on the wall in the room he was alone in. It automatically called the Secretary of Defense at the Pentagon. "Stop the bombers."

The Secretary of Defense was speechless.

"You hear me stop the bombers. I don't want to pursue this. Not right now! Abort! Abort! I repeat abort this mission!"

"Yes Mr. President."

The mission was aborted. A secret service agent walked into the room an hour later. "Mr. President, I guess you took Yusuf Al-Qaradawi's advice." He spoke.

"Excuse me?" President Riley replied.

The secret service agent fired three shots with a silencer on his 9mm into the President's chest then one in the center of President Riley's forehead once he hit the ground. All the people that remained in this secret hiding place who were part of this massive terror cell quickly exited the scene behind everyone's back and headed towards Bomback's headquarters without the other people inside President Riley's hiding hole noticing they were missing in action.

The authorities set up a new work site in another location. They were all outside under a tent. They were standing around talking.

"What's the plan?" Captain Beckham walked up to Jim, Sean, and General Turner.

"We have to get Robbie back." Sean explained

"Where have you been?" GBI Agent Turner asked.

"I have been associating with the SWAT director. They are dropping like flies…

"There are more troops coming." The General spoke coldly.

"How are we going to find Robbie?" Sean asked very concerned.

Everybody was depressed. Billy was out of commission and Robbie was kidnapped. Simply Priceless and Sophisticated Intimidation are God only knows where? Nobody knew what was going on. It was a state of mass confusion and panic unlike any other. It was terrible. Atlanta was a city under attack, and the good guys not knowing where the terrorist would strike next was at a major disadvantage. The terrorist group seemed to be growing in numbers by the seconds. The terrorist multiplied like rabbits. More groups kept joining the cause.

"You ever going to let me back in the game?" Billy asked.

"No." Ashley burst into laughter. "Well maybe." Ashley smiled.

"What does this maybe mean? With women maybe can be yes, maybe can be no, or maybe can, well actually. mean, maybe that they will think about the subject at hand." Billy tried to kiss his wife's lips, but she turned her head. "Don't be like that."

"Well, you are mean to me by not letting me go out and play."

Ashley and Billy seemed like a bunch of teenagers staying up late at a slumber party as they cuddled and went back and forth with their dialogue in Dr. Rod's spare bedroom.

"How about you get down there and…..

Ashley pointed at the end of the bed as the bedroom door slowly opened and what would have been a romantic moment was interrupted.

"Sorry to interrupt a Kodak moment but I need to explain what happened to you Ashley." Dr. Rod came into the room.

Billy and Ashley looked at Dr. Rod very interested.

"You had some sort of bipolar episode of mania. Bipolar can kick in when a person is confronted with certain stressors. There is no single factor that causes bipolar disorder but yours is unique. I don't believe it is bipolar 1 or bipolar 2. It is possible that genetic factors during the process of your creation had a disturbance with your brain chemicals such as your neurotransmitters which provide a biological basis for making a certain group of people vulnerable to bipolar. Neurotransmitter disturbances play a major role in this disorder since neurotransmitters are the chemicals that pass messages between various areas of our brains. Research shows that these individuals with manic depressive illness have an imbalance in these chemicals. Our brains are producing either too few or two many of these chemicals. Very often there is also an overproduction of the stress hormone cortisol. Seeing the fact, you are very stressed because of this massive attack on the city with these terrorists your bipolar or your brain-based problems which is in the bipolar spectrum, which were in hibernation all these years has come out. I will give you some medication to use which will be effective in treating your brain-based problem. It will even out your chemical imbalance. How exactly this medication will affect you I don't honestly know?"

"Will it hurt her?" Billy asked stressed out.

"She will be fine

Dr. Rod continued "The main problem with this Ashley is the equation of stress. Stressors and trigger that tip a person with a biological vulnerability to manic depression over the edge into an episode of depression or mania. I don't believe you will get as much depression as you will mania with your chemical imbalance Ashley but if you go into a huge mania episode your body will shut down like it did. Therefore, I want you to always carry your medication with you. I will meet with Angie my main nurse who is into science because she is also a scientist to develop a special medication to cure the mania high instantly when it strikes. It won't be done overnight but the Geodon injections will work for now. As soon as you start feeling the manic episode coming on give yourself a shot in the knee right away! Like instantly Ashley. I am serious. I don't want to see you get hurt because based on what I notice all your superpowers will seize to exist, and you will be a normal human, with normal human weaknesses. Basically, I am telling you Ashley if they shot you in the chest multiple times then you could die if you weren't taken to the hospital, and hopefully the ER doctors can save you. again" Dr. Rod paused.

"I can't quit being a superhero. I live for it. I am not really the house mom type." Ashley stopped talking because she was about to cry.

Billy noticed her facial expression right away. "No baby, don't cry, please. I love you! We will get through this just like we have anything else." Billy got on top of his wife and wrapped his arms around her. He held her tight. She was hard like steel. Billy could just lean against her because he couldn't move her. He tried to kiss her, but she put a shield up between them after pushing him lightly off her.

"What am I to do doc?" Ashley said sternly.

Her moods were bouncing back and forth. She wasn't on an even kilter at all. It was terrible news for Simply Priceless. She couldn't deal with the fact she might have to quit being a superhero. At least that is what she thought till Dr. Rod said "Ashley calm down, I called Angie and she is working on the injection right now. She should have it to you within the next seventy-two hours."

"Really?" Ashley was excited and removed the shield and let Billy hold onto her again. He just rested his head on her shoulder.

"Ashley it is not a guarantee. We might need your help in the process. All of us in this room know you created the injection to keep roses from affecting you. This is just another obstacle of life. We will get through this. Will you just trust me and try to quit worrying? Any stressor can affect a normal person with bipolar such as financial problems or troubles at their job. Frequently the people regular non super humans obsess internally. Do you? Honestly, we can stress ourselves through the way we think about and interpret the events in our daily lives."

"I'm not stressed in my normal Ashley Coatman life. I am not really stressed as Simply Priceless but with these terrorists I don't know how to stop them, but I know I will. Honestly, I am just worried about Billy, and I miss him being involved with the crime fighting."

"Really?" Billy smiled.

"Yeah." Ashley kissed the top of her husband's head.

"Well, I am not exactly sure what caused this bipolar spectrum but like I said the leading theory I have is something went wrong in your brain when it was developing by the various DNA involved in creating you. I don't think this will affect you much but with bipolar when the certain chemical that has caused your chemical imbalance to come out goes too high you will develop mania. In normal, not saying you are not normal but in the average human with the chemical that cause their bipolar drops too low they will go into severe depression. Like I said it is my diagnose that you will go into mania at times you are very, no we are talking severely stressed like over your husband when a major attack is happening on the city." Dr. Rod finished his long explanation to Ashley "Simply Priceless" Hatch-Coatman's diagnoses.

"When can I get back to work?" Ashley Hatch-Coatman asked in one hundred percent Simply Priceless mode.

"What are you going to do about worrying about Billy?" Dr. Rod asked

"Yeah, baby what are you going to do?" Billy asked.

"I will take him with me to the place everyone is plotting strategy. He can stay there and work on stopping this problem. Then I will know he is involved, and I will be happy. Then he should be happy because he is back in the game. You would like that won't you baby?" Ashley spoke excited.

"Yes Princess. If you promise not to worry about me. I don't want you hurt." He kissed his wife's neck then lightly bit the bottom of her earlobe.

"I'll be fine! Just get my injections that I will have to use before I get my special injections." Simply Priceless order.

Dr. Rod went to do what Ashley Hatch-Coatman in Simply Priceless mode commanded out of him. He knew Simply Priceless was ready to get back in the game.

"Now baby put my shoes and socks back on and do it fast!" Simply Priceless commanded her husband.

Billy didn't say anything. He just did what his wife asked out of him, and he got Simply Priceless footwear back on in time for Dr. Rod to dismiss her. Billy and Simply Priceless thanked Dr. Rod. Dr. Rod brought her a syringe holder which she strapped around her waist. It was a small holder that held six syringes on both sides. It wouldn't get in the way of her crime fighting. It was like two pockets the size of a syringe. It had six slots to put the syringes in. Dr. Rod gave Ashley the medicine and she put the injection in each holder. Then she flew Billy back home. He got his 9mm, and Simply Priceless used her psychic ability to find the base camp. She then flew and landed Billy down there

"You better go to Five-and-Dime Home Specialty Shop and get a door after we wrap this mission up." Ashley whispered in Billy's ear." Then Simply Priceless immediately took off to find Sophisticated Intimidation not waiting for a response.

The new terrorist recruits were at a separate warehouse than the main terrorist compound. It looked like a prison. There were several cells. There was a workout area. There was a designated smoking room. It had a concrete floor which had blood splattered over it. There have been various police officer murders and disappearances which resulted in them being brought here tortured, and their disappearance were unsolved and being investigated by Atlanta PD, GBI, and FBI.

The men were lined up in front of a stage. "Men you were brought here for a reason. All of you announced you would accept Islam. Is that true?"

"Yep! Yep!" The men shouted.

"Good. We are involved in a war. A war which will be won by us. We will take over and crush this great country known as the United States. We will kill anybody and everybody that tries to stop us. We will especially kill those that choose not to accept Islam. A nuclear bomb has been set inside the Georgia Aquarium. That will go off whenever I choose because I hold the detonator around my neck. Isn't this exciting and better than prison?" Bomback explained.

"Yep! Yep!"

Bomback then made the men take the oath of allegiance called hilf al-mutayyabin. The men said…

"Many of the sheikhs of the faithful tribes in the Middle East. We swear by Allah…that we will strive to put a stop to the great snake of the United States, and we will cut its head off to end the oppression to which what our people are being subjected by the malicious United States Government and by the remaining occupying crusaders who are here to help our military in a goose hunt, to assist the oppressed and restore their rights even at the price of our own lives… to make Allah's word supreme in the world, and to restore the glory of Islam…"

"Now men I want you to go take these chemical bombs and plant them where nothing happened yet." Bomback ordered 2as the loading dock door opened and there were four vans full of chemical bombs. The chemicals in the bombs were Tabun which is a nerve agent, Methyldichlorosilane that is a blister agent, and cyanogen chloride that is a blood agent. The men loaded up in the vans and took off. All except Prodigious.

He was sent into a room with the traitor to Bomback's group. The man was standing with his hands bound behind his back. Prodigious pushed the traitor down then stomped the guy's chest which broke his ribs. Prodigious picked the traitor up and threw him against the wall. That broke the guy's back. He was now paralyzed.

The giant began punching the terrorist face breaking every bone in the guy's face. Finally Prodigious snapped the man's neck. Prodigious then walked out of the room like he did not just commit a brutal murder with his bare hands.

"Is it done?" Bomback asked.

Prodigious just nodded. Prodigious never speaks. He hasn't spoken a word since he was thirteen years old and killed his mother, sister, the infant his mother was babysitting, and the family dog. He walked past Bomback and outside listening to sirens.

In his palace Emanuel Reed was meeting with Ockmed Hussein. The men were smoking Cuban Cigars and drinking expensive scotch. They had the world news on watching the chaos at hand.

"Nice, isn't it?" Emanuel Reed said.

"It was my idea." Ockmed replied.

"I'll give it to you. I didn't think you could pull this one off." Reed laughed.

"It's not over with yet. The nuclear bomb still hasn't gone off and neither has the chemical weapons."

"True. True." Reed replied.

"Well Reed, you know it is just a matter of time before they come after us. The CIA will get onto us." Hussein stated with an evil grin.

"I'll take care of the CIA." Emanuel Reed stated with confidence.

"What's this I hear about a guy killing people at your compound?"

Emanuel Reed thought for a second. Then got an angry look on his face. His dark complected face seemed to turn red.

"Sorry Mr. Reed but I am just saying I am not ready for death."

"I don't like what you are implying. It was a fluke. The United States will not come after us especially with my man being President of the United States now." Emanuel Reed laughed his ass off to put it in internet chat te8rms.

"What are you talking about?" Ockmed asked sitting his glass of expensive scotch down on the desk.

"Coaster!" Reed yelled.

"Sorry?"

Ockmed got a coaster and sat his drink on it.

"But what do you mean?"

"The Speaker of the House Alborz Al-Mughassil." Reed laughed hard.

"You're shitting me."

"Nope. "

Emanuel Reed knew he had things his way. Ockmed Hussein believes he is in control because his money helped finance this operation, but it was Emanuel Reed who got the terrorist together. All the men are on his payroll. He is just using Ockmed for his money, and he was about to show him that.

The terrorist from President Riley's hiding spot arrived at Bomback's original hideout which he was back at with the Four Gods while Alborz Al-Mughassil was being flown on Air Force One. They swore him into office up there. His first command as President of the United States was to surrender to the demands of terrorist and hand over the Blood Money. It wasn't a favorable decision between people of the United State Government, but he acted the part saying this violence must stop.

<u>Beat into Submission?</u>

President Alborz Al-Mughassil began a telecast from Air Force One asking for the men responsibly for the CNN broadcast about Blood Money to contact him. He said he is ready to compensate them in the agreeance that the chaos will quit once the terrorist receive their Blood Money. He explained for them to contact the Pentagon, and the Pentagon could patch their leader through to him to make the arrangements. General Turner got messaged on the CB Radio by the Secretary of Defense. "General Turner abort the mission temporally. Call all your troops back and tell them to stand down. President Al-Mughassil is going to pay the terrorist what they are asking."

"Wait what?" General Turner spoke.

"You heard me General. I don't like it either."

"What are you going to do dad?" GBI Agent Turner said.

General Turner stewed while on Air Force One the following conversation took place "President Al-Mughassil we have those responsible for this on video chat."

The President shooed his personnel from the room.

"You ready to comply with our demands?" Bomback acted.

Nobody was in the room but President Al-Mughassil.

The remaining people on the plane were only secret service agents.

"What are we going to do?" A secret service agent spoke to the man in charge.

The head secret service agent's cell went off. He answered. "Can do." He replied.

"What's going on Scott?" another secret service again asked.

"That was the Secretary of Defense. He just ordered me to tell all of us to restrain this so-called President because once he transfers all this money over that he had created an act of treason. If we are going to win this game, we must step everything up a notch!"

President Al-Mughassil sent Bomback the money and opened the door only to have six Glock 9mms in his face like the Men in Black stick their memory zap gizmos into people's faces in that franchise to wipe innocent's memory. "What's going on guys?" Alborz Al-Mughassil put his hands up.

"Alborz Al-Mughassil you are under arrest!" Scott yelled then kick Alborz between the legs. Alborz stumbled back. Agent Burk holstered his weapon then slammed the President against the wall. He pinned him against the wall. "Who are you working for?"

"What do you….

Scott slammed the terrorist ally's face into the wall then slung him to the ground. Agent Burk stomped the traitor's chest knocking the wind out of him. The Presidential traitor fell to the ground.

"You won't stop them you know. There are way too many of them."

"Get up!" Scott yelled.

Agent Burk picked Al-Mughassil up. He grabbed his jugular and pressed him against the wall. He then began to beat him in the head with the bottom of the handle of his gun.

"Don't kill him, Scott!" Another agent yelled.

Alborz Al-Mughassil forehead was split open, and his eyes were black and swollen shut where Agent Scott Burk hit him in the face with the handle of his gun. The President of the United States only by title wore a crimson mask. Alborz Al-Mughassil was breathing his last breathes. Scott dropped him to the ground unconscious

Agent Scott Burk handcuffed the traitor securely to a chair. Then another agent found duct tape and taped the sleazeball into place. Scott called the Secretary of Defense back he asked him what the plan was. The secretary said the plan was simple to fly him around on Air Force One till it is decided who's with the United States, who's against the United States, and where a safe place to land would be not knowing where the terrorist will strike next.

Mission Impossible

After the turncoat President of the United States was turned into sleeping beauty The Secretary of Defense got back in touch with General Turner. "General Turner the mission is back on ignore that last directive."

About that time Little Jim's cell phone went off. He looked down at his Caller ID. It was Emma. He got as far away from people as he could and answered the phone. "Hel…

"Jim." Emma said in tears.

"Baby calm down. Where are you?"

"CNN Center…

"I thought you were in Florida. Hold on I will come get you." Jim said trying to hold back fear.

"There are men here Jim. Real bad men and they have guns."

"Where you are?"

"I'm in one of the editor's offices underneath their desk on the third floor. They are right outside the door. Jim I….

The call suddenly dropped.

"Emma! Emma!"

Jim tried calling her back, but he had no signal on his phone.

"All communication is down again." Sean said walking over to Jim.

"Not right now!" Jim yelled running to his GBI vehicle and taking off toward CNN Center. He knew he had to do this himself because he couldn't risk a group of men going in there blowing the place to hell and hurting the love of his life in the crossfire.

He made it to CNN Center and got out of his vehicle. He went to the back of his GBI vehicle, and grabbed a pump shotgun, and some smoke grenades. He entered a unmonitored backdoor to CNN Center and took the stairs up two floors. When he turned the corner to go up to the third floor, he saw one of the terrorist smoking. The terrorist spun around with a cigarette in his mouth going for his weapon when Jim shot him in the chest with the shotgun. The man fell dead. Jim went up to the door of the third floor and pulled the pin to one of the smoke grenades with his teeth and tossed it in the room. Terrorist began firing toward the door. Jim ran down to the second floor until the gunfire stopped. Then Jim ran back up to the third-floor door, and he opened it and investigated the room. The room was still full of smoke. He got down on his knees and began to crawl behind a desk. He saw a terrorist trying to find his way around moving toward him. Jim fired a round of the shotgun into a terrorist's face, and he fell backward over a desk. Another terrorist was coming the other direction and met the same exact demise.

He stood up and fired two more quick shotgun shots into another terrorist that was coming in that other direction. He was out of shotgun rounds. He didn't grab any extra shells. He pulled his 9mm and continued his rampage.

Jim found a group of hostages. "I'm with the GBI. Where's Emma?"

The smoke began to clear. "She's in Jamie Robinson's Office."

"Ok take the stairs go outside and go to my SUV. I have a CB Radio. Contact FBI Agent Sean Black. Tell him where you are at. Then hide and wait. Help will be here shortly."

Jim stood up as the hostages ran toward the door. "Jim!" Emma yelled.

He turned around only to se2e Emma being drug to the elevator by Makin. Jim took aim but was attack from behind. He fell forward onto a desk. His gun fell out of his hand. The terrorist slung Jim to the side, and he fell over a chair. Jim rolled onto his back. The terrorist took aim with his AK-47. Jim kicked the rolling chair into the terrorist leg. It made him fall frontward. The cunning GBI Agent grabbed the man's AK-47 and twisted it around choking the man with the strap. Jim got up to his knees.

"Where is he taking her?

The terrorist spit at Jim. Jim unloaded some clobbering blows punching the man in the face. "Where is she!"

Jim pulled the man to his feet, and he stood up too. He kicked the man in his leg shattering it causing the man to fall. The GBI agent removed the AK-47 from the man's head then unloaded the clip into the terrorist legs. The terrorist laid on the ground crying. Jim picked up his 9mm and shot the man in his arm.

"Now tell me where she's at?"

"I don't know! I don't know!" The terrorist cried.

"Then there's not much reason to keep you alive." Jim replied

"Wait. This group has many hiding spots. I can tell you the only one that I have been at."

"That could help." Jim said coldly.

The man told Jim the address then as soon as he finished the GBI Agent unloaded what was left of his 9mm clip into the man's chest. He then went downstairs where he was met by Sophisticated Intimidation. Jim told Sophisticated Intimidation that the terrorist had Emma.

"They also have Robbie."

"Yeah, but I got an address." Jim gave one of Atlanta's superheroes the address.

"Then let's go." Sophisticated Intimidation said quickly then grabbed Jim flying towards that address as military members and police tactical team members were bringing the CNN Center hostages to safety.

It's Time To Play A Game

Jim reloaded his 9mm after Sophisticated Intimidation and him made it to the location. He had extra clips in a clip belt he was wearing. At the location there were two guards outside speaking Arabic to one another smoking blunts. The marijuana smell was very potent. The guards laughed to themselves cutting up. They had no clue what action was about to take place. They would be better off if they saw the face of the devil himself than the hell that was about to be unleashed on them.

"Ready" Sophisticated Intimidation asked.

"I was born ready."

Jim began to slowly approach sneaking up on the guards as Sophisticated Intimidation took another route. She flew faster than every football tackling player who was taking their opponent down. She hit them so hard when they fell and hit the pavement the guards broke their backs Jim finally made it up to where Sophisticated Intimidation was.

Jim spoke seeing Sophisticated Intimidation's work "That's one way of doing things."

Sophisticated Intimidation didn't respond. She just did one swift forceful kick to the warehouse door. The door was knocked off the hinge and flew all the way across the warehouse bouncing off the far wall. Sophisticated Intimidation entered but she was greeted by gunfire. She sheltered Jim as he began to return fire.

He shot down two men. He saw a third reloading. Agent Turner ran and tackled the guy. He began to beat the man's head against the concrete floor after disarming the terrorist. Jim shouted to the man asking him where Emma was located. The man spit in Jim's face and began to cuss Jim in Arabic. Jim punched the guy square in the nose. Blood splattered all over the man's face, and Jim's fist.

"Now tell me where Emma is?"

Jim had tears of frustration forming in his eyes, but he knew now wasn't the time to cry. Not only would that be very non heroic, but it wasn't the place or time to get distracted by normal human emotion.

The man smiled a mouth full of blood-stained teeth. Then he pulled a micro cassette player from his pocket, and pressed play.

Jim listened as the tape began to play.

"You will follow my instructions if you wish to see your blonde-haired friend. I must say the carpet doesn't match the drapes. Go to the National Science Museum to the snake exhibit, and you will find your next clue."

Jim put a bullet in the man's forehead then left. He went outside and found a jeep Cherokee with the keys in it. He got in and sped to the National Science Museum before Sophisticated Intimidation even realized he was gone.

Sophisticated Intimidation was battling a lot of people at once. She got angrier by the minute and people shot at her and attempted to stab her. Within a matter of moments all the men were laid out. She found steps up to an upper office. At super speed she ran up the steps and jerked the office door open. She was relieved when she saw Robbie in there tied to a chair. She undid his binds and then removed the gag from his mouth. He was out cold.

"Robbie! Rob!"

Cali "Sophisticated Intimidation" Cooper soon to be Cali "Sophisticated Intimidation" Brewer had a rush of fear come over her. Was he ok she thought? She scanned his body with her x-ray vision. He was alive and everything was in proper order. Cali kiss Robbie, and he opened his eyes.

"Baby?"

"You ok Rob?" Cali asked.

"Get me out of here." He ordered.

"Yes sir." Sophisticated Intimidation picked up Robbie and flew them out of there. She flew them back to base where she gave General Turner the location of that warehouse. General Turner sent military troops over to the warehouse Sophisticated Intimidation gave the address to for the General's troops to take the terrorist who were still alive but wounded into custody. All the terrorists that were alive at that location were still knocked out. The military handled their business and took the terrorist into their possession.

Snake in the Grass

Jim made sure his 9mm was loaded before he approached the front entrance. A terrorist walked by the front glass door. Jim fired three rounds through the glass and into the guy. The terrorist fell through the weakened glass entrance. The terrorist body got hung up in the glass entrance. Jim disarmed the guy of an AK-47 and a hunting knife.

All he thought about was Emma. Jim had to find her! He loved her so much! He wanted her back. He never wanted the breakup anyway. It crushed him. After the breakup he just buried himself further into his work. That's all Jim could deal with.

Jim's thought process was interrupted by gunfire. He fired back killing one, and seriously wounding the other terrorist.

Jim thought what are these sand bastards doing at the National Science Center? Jim hated he was thinking and saying such racist remarks. There weren't too many terrorists there GBI Agent Turner noticed quickly. He didn't kill anybody else. Surprisingly GBI Agent Turner was outside the giant snake exhibit before he knew it. He peered through the glass window. There were five terrorists standing armed, and somebody tied to a chair with a bag over their head.

Jim knew that hostage had to be Emma.

"I found her." He said to himself.

The giant anaconda exhibit is the center giant aquarium. It is a round room with all glass walls. There is only one way in or out. Jim kicked open the door and fired the rest of the AK-47 rounds into two the terrorists. He then jumped and rolled pulling out his 9mm firing two rounds into a third terrorist. He then pulled the knife and tossed it into a fourth terrorist's neck. Then Jim was kicked in the face.

The fifth terrorist twisted the AK-47 strap around Jim's neck choking the life out of him. As the terrorist was chocking Jim the terrorist was kicking Jim. Jim dropped his 9mm. The terrorist began to cuss Jim in Arabic. The terrorist was shouting to Allah for strength and shouted, "Death to America."

Then the terrorist tossed Jim against the glass window with enough forced it cracked the massive glass.

Jim quickly removed the AK-47 got up and punched the terrorist in the eye. Then judo slung him into the glass viewing window. Snakes were going everywhere. There were multiple anacondas of different sizes. Jim is afraid of snakes, but he had to cope to get Emma out of there. He began to kick the terrorist. The terrorist pulled out a knife and jabbed it into Jim's foot then threw sand into Jim's face. He fell to the ground. Jim's face began to get bit by some snakes. He slung them off him and gained access to the knife he originally used.

He threw the knife into the terrorist's leg. Then he got up and grabbed the terrorist. He began to put a beating on him. He slung him into a tree in the exhibit then slammed the terrorist face first into a giant log. Jim slung the terrorist back into a giant pool for the snakes to go in. It wasn't deep. The pool was just deep enough for bigger snakes to lay in, and there was currently a bigger snake soaking in.

Jim ignored the snakes and held the terrorist head under water till he drowned. Then he picked up his 9mm. He removed the binds of Emma or so he thought. When he removed the pillowcase, it was a Middle Eastern woman dressed in the same clothing Emma was wearing. She kicked Jim between the legs then pushed him to the ground.

She picked up the chair and broke it over Jim's back. Jim was crawling slowly getting bit by snakes as she kicked him and cussed him in English. Jim finally was able to kick the woman in the knee shattering it. He then picked her up and threw her over his shoulder.

He tossed her at the biggest snake in the exhibit. The massive reptile monster curled itself around the woman and proceeded to eat her. Jim walked back out of there and got his gun. He saw another micro cassette recorder on the ground that was taped underneath the broken chair.

He pressed play. "Next phase in this game is you dealt with slimy things that slither so now it is time to deal with blood suckers. Go to The Brood and speak to my main source of gaining soldiers of death Prince Izic Obayifo." Jim got some extra ammo off the fallen terrorist and proceed to the next step in the game of death.

Family Reunion

Simply Priceless flew back to base camp and got there exactly when Sophisticated Intimidation got back with Robbie. Robbie took a seat next to Billy.

"Sis you ok?" Sophisticated Intimidation said running up to Simply Priceless and giving her sister a hug.

"I'm fine. Long story but I am fine."

"What's the plan of action?" Sophisticated Intimidation asked looking for guidance.

"I am going to follow your lead Sophisticated Intimidation." Simply Priceless spoke giving up control to her co-captain.

Sophisticated Intimidation told Simply Priceless what they needed to do knowing in the back of her mind that she better dot all of her Is and cross all her Ts since her sister is making her take the lead on this part of the mission. Before Sophisticated Intimidation knew it; she didn't have a chance to rethink her plan of action because off they went.

Back to the Mayhem

A van parked itself directly in the center of the city. The men inside this van were all dressed in police uniforms. The van was perfectly secluded in an alleyway. The men got out after setting the timer and vanished like Casper the not so friendly ghost.

<u>Be Careful What You Say
You'll Give Yourself Away</u>

Agent Johnson was inside the private ball that was co hosted by Emanuel Reed and Ockmed Hussein. Neither man was in attendance even though they were co-hosts neither man would attend if their life depended on it. All that was there were lackeys, their family, friends, and some of the higher ups but only some of the higher ups were there. A waiter came by with a tray full of margaritas. Charlie grabbed himself a frozen margarita and examined the room.

He looked in every direction becoming aware of his situation. He knew he had to be careful who he talked to. He had to be careful what he said, or he would give himself away. He knew the rules of the game because yes, he has played this game before. He has been in this situation several times before actually.

I've made it this long under these conditions he thought. These predicaments don't get any easier he continued to think as he took a sip of his frozen alcoholic drink.

Finally, he zoned in with full concentration on a very tanned blonde in the corner of the room. He knew Ockmed Hussein, and Emanuel Reed were pimping in this country, and thought of themselves as lady's men based on their criminal work up.

Like a predator to its prey Charlie made his way across the room to the woman as graceful as a figure skater. He got up to the woman and stood right behind her. He took a glass of champagne off a tray then tapped on her shoulder.

She looked over her shoulder. "Yes."

"Here you go my lady." Charlie extended the glass of champagne to the blonde that turned and faced him. She took the glass out of his hand and took a sip. She then started to walk off coldly. Charlie touched her shoulder, and she stopped.

"What can I do for you?"

"How about we have a chat?" He asked.

"Then step out into the hallway with me" she said.

They walked out of the ballroom and into a massive hallway.

"You're American. What are you Allah's Jihad Destroyers of Destruction accountant?"

Charlie laughed because he knew he was treading on thin ice.

"Just consider me an advisor for the Allah's Jihad Destroyers of Destruction. I am overlooking their best interest." Charlie replied.

"They are a bunch of pricks I think personally."

"I agree so what's your name?" Charlie asked.

"Abigail Chase."

"The name is Williams, Steve Williams." Charlie tried speaking in a British accent.

"Cute but I thought those movies sucked Steve Williams. I don't recognize you so what are you doing here?"

Charlie or Steve wondered what to say. He had no clue what to say and was rambling inside his mind of the correct choice of words.

"I'm a party crasher let's say but I am a bit bored and am going to head back to my hotel room. Would you care to join me?" Charlie extended his hand.

Abigail took hold of Charlie's hand when suddenly a band began to play some classical music.

"Let's dance." Abigail said wrapping her arms around Charlie's back. Then they began to sway back and forth.

Abigail leaned and whispered into Charlie's ear "Want to tell me who you really are?"

"How about you first."

Abigail thought then replied, "We can't talk here."

She grabbed Charlie's hand and lead him up a back set of steps only a select few knew about. A guard gave her the heads up for her to proceed. They went upstairs and got into a massive bedroom.

You Let The Wrong Words Slip By Kissing Persuasive Lips

Charlie knew what he had to do. Abigail sat on the edge of the bed in Abigail's hotel suite. The CIA Agent walked up in front of her. She leaned up and brushed her fingers down the side of his face, and then tapped the tip of his chin.

"What is an elderly man like you doing in Iraq?" Abigail joked.

"I am far from elderly." Charlie said touching both sides of her face then leaning in and kissing her lips. She leaned all the way down on the bed, and Charlie got on top her. He pinned her hands down by her wrist. He began to kiss the side of her neck then climbed up on top of her straddling Abigail. She leaned up, and he removed her top. Abigail began to unzip his pants when there was a knock at the door.

Charlie got up and pulled his gun out of his ankle holster. Fear quickly ran across Abigail's face. He opened the door barely even a crack, but nobody was there. He turned around and held the barrel of the gun towards the ground.

"What are you doing?" Abigail asked with her hands in the air.

"I am not going to hurt you. See I am putting the gun down." Charlie laid the gun on the dresser. Abigail got up and kicked him between the legs then tried to run out the door. Charlie grabbed her by her left arm jerked her back, pushed her onto the bed, then slapped her.

"Don't make be bend you over my knee, spank you, and dump your ass in the floor."

"What do you want? Don't kill me!" Abigail started getting loud.

"Shh. Lower your tone. I just want to know where is, Emanuel Reed? I know you are aware where his main base is, and you are going to tell me."

"He would kill me." Abigail spoke breaking down in tears.

"I won't allow that to happen. I will pass you off to my men, and they will take you out of the country. You will get permanent salvation and salvage in the United State of America. We will set you and your family if you have one up in any state you choose. In any city in the country, and we will set you up for life financially! All you must do is tell me where Emanuel Reed is, and I will make it happen like….

Charlie snapped his fingers

"Like that." He finished.

"Ok. I'll show you on a map just take me out of this hell hole."

"Come on let's get out of here."

"I know who you are." Abigail said.

"Who might that be per say."

"You were at my men's compound."

"Going to scream for help now because I can have you on the floor dead in a matter of three second."

"No. Come here."

Abigail reached into her large pocketbook and handed Charlie a red folder. "In there is a lot of the information on the United Nations attack. They are shuffling their teams now. I don't agree with this, and I want out."

"Why not get out?" Charlie asked concerned.

"They have my sister. They will kill her if I don't entertain Emanual Reed. I am his official sex slave." Abigail explained.

"I can get you out. Where's your sister?"

"They have her at his main palace. She is locked in the basement. I have only been allowed to see her a few times." Abigail began to cry.

"I will get you out. Where are you from?" Charlie asked.

"South Dakota."

"I'll get you back home. Trust me." Charlie reassured.

About that time Abigail's name was being called. "You got to go."

"Where will I find you?" Charlie asked picking up his weapon and inching his way toward the window.

"I stay here. This entire floor is mine."

"Abigail!" A guard yelled.

Charlie rushed toward the window and climbed out. He mouthed to Abigail that he would be back. The spy climbed down a few floors. Then he dropped the file safely into the dirt below before he fell down into the swimming pool. He quickly got out soaked and got the file and escaped before being noticed.

<u>Blood Suckers</u>

Jim road over to Atlanta's famous The Brood nightclub. This vampire nightclub was now owned by Prince Izic Obayifo. The Brood was bopping as usual. Jim walked inside. It was like a giant rave. People running around waving green glow stick lights. Everyone was dressed in gothic attire. Most had their face painted or covered in some fashion. There were men kissing men, women kissing women and straights kissing, along with three or four way kissing. People were passing ecstasy to one another by their tongues into their partner's mouth. The smell of marijuana was very potent in the club.

As soon as Jim got a handle on the place someone placed their arm firmly on his shoulder. Jim grabbed the person's arm and twisted it. He kicked the man in the chest. The man leaned over with the air knocked out of him, so Jim followed the kick to the man's chest up with an axe kick to the back of the man's head knocking him to the ground. Jim just took out The Brood's head of security. Jim still firmly had The Brood's head of security's arm twisted behind his back and had his left foot pressed firmly against the back of the man's head.

"Where is Prince Izic Obayifo?" Jim asked coldly as the man cried

"If you wanted to talk to me, you should have just asked." A man matching Prince Izic Obayifo's description announced.

Princess Izic stood there in front of Jim. The prince was a very unique sight. Prince Izic appeared to be oriental. The prince was under six foot tall with ice blue dreadlocks and his eyes tattooed blood red. He was physically fit for his short demeanor. He wore what appeared to be Tibetan clothing, and Princess Izic appeared like something straight out of the dark ages as Jim noticed all of Princess Izic's tattoos that were displayed where his clothes didn't cover his heavily tattooed body up.

Jim released the head of security's arm peering at this unique clown who came on the scene of this ass whooping Jim was placing on his nightclub's head of security.

"Prince Izic Obayifo I believe you have information that I need to know. Do you have somewhere quieter we could talk?" Jim flashed his 9mm.

"Follow me into my office." Prince Izic Obayifo calmly spoke not fazed by the GBI Agent's weapon.

Jim walked into Prince Izic Obayifo's office. The walls were painted to appear to be bleeding. There were neon lights and black lights everywhere. Jim saw a group of girls chained to the wall by a collar. They were hissing at Jim and jerking at their chains.

These women against the wall would remind you of Dracula's brides.

There was another girl inside a cage.

"What the hell is this?" Jim asked

"Some fans." Prince Izic Obayifo said with an evil smirk.

Red liquid began pouring out of what appeared to be like small sprinklers from the ceiling.

A man entered the room approached Jim. He was a huge man who appeared to be the size of a professional wrestler. He was dressed in all black with a red tie. His face was pale. He had glowing green eyes, long black hair, and sharp pointy teeth.

"Is this the welcome committee?" Jim asked.

"You really think you will get the info on your girl that easy. Boy how I would love to get a taste of her." The prince laughed.

Jim reached for his gun but was grabbed at the wrist by the muscular man. He bent Jim's hand back which caused the federal agent to drop his gun. The man then pressed Jim over his head and dropped him down on the prince's desk. The man tried a double handed club to Jim's face, but Jim kicked the man in the face.

Jim stood up and shoulder bumped the guy football style. Then Jim kicked the man between the legs. The low blow didn't affect the guy. He tossed Jim over in the corner where the chained vampire girl began to claw his face. The man wrapped the girl's chain around Jim's throat.

He was struggling to breathe. The prince laughed maniacally. There was a cup of some sort of scolding hot liquid steaming on the prince's desk. Jim reached out for it. He was fingertips away. His face was quickly changing colors, and he was about to go lifeless.

Jim finally grabbed the cup. He splashed the contents into the massive man's face. He screamed and let go. Jim got out of the chain and grabbed the man's skull and began to smash the man's face into the cage till the man laid there out cold and a bloody mess.

Jim picked up his gun and fired a round into Prince Izic Obayifo's right shoulder. He fell backward into a desk chair. Jim fired another round into his attacker's left leg.

Jim was bleeding from the face where he was clawed by the vampire girls. He was sore but his pain wouldn't compare to what he was fixing to put Prince Izic Obayifo through. The prince sat there in pain as Jim found two pairs of handcuffs and cuffed the vampire prince to the chair. Jim then locked the door.

"Where's Emma?" Jim yelled.

Prince Izic Obayifo didn't say anything. Jim punched the guy square in the face and then the mouth. The prince was in laughter. He must be a machoistic Jim thought. Jim shot him in both feet. Then he tried another method. Jim didn't care anymore. He was going to do whatever it was he had to do to get Emmal back. He fired wounding shots into the chained girls. The girls lay there crying in pain as they bled from their wounds.

"No! No!" Prince Izic Obayifo yelled.

"Where is she!"

"There is a Portable DVD player in the bottom right drawer. It is your next clue." Prince Izic Obayifo explained.

Jim opened the drawer. Snakes were inside that bottom drawer crawling. Jim jerked the drawer out of the desk and poured the contents on top of the desk. He then played the DVD. The next clue would bring Jim to a toy manufacturing factory. I hope this ends soon Jim thought. Jim found a knife in the drawer. He picked it up and slide a button and a blade popped out.

Jim had a sadistic look flash across his face. Jim undid Prince Izic Obayifo pants and pulled out his penis. He then slowly but surely began to cut the prince's member off as Prince Izic screamed in pain. Once it was off Jim

shoved Prince Izic Obayifo own penis into the prince's
mouth till he choked on it. Then Jim left for the toy factory.

<u>To Everyone He Meets He Stays A Stranger</u>

Charlie met with Steve and handed over all the documents. He knew he had to finish this mission and he was a man on a warpath. Charlie made a promise to Abigail to get her and her sister out of there. That was exactly what he was going to do.

"I need your help, Steve."

Steve ignored Agent Charles Johnson's sincerity and smarted off "What no fat jokes."

"I want to get out of this stupid country alive. We have one last thing we need to do. There is one last place to go." Charlie ignored Steve's statement trying to remain professional.

"Where?"

"Emanuel Reed's main compound. There we will find the remaining pieces of the puzzle."

"Just us?" Steve replied.

"Who else do you think?" Charlie smiled.

"OK. I will get us some ammo."

Steve left and gathered some weaponry. He was back in about two hours. Charlie and Steve got dressed for combat. Charlie and Steve resembled a couple of the Expendables from the Sylvester Stallone Expendables Franchise. Both men knew this could be their last run. One last ride to the depths of hell to stop another mad man.

"Got the chopper?" Charlie asked.

Steve nodded.

"Fly me back to the ball I have to pick somebody up."

At Reed's compound Mel and Jenna were tossed into the basement holding area. Mel was beaten down badly. Both were restrained! Reed's men set up a roadblock down the road a little way. There was no way to get around it. The number of men that were there was astronomical.

Mel had his wrist restrained behind his back. One of the terrorists began beating him with a Singapore cane. He was weeping like a baby. The man knocked Mel's feet out from under him. The guy even hit Mel over his head with the hard Singapore cane. That strike split Mel's forehead wide open like an Extreme Championship Wrestling superstar. Mel fell face down on the floor and the terrorist began to beat Mel's back.

Jenna, Abigail's sister, was screaming and crying over the horrific act that was taking place against Mel. Finally, the guard when he got bored playing with his prey like a cat to a mouse left the room and left Mel lying in a bloody pool.

Charlie and Steve took to the air. Steve flew them over to where the ball was held. As Steve held the chopper steady Charlie pulled a rocket launcher and fired three rockets into three windows on that floor that he was on with Abigail earlier.

Charlie laid down the rocket launcher and announced, "Be back in three minutes." Charlie said jumping onto the balcony. Charlie pulled a 9mm. He walked into a living room area. He began to shoot guards down left and right as they ran down the hallway in a panic.

"Abigail! Abigail!"

Charlie shot and killed two more guards as black smoke filled the hallways. Charlie walked out into the hallway. He saw Abigail being held by a man with a gun. It was Emanuel Reed.

"Who are you American?" Emanuel asked.

"Your worst nightmare sleazebag."

"You want to take me in?"

"No, I rather just kill you." Charlie took a step forward that measured an inch.

"I don't think so."

"What is the plan?" Charlie asked

More gunfire erupted Charlie jumped into another room.

Emanuel Reed yelled for his men to kill the American in Arabic. Abigail did a mule kick nailing Reed between the legs. She then took off toward the bedroom Charlie came in from. Charlie killed three more guards then shot Reed in the kneecaps.

He kicked Reed's weapon out of the way.

"Now tell me what is going on?" Charlie said.

"Just kill me American."

"I plan on it. Now tell me what I want to know!" Charlie yelled.

"I am not going to tell you a god damn thing!"

Charlie stepped on Emanuel's throat choking the life out of him. Abigail came out into the hallway. "Upstairs! His office is upstairs, and all the information is there."

"Thank you." Charlie said firing the death round through Emanuel's eye socket.

Charlie ran towards Abigail. He picked Abigail up and carried her outside. Charlie helped Abigail into the chopper before Charlie got into the chopper himself and told Steve where to fly. Steve flew them up to Emanuel's office window. Charlie went inside. There was a black duffle bag in the corner of the room. He poured the contents of that bag to the floor then loaded up Emanuel's laptop, files, CDs, and anything else of importance. He then jumped back in the helicopter with all the intel he gathered. Steve flew them to Reed's main compound.

"How do I get in this place?" Charlie asked.

Abigail instructed where Reed's bedroom was located.

Steve flew over that bedroom window, and Charlie attached a line. He then jumped out of the chopper and down repelling through the bedroom window.

He exited out into the hallway and killed two guards. Then he ran swiftly down a spiral staircase. Charlie was knocked down from behind. He began to wrestle with a guard. Charlie head-butt him then rammed the guy's nose bone through his skull. Charlie got up and worked his way to the basement. The palace was mostly empty.

All his guards were where the ball was being held. That location was burning to the ground. Charlie killed a few more then made his way to the basement. He killed the guard on the outside of the prison door and removed his keys. Then he went inside. Mel was leaning in Jenna's lap.

"Ready to go home?" Charlie asked as he began to save the captives.

"Who are you?" Abigail's sister asked.

"I am your hero."

Charlie threw Mel over his shoulder and carried him back upstairs as everyone else ran behind Charlie. He ran out the backdoor where Steve lowered the chopper down, and they loaded up and flew to Kuwait to the safe point. Charlie had enough information to get a genuine idea of the terror attacks that were going on in America in particular the city of Atlanta.

CIA and the Kuwait army sent in troops to rescue those kidnapped at Emanuel Reed's where Mel and Jenna originally escaped from. Charlie boarded a plane shortly that night with Steve and flew back to the states. Charlie never revealed his name to those he rescued.

Once him and Steve got back to the United States they went straight to the pentagon and began to go over the information they had at hand.

<u>Stop The Mayhem</u>

Sophisticated Intimidation and Simply Priceless landed outside Emory hospital. The hospital was on fire. There were burning cars in front of the hospital. Bodies laid everywhere like a great war movie. Sophisticated Intimidation quickly flew around the hospital blowing freeze breath which put the fires out. Then Simply Priceless and her walked into the ER lobby. There were more bodies inside. A terrorist came running towards them. Simply Priceless stepped to the side grabbed the guy and slung him through the front glass sliding door entrance.

All Sophisticated Intimidation and Simply Priceless could hear were screams. Patients, doctors, nurses, and candy stripers were being held hostage.

"Want to split up?" Simply Priceless gave her sis the option.

"Can you handle it on your own?"

"Cali!" Simply Priceless excitedly spoke.

"Stupid question I'll take the high road." Sophisticated Intimidation took off through the ceiling. She flew up to the fourth floor since there wasn't anything but dead bodies that could be found on the second and third floor.

Sophisticated Intimidation came up in the middle of a giant examination room. There were several gurneys. Some the gurneys had rotten corpses on them. It was something straight out of a zombie movie and stunk worse than drainage from a human parasite elision. Sophisticated Intimidation's super smelling sense wasn't helping matters. Two men ran into the room after her.

Sophisticated Intimidation kicked one in the stomach, and then grabbed the other by the back of the head. She slammed that guy into a metal body storage bin. The man's face split open like a banana. She then slung him across the room. He hit the wall with his head pointed toward the ground, and his back hitting the wall.

Sophisticated Intimidation then kneed the guy she kicked in the gut between the legs and bashed him headfirst into her knee. She then exited the room into a hallway. She proceeded down the hallway slowly but surely.

Meanwhile Simply Priceless was in the basement. She already subdued five armed men. She snuck up on these terrorists who were in the basement sitting around a round table playing a high stakes poker game. Simply Priceless called their bluff and showed them who had the higher hand as she destroyed those terrorists with ease.

Simply Priceless made it up one floor using the steps. An armed terrorist was coming through the door. Simply Priceless kicked the door slamming the door onto half the terrorist body. It destroyed his arm and dislocated his shoulder. Simply Priceless grabbed the man's injured arm and slung him down the steps. The terrorist rolled down the steps which caused his neck to snap. Simply Priceless then stepped into the hallway and was met by several bullet rounds lighting her chest up, as the bullets just exploded when they hit her suit.

She clapped her hands in front of her loudly and a sonic boom erupted. A blue lightning type flash exploded between her hands, and the men were knocked backwards only to be completely unconscious.

Sophisticated Intimidation made it to an office area after taking the stairs up another floor. The walls were wooden, and the floor was a bluish marble. All that was heard was Middle Eastern spoken language. Sophisticated Intimidation knew exactly what they were saying. If Sophisticated Intimidation heard a word spoken in another language, she saw the meaning of the foreign words in her mind. She saw the spoken foreign language inside her head kind of like a TV that has closed captioning displayed.

She walked up behind one of the terrorists and grabbed one of the men in a headlock. Sophisticated Intimidation began to speak a Middle Eastern tongue to the other man who she didn't have in a headlock. The other terrorist trembled in fear as he had an AK-47 pointed in Sophisticated Intimidation's direction.

"What are y'all's next plans?"

The man spoke back "Fuck you. You bitch!"

Sophisticated Intimidation threw the terrorist she was holding into the other terrorist who was standing. When the terrorist collided, they both went backward at a super speed, and through the wall at the end of the hall. At that time Simply Priceless flew up through the ceiling, and onto the other floor.

At the main terrorist hideout Bomback passed a detonator to one of the Four Gods for him to do the honors. Simply Priceless sensed what was going on as she flew upward to meet up with her sister.

"Come on Intimidation this place is about to blow." Simply Priceless ordered.

"Where do we go from here?" Sophisticated Intimidation asked not realizing the urgency.

At that time the structure rumbled as a giant bomb blast went off in the center of the city. Simply Priceless and Sophisticated Intimidation shook back and forth then flew out the window as the hospital building collapsed.

<u>Wonderland</u>

Jim made it outside the toy factory in record time. He was sore and still railing from his attack in the vampire Prince's office. He knew he couldn't stop now. He knew he was a little closer to Emma. He made sure he had enough ammunition then proceeded toward the building. Jim went to the side entrance. There was a terrorist outside smoking. Jim fired three rounds into the guy's chest. Blood exploded from the terrorist's chest as the man fell backwards and rolled down the steps. Even though he was already dead from the gunshots his neck snapped as he rolled down the concrete steps.

Jim entered that side entrance. There were toys all around. Everything from action figures to giant teddy bears. The warehouse would remind you of the toy warehouse keeping the Good Guy Dolls in Child's Play 2.

The federal agent turned a corner. There were three terrorist standing smoking. There was a cart full of action figures. Jim gave the cart a swift push into the group. Then he fired three rounds into their skulls and blood went like hairspray mist through the air.

Jim then began taking gunfire. He took off running up a set of steps to another level. The agent hid behind some giant boxes and began to return fire. All that could be heard was gunfire, and people cussing in a Middle Eastern tongue. Jim saw somebody walking below. He climbed upon the guard rail and jumped onto the guy. He slammed the guy's face into the concrete floor.

"Where's Emma?" Jim yelled.

The man spit in Jim's face. The terrorist's action only pissed Jim off and caused him to fire five slugs into the man's side. Jim got up and heard screaming over the intercom.

"Jim. Jim." Emma screamed.

"Emma! Emma!" Jim took off running. He killed three more terrorists till he found the steps up to the intercom room. Jim changed to a full magazine before he ran up to the top of the steps, and kicked the door in. When he got inside Emma was nowhere to be found. There was only an audio tape of her calling out her loved one's name.

He saw a box sitting on top of a corner table. He walked up to it and lifted the lid to the birthday box. When he looked inside, he saw a timer counting down. It was just under three minutes. Jim pulled out a portable DVD player. He flipped it up and pressed played. It was a black screen Then somebody speaking Arabic began to play, and the caption across the screen read.

One last time to the Atlanta Zoo. There you will find your monkey. I don't want her, but she obviously has caused you a lot of grief. Maybe when you find her you will put her out of her misery. Come to the hippopotamus exhibit, and there you can have this cow back.

Jim took off running. He tripped going down the steps and twisted his ankle and busted his forehead open on the concrete floor. He pulled himself up and took off running even though his ankle gave him shooting pain. He was about outside nearing his vehicle when he was shot from behind. The bullet entered the back of Jim's left shoulder at the same time Jim fell to the ground. The man that shot him kicked Jim in the side.

Jim looked up and the man who was putting the assault on him was Bomback. Suddenly boom! The bomb in the intercom room went off. The fire quickly engulfed the wall. Jim was being beaten bad by Bomback

"These people couldn't do what I needed right so I had to do it myself." Bomback yelled then punched Jim in the right side of his face.

"You know I raped that bitch! She is such a filthy slut! Who loves to suck dick."

Bomback statements enraged Jim. Jim pulled the terror leader's feet out from underneath him. Then he snapped Bomback's right ankle He climbed on top of Bomback and began to unleash a whirl wind of punches. It was hotter than hell in there as the fire spread. Jim began to slam Bomback's head into the concrete.

Jim got up and picked up his 9mm. "Is she really at the zoo?"

Bomback didn't answer.

Jim fired a shot right beside Bomback's head. Bomback nodded yes in fear. Jim read Bomback's eyes and could tell Bomback was scared as Agent Turner fired a round in Bomback's stomach. Blood was pouring out of Bomback's wound as Jim limped out of the toy factory about to head to what he hoped would be his final destination where the yellow brick road to Emma hopefully would end at the Atlanta Zoo.

Bomback passed out from his round to the gut and the massive blood loss that occurred from such a gut wound. Unaware of what was taking place due to being unconscious Bomback's legs began to catch of fire. Bomback had a little bit of life left inside him as his body was fully engulfed with flames. Bomback burned to death before the bullet wound killed him.

The Great Debates

The Presidential Candidates took their final spots behind each of their individual podiums getting ready for one of their final Presidential debates. John Bill from the Naples Daily News was the moderator for this final Presidential Debate, and he had his questions all laid out.

The news cameras were rolling, and their debate was getting ready to be telecast all over the United States. It was a tense matter of moments. John Bill sat at his assigned desk as the main new correspondent went over the details for that night. All the candidates were nervous and were holding their breath.

Finally, the lights fired up, and the show was about to begin. There was a packed crowd inside the venue. However, everybody was on edge but with the recent events who wouldn't be on edge because the debate was prone to terrorist attack.

"Ok let's get started. The first question comes from Ross Bender and he asks what are you willing to do about the massive debt crisis the United States has found itself in?" John Bill asked.

Four Noutes Stepping Up Their Role

As the Presidential Debate took place the terror unit were still intact even after losing Bomback who was one of their key leaders. The Four Noutes were about to step up in a General Role! The Four Noutes had their manager addressing the crowd of terrorists that remained to be used on various operations by the Four Noutes. None of the people at the debate including the Presidential Candidates knew that more shit was going to hit the fan before everything simmered down stick!

"I am the spokesperson for the Four Noutes. They have a master plan to finance further operations. They have tech teams in place to drain every Atlanta checking and savings account which the money will be placed into an undisclosed bank account looked over by the Four Noutes." A mysterious younger Middle Eastern man who was the Four Noutes manager spoke.

The terrorists in the room cheered. Everyone felt in their hearts that the Four Noutes had their best interest in mind.

The spokesperson began to speak again,"Everyone will get their payday when the blood money has been paid on top of what we receive from the infidels."

All the men cheered again! The Four Noutes came out and gave some further instructions about further attacks. Then each group scattered like roaches when the lights come on in order to act out each individual attack!

<u>Revenge of the Techno Geeks</u>

The men and women who escaped in the limousine from the original technological base camp set up by the terrorist were sitting in another warehouse office. This other warehouse was set up just outside Atlanta. The women were rubbing and kissing the men's feet inside that location.

There was a woman named Elizabeth A'ishah. She was a very obese Caucasian woman. She was very lonely and found her husband Hamza on an online dating site. She converted to Islam practically immediately after meeting Hamza based on Hamza's commands for her to do so. She didn't even protest. She completely remodeled her believes and submitted to the word of Allah. It was sick in most people's eyes how she can be submissive to a Middle Eastern man, and abruptly switch from Christianity to Islam. It was a bit whacky if someone asked most people. A lot of her friends believe she went fruit loops; you know a little coo coo for coco puffs; in other words, totally insane.

This warehouse had people running around like those yellow minions from those minion related cartoons. There was a lot of Middle Eastern men running from workstation to workstation. A lot of men ran out like chickens with their head cut off unaware of what to do. It was very chaotic.

As has already been mentioned it is so annoying to call a credit card company and be patched through to a Middle Eastern call center. Why there is all the outsourcing is very hard to understand. It is hard to understand these people. Then they seem to get annoyed when a person can't understand them. It really pisses people off and they wind up cussing at the customer service agents, and the customer service agent disconnects the call. Then the customer must call back and go through the process again. It is so stupid.

The men worked hard to set up the transfer to take place in exactly the time when everybody in the city of Atlanta should cease to exist.

A "Friendly" Trip To The Zoo

Jim gathered some ammo and traded up on machine guns. One last dance he thought or at least he hoped. He didn't know what to expect. Was Emma dead he thought. He swallowed hard in pain from all his wounds knowing he had to hope and pray for the best. He wanted his girl back. He had to feel her warmth when he would hug her. He loved hugging her tight and kissing the top of her head. The fruit sensation that filled his nostrils when he would smell her hair was fabulous.

He made his way to the zoo. He came in at the east gate. There was nobody around. Jim didn't know where to go so he looked at one of the posted maps to find out where the hippo exhibit was. Jim took off in that direction.

It didn't take long for him to be under fire. He dove over in a dirt area and hid behind a giant tree. Jim had no clue where the shots were coming from. He glanced but didn't see anybody. It was a sniper. The sniper peered through his scope at the tree waiting for Jim to make his move.

He knew he had to find another way to get to where he needed to go. He looked to his left. There was a high wall. It was high enough it would shield him from the sniper's fire. Jim took off and jumped the barrier and fell in the animal exhibit.

"O shit." Jim said as he looked around and saw numerous alligators and crocodiles. He saw a door all way across the exhibit. Jim was breathing deep. He didn't know how to approach this. Before he could even react, he found himself in the air.

He was sat down and looked behind him. It was Sophisticated Intimidation. "Figured you might need some help."

"Thanks, I am no crocodile hunter."

Jim's joke didn't last long till they began to take heavy gunfire. Jim dove behind a bench as Sophisticated Intimidation blew which caused the round to fly back into the men.

"Come on Jim" she said.

Jim got up and they took off running. Every few minutes they encountered more gunfire. Jim fired back and killed or severally wounded several of these armed goons. He was boiling. He was pissed. He wanted his girl back even if they did fuss and fought but that was mostly over marriage. Jim knew he couldn't let his head get clogged with memories or wishes or hopes. He knew if he got into his own head too much, he would wind up dead. Jim was wound tight. He was reaching his breaking point.

They made it to the hippo exhibit. "I'll go in first." Jim demanded.

Sophisticated Intimidation motioned her hands directing Jim to go inside. He went inside and nobody was in there. "What! What! What!" Jim ranted. The only thing that was in the room was an audio recorder taped to the hippo viewing glass to see Penelope underwater. Which she was under water.

Sophisticated Intimidation came into the exhibit just as Jim pressed play on the tape.

"It's not quite so easy. Don't worry she has company which is unarmed. There is a master plan which will become clear as further attacks take place. This is not

Then the recording abruptly ended. He looked around crying. He couldn't focus. He knew it was too good to be true for the joyous zoo trip to be the end of it. Sophisticated Intimidation looked around. She found an envelope in the corner on the room. She used her x-ray vision to look in it as Jim got some more ammo from dead terrorist pants.

"Calm down Jim. Emma is alive based on the knowledge inside this envelope." Sophisticated Intimidation explained as she handed Jim the envelope.

Jim opened the envelope and pulled out a letter. This was a letter written in Emma's handwriting and wasn't the average love letter, but it was an invitation to the main event a few days from that moment.

Jim read Emma's loving words as Sophisticated Intimidation envisioned the moment the terrorist watched over Emma as she wrote out her love letter followed by the invitation to the main event that the terrorist invited Jim Turner to.

Sophisticated Intimidation saw the anger in Jim's eyes as he folded up the piece of notebook paper with the handwritten love letter slash invitation on it and stuck it in his back pocket.

"Okay. It is the halftime show. I will make sure you are where you need to be when the time comes. Are you ready to blow this joint?" Sophisticated Intimidation asked nicely.

Jim gave a nod then Sophisticated Intimidation picked him up and off they went.

<u>Admission</u>

Jasper was sitting in the Navigator owned by CTU when his cell phone went off. He looked at the caller id on his Blackberry, and the number was not registered. Jasper answered anyway. Before he could say a word

"Daddy…

The phone was jerked away from Brittany's head.

"Britt! Brittany! Baby!"

"Aww how sweet somebody actually gives a care about you. You know Jasper. Can I call you Jasper? Anyway Jasper…

"Who the fuck is this." Jasper asked.

"Doesn't matter who I am. Your decision in the next hour will make or break your daughter's life."

"What do you want?" Jasper asked trying to hold it together.

My brother he's in custody and my Four Gods would like him back," The man said.

"Who's your brother?"

"Malachi Hassan. He is in custody at a CTU location in Rome, Georgia which nobody knows about. Yeah right!" The man shouted then burst into laughter.

"Ok what do you want me to do?"

"I want you to go get him out and bring him to the Greensboro Bats baseball stadium once he is secure you will receive directions on how you can get this bitch back." The man disconnected the call.

"Shit!" Jasper yelled then slammed both hands down on the steering wheel in a fit of rage. He shook the wheel like a rag doll then placed the car in drive and sped off.

<u>Deep Shit</u>

Jasper made it to the CTU location Malachi was located at. Jasper was well acknowledged on Malachi Hassan; why because he caught him. Now he just had to figure out how to bust him out. Jasper knew he was in deep shit! How am I going to get him out? Jasper thought to himself. Then he got out of the car. He walked up to the front gate, and showed the guards his ID. One of the guards swiped his access card, and the double doors opened. Jasper walked up to the front desk.

"Hey. I am CTU Agent Jasper….

"I know who you are. You are a legend." The young girl spoke ecstatic.

The receptionist had long blonde hair and blue eyes. Jasper had tears trying to build up in his eyes because she reminded him of Brittany.

"I need to speak to Malachi Hassan."

"You know he is getting ready to be sent to a CIA prison in Syria, right?"

"I heard but it is very important I speak to him. I just need five minutes."

"I am sure that can be arranged for a legend like you."

The secretary got on the phone and before Jasper knew it, he was ushered into a room where Malachi Hassan was sitting chained to a chair.

"Good to see you, old friend." Jasper spoke coldly.

There was a guard in the room.

"You can leave us be." Jasper told the guard.

"You sure?" The guard appeared confused knowing Hassan's terror status.

"I wouldn't of told you if I wasn't! Now get out!" Jasper raised his voice.

The guard exited the room, but Jasper moved to force the guard to bump into him, and he pick pocketed the guy taking the key to Malachi's chains. When the guard left Jasper stuck a chair underneath the door handle blocking the door from being opened.

Jasper quickly unchained Malachi. He released everything but Hassan's wrist restraints. Jasper pulled his gun. "If anything happens to my daughter, I am killing you first, now come on!"

Jasper reached his hand into a secret compartment in the wall and pressed a button. A panel in the wall moved unveiling a secret passageway. He knew he only had a matter of minutes before the CTU officials at the facility knew he was gone. Jasper knew his five minutes was about or probably were up, so he had to hurry fast.

Jasper and Malachi sped walked. Jasper had his gun on the back on Malachi's head the entire time. He felt like a rat in a maze when he heard an alarm sound.

"Move fuck face!" Jasper yelled to Malachi.

Jasper made it out another door and into a hallway. He and Malachi stealth like slipped past two guard who were talking amongst themselves. They made it to a doorway. Jasper knew his plan were going to work. He swiped the key card that were on the keys he "borrowed" from the guard, and the door opened. He was in the parking area for the CTU vehicles. Jasper and Malachi creeped as Jasper kept pressing the unlock button attempting to find the car this guard drove.

Sweat built up on Jasper's forehead. He knew he had to act fast if he ever was going to see his daughter again. He knew Brittany was a wild child, and he knew she was up to something being able to buy whatever she wanted all the time when she didn't have a real job, and he didn't give her money every time she wanted it for clothes or anything that wasn't needed at that time such as food or gas money. He bought her clothes when she needed them not when she just wanted them like a new outfit to go out partying in.

Jasper wondered if his daughter was a prostitute. The thought crossed his mind but at that time the only thing he was concerned with was getting her back. Finally, he heard the click of a lock unlocking. He opened the door for Malachi, and he got in. Then he went around and got in the driver's seat and sped off hoping to get the hell out of dodge before an all-points bulletin was put out on him!

Guy Talk

"What are you and Ash going to do when this fiasco is over with?" Robbie asked trying to make small talk.

"Whatever she wants to do." Billy answered trying not to laugh.

Thing was Billy knew it was whatever his wife wanted to do because Billy knew his place inside his family dynamic. Ashley called all the shots both on the battlefield as Simply Priceless and at home as Ashley Hatch-Coatman the loving wife and mother.

"Have you heard of the term whipped?" Robbie laughed.

"Have you heard of the terms, punched, kicked, and slapped?" Billy replied with a glare. Billy fired off an attitude out of embarrassment because he knew he was whipped. Billy knew he was whipped unlike any other time in his life with any other girl who has ever been in Billy's life.

"If it means anything I am going to do whatever Cali wants too." Robbie spoke the truth trying not to laugh because even though what he said was true Robbie spoke that last sentence in the most sarcastic way possible.

"You don't have to tell me that." Billy laughed.

"I love her man, and she must love me. I mean she has saved my ass enough."

"They save us just so they can gripe at us." Billy laughed.

"That's the truth."

"Yes, it is" Billy replied.

"We love them though. When did you know Ashley was going to be the woman you married?" Robbie asked with curiosity.

Billy thought business is about to pick up before he began to speak. "It's hard to say. We had such a love hate relationship. I loved to hate her for not saving my former partner Detective Bear. Before I knew it Captain Mitchell had us partner up. Which I thought was very unusual since Simply Priceless isn't on the department's payroll."

"Yeah?" Robbie said.

"Well, my house got destroyed. I about got killed. I woke up in my guardian angel's arms sailing through the wind."

"Yeah?"

"She let me stay with her. She even bought me new clothes. The fact she could be so good to me, after, well, after I treated her so poorly. It was amazing. Seeing her walk around dressed for bed and lounging didn't help matters. Then one night. Well. Let's just say, well."

"You had sex." Robbie finished Billy's thought.

"I fell for her way before that night we released all of our pint up sexual energy but that sexcapade was the icing on top of the cake. She by far was the best girl I ever slept with, and then when she almost died on me. I knew I had to hold onto her forever. I couldn't imagine my life without her." Billy finished.

"I couldn't imagine being in that predicament. Seeing my girlfriend die or near death."

"It's not fun at all." Billy spoke direct and to the point.

"I know Ashley loves you." Robbie said in a serious tone with a serious look on his face.

"I love and worship her." Billy admitted that his wife was his kryptonite.

'That's good baby." Simply Priceless said walking up behind the guys with Sophisticated Intimidation in toe.

Billy sat in fear wondering how much his wife heard. He also didn't know if she was reading his mind. All he thought about was did she know that he secretly looked down at her feet when she walked by him before they had sex. Did she know he loved to watch her transform from Ashley Hatch to Simply Priceless or did she know that he enjoyed watching her as she did her toes on the couch while they watched TV. They became comfortable around one another quicker than expected after Billy moved in with Ashley years ago. Ashley knew all the things Billy was wondering if she knew, and Ashley knew that Billy didn't know that she enjoyed using her X-Ray vision and peeking under Billy's shirt any free chance she had.

She loved her boy toy, and he loved her, and both were ready to get their lives back to normal.

The group regrouped and began to plan their next phase of action.

<u>Change of Scenery</u>

Sean got a phone call from FBI Director Rollands, and the FBI Director ordered that Sean must leave Atlanta and immediately fly to Greensboro, North Carolina due to the situation with Jasper. Agent Black didn't want to leave his crew, but he had no other choice. A helicopter landed and off to the air he went without telling anybody bye.

Sean landed in Greensboro about an hour later and was rushed to CTU headquarters. There he was briefed on the situation with Jasper.

"I know people like him. Why don't you just back him up." Sean replied.

"We can't have rouge warfare."

Sean grabbed the CTU Director by the collar of his neck "Listen here you son of a bitch. Atlanta is a warzone, and I am sure you heard about that. Now listen asshole I know this shit is connected. Now if this Jasper can put a dent in their system, then so fucking be it!"

"Ok. Ok. I gotcha."

<u>**"Take me out to the ball game,**</u>
<u>**Take me out with the crowd.**</u>
<u>**Buy me some peanuts and cracker jacks**</u>
<u>**I don't care if I never get back,**</u>
<u>**Let me root, root, root for the home team,**</u>
<u>**If they don't win it's a shame.**</u>
<u>**For it's one, two, three strikes, you're out,**</u>
<u>**At the old ball game."**</u>

Jasper drove almost 7 hours before he pulled into the Greensboro, Bats baseball field parking lot. Jasper pulled up right in front. He pulled his gun and pressed it against Malachi's temple forcing his head up against the glass window from where Hassan sat in the passenger seat asleep the entire drive from Rome, GA to Greensboro, North Carolina.

"What do I need to know? What kind of death trap am I walking into?" Jasper yelled.

"They are going to kill us both."

"Who's they?" Jasper asked.

"Atlanta…

A bullet pierced the window and blood and brain fragments splattered all over Jasper's face from the rifle round that pierced Malachi's head. The bullet was fired from a sniper that was out of sight,

Jasper opened his car door and slid out just as machine gun rounds pierced his ride. He took off running and dove behind some other vehicles in the parking lot. All Jasper thought about was his daughter. He knew her life

was on the line. Two terrorists walked up to where the CTU
Agent was hiding.

Jasper stood up and fired three rounds into both
their bodies.

"Jasper!" An Arabic man spoke over the stadium's
loudspeaker.

Jasper listened with interest.

"We won't hurt you. Come out unarmed with your
hands up, and we can discuss this." The man explained.

"Daddy!" Brittany yelled.

Jasper knew he had no choice. If he had any hope of
seeing his daughter alive again, he must comply with the
directive of these mad men.

Jasper stood up and tossed his weapon. Three men
walked up to him, and one tazed Jasper. He woke up about
fifteen-twenty minutes later. Jasper found himself on the
pitcher's mound with his hands cuffed behind his back. A
helicopter landed in the backfield.

"Daddy!" Brittany yelled as she was being led to
the helicopter.

"Baby!" Jasper yelled.

There was a man pressing Jasper's own 9mm firmly
against the back of Jasper's head. Brittany was loaded into
the helicopter with the terrorist who was leading her to the
helicopter and once that helicopter was in the air and out of
sight the stooge that had Jasper at gun point asked in
Arabic "How does it feel to get killed with your own gun."

Jasper quickly spun around and knocked the man's
legs out from under him. The man fell and dropped Jasper's
weapon. Jasper wrapped his legs around the guy's throat.

"If you don't know English you better learn it quick! Where are they taking my daughter?"

"Atlanta, Georgia then Washington DC!" The terrorist answered.

"Where at?"

"Our base camp is out of an old carpet store building. It used to be known as Carpet Gallery on West Market Street. Go there all my unit's operation info will be there."

"Thank you!" Jasper snapped the man's neck then slipped his cuffs to the front of him by bringing his legs through. Jasper searched the man's pocket and found the handcuff key, and he let himself out of the handcuffs.

Jasper was alone in the stadium. He picked up his gun but still carefully left the stadium. He hailed a cab once he made it outside and got it to take him to the former Carpet Gallery store.

<u>Rug Man</u>

Jasper arrived at the former Carpet Gallery building. There were three entry points, there was the front, the back where a loading dock was located, and a side door. The front entrance entered the former showroom.

The rouge CTU agent watched from across the street. The neighborhood had gone to pits over the years. Bloods, Crips, and various other gangs ran rapid through the streets. That area appeared like an apocalyptic future Mad Max or Escape from New York movie setting. Jasper could hear sirens and blood curdling screams all around him. He knew he had to keep his game face on.

All he could imagine was Brittany's face as she was being led to the chopper. Tears built up in his eyes as he thought of his daughter and how scared she must be. Jasper knew he had to maintain his composer, however.

"Hey white boy."

Jasper turned around and stared at a tall muscular black man who was holding onto a pink leash which had a white guy on the other end in a collar.

"I have no issues with you! So fuck off!" Jasper sternly spoke.

"I have an issue with you bitch! I have another leash and collar with your name on it. Ain't that some shit?" The black man said before he spit at Jasper's feet.

Jasper heard enough. His daughter's life was more important than dealing with some street thug. He kicked the guy in the chest. The black man bent over. Jasper hooked his head then threw all his own body weight up breaking the man's neck.

"Now do you want some?" Jasper asked the white guy who just undid the collar and ran off.

Jasper made his move. He safely crossed over four lanes of traffic and began to go toward the back of the carpet store. He got to the back and saw two armed thugs loading up a moving van. Jasper fired two rounds into each of them. Then he shut the back of the moving van with the two-armed thugs in the back of the moving van bleeding out. He hoped into the driver's seat. The keys were in the ignition. Jasper cranked the van and drove around to the front of the building.

The front was paneled with glass. Jasper floored the gas like some Nascar racer and drove right through the front door running over about five men leaving the rest scattering. Jasper dove out of the van as bullets began to fly inside the van. He found as well of a secure place as possible to station himself and return fire. He shot one man in the throat, another in the chest, and a few in the head.

Then gunfire began to dwindle. Jasper moved locations. His adrenaline was flowing, and the blood was rushing through his veins. He felt like some professional wrestler getting ready to wrestle a match at the biggest pay per view in sports entertainment.

The coast seemed clear. The few remaining terrorist stooges hauled ass and left Carpet Gallery running off knowing the police were likely on the way. He got up and walked toward an office area behind an island. He walked to the main office where a giant desk sat. In the corner was a surveillance system, and several broke filing cabinets with paper scattered everywhere.

He saw a file on the desk labeled Desert Heat. He knew what this was. Jasper was part of this mission which took out a major terror leader over in Iraq. The man was dead. After all he should know he killed the man himself. Jasper began to go through the file and quickly realized this wasn't just any file. It was a CIA file straight from the pentagon. It wasn't a copy. It was the original.

The man Jasper killed son was still alive, and apparently a week before hand was rumored to have entered the United States via a Coyote through Mexico. Border Patrol never found the man's son however Border Patrol only found the Coyote dead. He was strangled to death by fishing wire. Jasper knew right away that this wasn't a by chance kidnapping involving his daughter this was a revenge plot, and he knew now anything was possible.

<u>Next of Kin</u>

The Four Gods were talking alone when Brittany was dragged into the room.

"Is this her?" Ahmad Abualsami asked

The men that dragged Brittany into the room nodded.

"And the wife?" Ahmad Abualsami gave a follow up question.

"We are working on that" another man said.

"Working on it?" Abualsami asked.

"We don't know where she is at."

"O' I see." Ahmad Abualsami pulled a gun and shot the man in his Adam's apple.

"Then I suggest you find her!" Ahmad Abualsami yelled at the top of his lungs.

Ahmad Abualsami was the son of the man killed by Jasper during the Desert Heat mission. A mission that went to par only Ahmad Abualsami wasn't there at that compound the day it went down as first planned or else he would be a corpse himself.

"When my dad gets here all of you will be praying to Jesus Christ for death! I can guran-damn-tee that."

"How sweet, get her out of here." One of the Four Gods spoke in Arabic.

A man came in with a news report "We have a location for his wife!" The man said.

"About time!" Abualsami stated cold as ice.

The terrorist continued to talk as Brittany was taken back to her holding area.

<u>Veterans</u>

General Turner alerted Billy that intelligence has notified him that something was happening at the Marta station. He explained to the detective that military forces hadn't quite made it to that area yet. They were held up by heavy opposition middle ways there. Simply Priceless and Sophisticated Intimidation listened as the General spoke and then before General Turner had a chance to give out his directive Simply Priceless and Sophisticated Intimidation spoke at the same time "We'll handle it."

There wasn't an answer from Billy or Robbie because suddenly their significant other swooped them up and took to the air.

They landed outside the Marta station. Billy pulled back the slide of his gun. He had an evil look in his eye. He was ready to be back in action. Robbie had the look of fear across his face. It was a very dangerous look to have to be in the predicament they were in. The look and feelings he had running through his blood were the type that would get himself killed.

Sophisticated Intimidation squeezed Robbie's hand and gave him a reassuring look. He returned the best smile he could. Then the gunfire erupted. Terrorist in biological suits were firing machine guns. Simply Priceless sniffed the air. She could smell the biological gas inside the bombs, and she knew they were going to go off at any moment. She knew her and Sophisticated Intimidation had to act quickly.

There was no question that this was probably the deepest danger Billy and Robbie had ever been in. If those bombs were to go off, they would be dead in less than thirty seconds. Their skin would just rot off their bones. It would be something straight out of an adventure movie. Talking about an adventure movie where they are looking for lost artifacts like the Holy Grail.

"Intimidation follow my lead." Simply Priceless ordered.

"When did you become my boss?" Sophisticated Intimidation laughed.

"When it came down to saving our men's ass. One more time." Simply Priceless gave a wink.

"Guys don't get shot and don't shoot the containers." Sophisticated Intimidation commanded.

Sophisticated Intimidation and Simply Priceless took to the air, and they began to defuse the chemical bombs. Billy and Robbie shot down as many bad guys that came their way. They were a two men rock band streaming up the charts as they killed terrorist after terrorist.

"What's the count now?" Robbie yelled.

"I believe I am ahead like always because you shoot as good as a grandmother hyped up on ensure.'

"You are always a critic." Robbie replied then fired four rounds into a terrorist's chest.

"Good boy six points" Billy laughed.

Sophisticated Intimidation and Simply Priceless were about done with the bombs but SP sensed something bigger on the horizon. There was no question something more was going to go down.

Billy was in a boxing match with one of the terrorists as Robbie was taking fire. Billy finally kicked the man between the legs and snapped the guy's neck. Shortly after a few more guns shots Billy and Robbie stood around over a pile of dead bodies as Sophisticated Intimidation and Simply Priceless landed with all the chemical biological weapons disarmed.

"So, what's next?" Billy asked.

The entire hero gang got together with General Turner and took the time to go over all of their intelligence in order to properly plan out the final act!

The Plot Thickens

Becca was leaving Push Yourself Gym late that night. She woke up aggravated that Jasper was gone, and she was pissed when she peered inside Britts room, and she was gone. The girl defied her every chance she could get. As she was walking a Middle Eastern man approached her. He introduced himself "My name is Sohum Naik please come with me."

"What?"

"Your husband sent me to meet up with you. I work at CTU." Sohum showed a fake badge, and like a kid to candy Becca got into the car and road off with the terrorist.

Becca was brought to where Brittany was held. The first thing the terrorist did was bind her wrist and ankles but not before removing her shoes and socks.

They brought her to a room where Brittany was being held. Brittany was duct taped to a chair, and one of the terrorists was playing with her feet. Becca was sat down in another chair and found herself being bound and gagged the same way as her stepdaughter.

A terrorist was drawn to Becca's feet stink. If it was a cartoon green stink fumes would be coming up from between Becca's toes. Her feet stunk so bad it was terrible. It would make any normal person with a foot fetish gag. The terrorist however loved it. He inhaled her feet stink like a guy snorting coke. He sniffed between every toe and licked the salty tasting sweat from her feet. She didn't shower after she got done working out. She never does till she gets home because she doesn't like using Push Yourself Gym's facilities. Becca cried harder than Brittany.

As a matter a fact Brittany wasn't crying at all. She was used to her feet being worshipped and she gave up on the fact of crying. It did no use she would still be there in that same spot. She just had to hold on to the faith that her father would be there to save her. That was her only hope. That sounds corny, and the line sounds like it comes directly from a sci fi movie, but it was true Jasper Martin was Brittany and Becca Martin's only hope. If he messed up in anyway, they would for sure be dead.

The terrorist had things in motion, but they didn't know Jasper was one step closer from crashing the party. Jasper has crashed many parties that bad guys has held. He has over seen many missions out of the country which some he did participate in. He settled down after his marriage to Becca. He mostly handled desk work but don't get the situation wrong Jasper Martin is a true bad ass and he will kill or be killed if he needs to.

<u>After The Carpet Instillation</u>

Jasper was planning his next plan of action, but he knew the business arrangement of the carpet instillation was about to close. He found a residential address that kept popping up throughout the various contacts in the files. Even though there was no name connected to the address Jasper decided to visit the address anyway. He figured if it was an elderly couple, he would just ask to borrow some brown sugar but if it was a terrorist or any other nasty guy, he would implant a bullet to their skull.

He picked some extra weaponry and a set of keys to a Viper outside. He got in that Viper and sped to the address. The address brought Jasper to a house in a residential multimillion dollar community. Jasper drove the Viper directly through the front door.

"Honey I'm home!"

There didn't seem to be anybody around. Then Jasper saw a man in a t-shirt and tighty whities run upstairs and hide himself inside another room. Jasper got out of the Viper and sped up the stairs. He kicked in the door just as the man who had black curly hair and was overweight was trying to get into a panic room. Jasper had his 9mm ready and shot the man in the ass. The man was in such a panic he couldn't enter his password for his panic room.

Jasper refused to ask any questions. He had nothing to lose besides the wound wasn't fatal. Jasper looked around the room and saw pictures of his daughter and pictures of her feet. "What the fuck" Jasper thought to himself.

"I want your name and I want your name now."

"John Omar Stevens."

"How do you know my daughter?" Jasper questioned.

"Your daughter?" John dumbly replied.

Jasper fired two shots in both of John's legs.

"Do you mean Goddess Brittany?" John yelled in tears.

"Yes, Brittany you dumb fuck."

"I met her on a BDSM Personals Website. She is my Owner."

"Where is she?" John yelled.

"I set her up with a group I have known for a while. You might know them to. They are going to give her to me, and I will serve her as my Goddess twenty-four seven." John burst out in an evil laugh.

Jasper fired a shot into John's right shoulder. "Now perv tell me where she is!"

John gave up the address and was met with a thank you bullet to the head. Jasper ran back downstairs hearing sirens in the background. He sped out of the rubble in the Viper and was met with police cars in the street. He took off and was now in a high-speed pursuit by the authorities.

He knew all these twists and turns were really pissing him off. He knew he was outnumbered, and he couldn't contact division for help due to the moles that are on the inside. All he knew was he had to shake those cop cars. He was aware of police protocol and knew they wouldn't pursue at full speed as long as there were other drivers around that could get seriously injured or suffer death. He swerved in and out of traffic in the fast-moving car. It didn't take too long for him to shake the cops.

The address the rug man gave him was back in Atlanta, GA. He had to get his own ride there. He drove into the airport. It was a local airport for local plane travel. It wasn't for big jets it was for helicopters and private flight. He got out of the Viper, and saw a man walk inside the small shack from his helicopter. He knew that was his moment. He crept over to the man's helicopter and looked inside the chopper. There were no keys.

"Shit."

The man came back outside a few minutes later smoking a cigarette. By that point Jasper was hiding at the side of the shack. Jasper chop blocked the guy then choked him out. Then he stole the helicopter keys. Three guys ran up to defend the guy on the ground. Jasper went into martial arts mode doing a jump front kick to the first guy that came up. Then grabbing the second guy's arm and slinging him over his own shoulder. Then Jasper had a boxing match with the much bigger guy that ended with a kick to the nuts of the larger guy, and a knee to his face. Jasper ran to the helicopter started it up and off he went back to the Peach State.

A Foot Fetishist Dream

Becca and Brittany were stripped down to their bra and panties and were placed in the middle of a living room. They were surrounded by armed guards and were about to be forced to do something neither one of them wanted to do.

"Suck your mamma's toes." A terrorist ordered then nudged Brittany's back.

"What?" Brittany shockingly said.

"You heard him." Another terrorist replied.

"Just do it Brittany." Becca said lifting her foot toward Brittany's mouth.

Brittany began to cry as she held on to her stepmother's ankle and took her toes into her own mouth. Brittany sucked on her stepmom's foot like she would suck her boyfriend's cock. She was crying the entire time.

Becca began to moan and rub her vaginal area. Brittany thought how sick as she noticed somebody with a video camera taping the sexual act. Becca took her other foot and rubbed it on her stepdaughter's face.

"Suck her toes." A terrorist commanded Becca like a movie director. It didn't take much convincing as Becca picked up Brittany's foot and began to lap on it like a dog.

Brittany had no enjoyment out of this. She was crying so hard her face was red. However, Becca acted like she was at Wonderful World theme park.

Brittany swirled her tongue around her stepmom's ankle. She then licked, kissed, and nibbled on it. The video was going to be hot and sexy. It wasn't the first foot fetish video these terrorists have shot. They filmed others with other kidnapped victims. They sold them all around the world on the Dark Web. The terrorist made a good bit of money doing this. They made enough to finance their operation.

Enjoyment showed in Becca's face as she rubbed her feet on Brittany's face.

"Suck baby, suck." Becca commanded her stepdaughter.

The terrorist laughed. "Break it up a second" a terrorist commanded.

Another terrorist came into the room and put a collar around Brittany's neck. It was a pink sparkling studded collar. He then tossed the leash to Becca. "Dominate her."

"My pleasure." Becca replied to the terrorist order.

Becca stood up as the camera's zoomed in on her.

"Get on all fours you little slut. You are going to pay for all the hell you put me through." Brittany got on all fours then was kicked harshly in the side by her stepmom. "Call me Princess Becca whore."

"Yes, Princess Becca." Brittany whined winded.

"Kiss my feet."

Brittany began to make out with Becca's feet. "Now thank me you whiny bitch."

"Thank you, Princess Becca."

Terrorist were masturbating in the corners of the room. As others looked like drooling dogs.

"Kiss my ass."

"What?" Brittany whined, and then was met with a back hand.

"Yes, Princess Becca."

Becca pulled down and stepped out of her panties. Brittany kissed her stepmother's butt. "Now toss my salad." Princess Becca commanded with authority.

"No! No!" A gunshot was fired into the air, and somebody shocked Brittany's butt with a stun gun.

Brittany screamed then stuck her tongue up Becca's ass. She licked around on the stinky thing and kissed as Becca pulled her butt cheeks apart.

After tossing her stepmother's salad to Princess Becca's enjoyment Princess Becca had Brittany get back to worshipping her feet. Brittany had an indescribable taste inside her mouth, and a reeking smell on her nose. Becca pulled Brittany up then slapped her around degrading her. She told Brittany what a filthy nasty bitch she was. Then Becca began to degrade Jasper. She wasn't acting either. She knew this was her way out.

"Can I stay with you, and we can make this slutty, whorish, slut puppy be my bitch forever." Princess Becca spoke to Sohum who was walking into the room to check on the activities that were taking place.

"Sure, if you marry me" Sohum answered honestly.

"Deal." Becca replied.

Becca and Sohum kissed, and then Sohum made Brittany sucked him off, and swallow his orgasmic juices.

Brittany couldn't imagine the feelings of how she was being treated and thought about all those slaves she had to do crazy things online. She had a hanger bitch that she referred to as her hanger fucker because he stuck a huge wooden coat hanger up his ass. He fucked his ass so hard with the coat hanger he had to go see a proctologist because it ripped his rectum apart.

Brittany was then forced to worship Sohum's feet. Sohum and Becca sat on a wooden table as Brittany worshipped both their feet from the ground on her hands and knees. Becca once she finished worshiping her new Alpha Couple's feet even worshipped Brittany's feet more in order to complete the foot fetish video they were filming for the Dark Web. This video would be a foot fetishist wet dream, and all the terrorists thought of were dollar signs.

<u>Surprise Party</u>

Jasper made his arrival at the location shortly after landing in Atlanta hours later. It was a brick warehouse. The scary thing is there was nobody around. Is this another dead-end Jasper thought? He landed the helicopter out of sight and got out. The CTU Agent ran to a ladder and climbed up onto the roof. There was a single guard looking in the opposite direction than where Jasper came onto the roof at. Jasper rushed the terrorist and knocked him off the side of the building. He fell quickly to his death crashing into the cars below.

There was a sunroof Jasper looked through. He saw several levels to the warehouse. There were iron bridges all the way across. There was a terrorist right below Jasper. He jumped through the sunroof and knocked the terrorist down. Then he immediately snapped the guy's neck. Jasper removed the man's machine gun. The machine gun was equipped with a silencer. Jasper went straight on the move. He was like a predator hunting human beings straight out of a sci fi movie. He looked down and saw multiple terrorists. He knew he would be majorly outnumbered, but he didn't expect to be this outnumbered.

Jasper had to jump into stealth mode. Meanwhile action was taking place on the other side of the warehouse. Sophisticated Intimidation and Jim teamed back up and were there going to work. Maybe both of them will find their loved ones, but nobody knew at that time. Jim shot down three terrorists as he made his way through the warehouse.

The Four Gods and the important officials to that terrorist group escaped to another hideout. Jasper creeped up on a terrorist and snapped his neck. Then he put two bullets in the chest of another terrorist. The last terrorist Jasper shot and killed stumbled back and fell over the guard rail. Jasper was able to make it down to the floor level when he was shot at by Jim.

"Hey, who the fuck are you?" Jasper yelled because he saw Jim was white.

"Jim Turner GBI."

"Got a badge?"

Sophisticated Intimidation stood beside Jim. "Yeah, I have one dick head and if you don't have a good reason for being here, I am going to suspect you are working with the sand people from Tatooine and I will shove my gun so far up your ass it will come out your nose."

"I am Jasper. I work for the Counter Terrorist Unit."

Sophisticated Intimidation checked Jasper's heartbeat using her x-ray vision.

"He's telling the truth."

Jasper came out from hiding with his hands up in the air. "You can shoot me, or we can work together."

"Jim cool your head he's one of the good guys."

At that moment Jasper jumped to the side and fired three shots into a guy behind Jim and Intimidation.

"Come on let's go." Jim said running over and pulling up Jasper.

The warehouse seemed to be emptying of bad guys. Jim and Jasper made it to the only part of the warehouse they didn't search. Suddenly Simply Priceless and Billy arrived on scene along with Robbie.

"You know we could have used your help like twenty minutes ago." Jim scolded in a sarcastic tone.

"Who are you?" Billy asked Jasper.

"Now is not the time for introduction."

The hero dream team moved forward to another part of the warehouse where at that time Brittany and Emma were visible hanging from a crane. They were bound with C4 explosive on their chest. There was an office above the hero's head and the office looked over the top of the crane that was inside the unfinished warehouse. This warehouse had a lot of different construction equipment all about and construction on this warehouse stopped a long time ago due to failure to have the funds to complete construction! Ahmad Abualsami walked out of the office holding the detonator to the C4.

"I will sacrifice myself in the name of Allah but all of you will come down with me."   The women were crying as would be expected.

Simply Priceless and Sophisticated Intimidation began to analyze the situation. They knew exactly what to do. About eight men came around the corner armed with automatic weapons with laser sights on the hero's chest.

"Ahmad Abualsami." Jasper said.

"I am glad to know we are on a first name basis. You killed my father."

"I know. How about you take me and let the women go."

"It's not that easy. You take from me then I will take from you."

Ahmad Abualsami began to put pressure on the detonator when Simply Priceless and Sophisticated Intimidation took off at the speed of light. The speed of their flight caused a wind to knock everyone down. Simply

Priceless grabbed Ahmad Abualsami and knocked him down. She then punched him so hard it knocked him down and tied him up. Sophisticated Intimidation took possession of the detonator. After Priceless had Abualsami all tied up she deactivated the C4 explosive vest and undid the hostages. Meanwhile Jim, Billy, Robbie, and Jasper shot down the eight men who were trying to get back to their feet.

The two true superheroes landed after they took the hostages to the nearest base camp within a blink of an eye. "You have about ten seconds now to get out of here. The whole building is wired to explode." Ahmad Abualsami spoke with satanic laughter.

Simply Priceless grabbed Robbie and Billy, and Sophisticated Intimidation grabbed Jasper and Jim, and off they went at lightning speed to the camp that everyone else was located.

The only reason Ahmad told them this was because if they ran there would be no way they could get out in time. He neglected to remember that they had a couple of superheroes on their side. Once they got safely in the air the entire place blew up, and pieces of the building went everywhere. They were at the camp within seconds. Once at basecamp Brittany told her father everything her stepmother did, and about Becca agreeing to marry Sohum and how her stepmother exited the scene with the terrorists under her own free will!

So, the adventure continues…

So, The Adventure Continues

Air Force One landed at LAX in Los Angeles, California. The pilot pulled into a private hanger where everybody was all alone. Scott lowered Al-Mughassil's gag. Scott had his gun drawn from its holster.

"Now asshole tell me all the details, or I will splatter your brains all over this plane. Do you know who Ahmed Elraei is?" Scott began his line of questioning.

"Right?" Al-Mughassil rolled his eyes as he spoke to a question that he knew would kill him if he answered correctly.

"Tell me! You dumb fuck!!" The Secret Service Agent yelled.

Out of fear of what Scott would do to him Al-Mughassil decided to answer Scott's question "He and I are in cahoots with the terrorist."

"And?" Scott sought out more details.

"The Four Gods have been broken out of jail, and everything is fixing to get majorly rough here in the United States. There is a nuclear bomb planted at a vampire goth bar in Atlanta called The Brood. They are out for revenge for our homelands, and they wanted money. Some of the members of this group wanted revenge on certain people. It is a mess." Al-Mughassil explained with defiant fear inside his voice.

"What's the plan." Scott asked boldly.

"Once everything takes place the Four Gods plan on robbing every national bank and Wall Street then they will go back to their countries as heroes, and the United States would have been sent back to the Stone Age. The Four Gods plan to burn the United States down before everything is all said and done! Even after the Four Gods leave the United States terror will continue to move across the United States including Alaska and Hawaii."

"So, all this is about money and revenge." Scott calmly.

"Yes."

"How's this for revenge." Scott fired a single shot to the center of the President's head.

Two other secret service agents stored Al-Mughassil's body in a storage compartment under the plane. Scott thought about having Air Force One head to Greensboro, North Carolina since that is where Ahmed Elraei would be. He ran the information he just received about the master plan that Mughassil spelled out by the other secret service agents so they would know the exact level of chaos they were about to encounter. He made sure those who weren't in on it wouldn't stay on Air Force One. Everybody was in for the good of their country. Air Force One was refilled with fuel and an across country flight was immediately underway. Scott was in fear. Along with everybody else. After all he hadn't seen any action since the Iraq, Afghanistan wars. He was in on this mission completely though. He knew what he had to do, and he was going to do it.

With his secret service squad behind him, he had his own little-small tact team since everyone had military experience, and most were military and then law enforcement of some kind before they came to work for the secret service.

Emma and Brittany sat by the superhero sister duo at a table under a tent. They were eating and trying to recoup from their ordeal. Jasper talked to General Turner who called the CTU Director over the Greensboro Division. Jasper gave him the briefing, and about an hour later Jasper brought his daughter to a safe house where he was one hundred percent certain that his daughter would be safe as he was sent back to Greensboro for a final push!

Meanwhile the Presidential Candidates were all in one big hotel suite at a different hotel than before. They were heavily guarded by both secret service and military personnel.

Senator Gonzales was alone in a separate area than the rest of the candidates. He was sitting on the edge of his bed when suddenly all the power went out on his side of the suite. Suddenly sounds of crashing glass was all that can be heard. Two men came into the room dressed in full tactical gear.

"Adios." One of the men said to Senator Gonzales before both men unloaded several machine guns rounds into the senator's chest. Blood exploded through the air as Senator Gonzales fell backwards onto the bed, and then rolled off the bed and fell onto the floor.

The power flashed all over the rest of the suite. Then the entire floor the suite was on went black. The military went on high alert as suddenly all that could be seen were red laser lights. Men, women, and the presidential candidates' children were being shot down as multiple terrorists entered the floor after repealing down from the roof.

The lights came on and everybody laid to rest except Senator Ahmed Elraei. One of the terrorists told the remaining Senator "Let's go" in Arabic. The terrorist staged a scene of pulling Senator Ahmed Elraei out onto the balcony. A helicopter was flying right beside the balcony, so the terrorist and the senator could load up into the helicopter and fly off.

Senator Ahmed Elraei was flown to the terrorist hideout in Atlanta. He knew the plan was he had been kidnapped by the terrorist in Atlanta. He even made a mock kidnap video which was aired all-across the United States, and Arabic television. The mock video said that Senator Ahmed Elraei would be taken to The Brood in twenty-four hours where he would be taken out or let go depending on if the United States paid the terrorist group more money than they asked for already.

Meanwhile Sean was notified on the situation about the presidential candidate's suite and was walking among a sea of dead bodies. He knew he had to get back to Atlanta, so he was flown back there immediately.

Scott saw the telecast of Ahmed Elraei being kidnapped, and he researched where The Brood nightclub was. Once Scott found out the location of The Brood, he had Air Force One diverted to Atlanta, Ga.

The Band is Back Together

Billy and crew knew this adventure wasn't over. They began to go over all the trace evidence. Rumors flew around about a nuclear bomb, and terrorist caught and interrogated mentioned such. Simply Priceless and Sophisticated Intimidation knew they had to get on top of it.

"We will be back soon babies. Remember Mommy is always watching over you." Simply Priceless and Sophisticated Intimidation said at the same time kissing their loved one's cheek then flying off.

"I love….

Billy and Robbie realized their loved ones were gone after saying love but then spoke to word "You" defeated.

Billy and Robbie went to talk to one of the terrorists which were in custody. They were driven in a hummer to the site where the terrorist was at. He was at a secret Atlanta PD location. Billy and Robbie burst through the door like a couple of Atlanta PI agents.

"Hey rag head." Billy said.

The Islamic man began to cuss the two Detectives in Arabic.

Billy punched the man in the jaw. The terrorist was chained to a chair. Then Billy kicked the man in the chest.

"Now you are going to tell me what is going on."

"Fuck you!" The terrorist yelled but Billy could sense a bit of fear inside the terrorist's voice.

"Fuck me. Fuck me. Fuck me!" Billy burst into laughter then quickly pulled his gun like some wild-wild west gunslinger and shot the man in his foot.

The man cried in pain.

"Now you better tell me what is going on before I work my way up shooting every inch of you till you are dead" Billy explained.

Some military agents knocked on the door. Robbie blocked them from entering by placing a chair under the doorknob.

"The broo. The broo."

"The boo what?" Billy asked then shot the terrorist's other foot.

"The vampires have the bomb! The vampires have the bomb!"

"What bomb dip shit." Billy asked.

"The nuclear bomb" was the terrorist last words because Billy fired two to three shots into the man's chest.

Robbie unblocked the door and Billy and his Atlanta PD partner walked out the door like nothing happened.

All Billy knew now was he was about to cross the line of extreme and deal with elements out of his norm. Vampires in movies were one thing. People living the vampire gothic lifestyle is another.

There was a motorcycle outside the secret prison. Billy hopped on "Let's go."

"What? On that?" Robbie spoke with fear.

"Get on or I will leave your chicken ass." Billy said starting up the bike.

"If you say so." Robbie said getting on.

Neither man wore a helmet as Billy sped to the Brood and Robbie hung on for dear life. Robbie was scared half to death. Billy drove like a champ though. It was a while since he been on a motorcycle, but he pushed this one to the limit.

They made it to The Brood. Billy parked the bike behind a dumpster in the back. They both got off the bike. Each pulled their weapon and made sure they were ready to rock and roll before they went inside.

Both went to the backdoor and slowly opened it up. Inside was dark, and a blood type colored fluid was spraying out of sprinkler located on the ceiling. There were several gothic people dancing around. Some had their mouth open and were drinking the red liquid from the ceiling. There were others feasting on one or more people at a time. It was like one big vampire orgy. One big vampire porn video in some of the rooms where there were people's breast and penises exposed. Not to mention people going down on women and biting them.

The dream team detectives went through the backdoor. "Go find out who runs this place I will stay here." Robbie spoke in fear. Robbie hated vampire movies. He just couldn't watch them. They scared him half to death. It was pathetic how a grown man like Robbie could get so scared over a vampire movie. Even with a black vampire killing superhero like Blade Robbie couldn't handle vampire movies. Cali loved vampire movies though and had to hold her baby close in order to watch them.

"Fine chicken shit."

Billy started to walk into the room, but he was blindsided by a giant bouncer. Billy fell to the ground with a bloody nose. He was dazed as he began to pull himself back up on the bouncer's legs! The bouncer who was a rotunda interlocked his hands together then slammed his hands down on Billy's head.

Robbie was frozen in fear. Billy fell to the ground. Then he did a spinaroonie like a dreidel top and tripped the bouncer up. He fell to the ground, and Billy kicked him in the face. Another bouncer came and kicked Billy in the side. Coatman was wondering where Brewer was. Billy got back up and football tackled one of the bouncers through the nearest wall.

Robbie came out of the back, and gave a death shot to the original bouncer. Billy jumped and slid across the floor through the blood that was spraying from the sprinklers. The blood puddled up from not being drained quick enough down the drains in floor. The floor drains recycled the blood bringing the blood back up to where it once again could spray from the ceiling sprinklers. Billy grabbed his gun and flipping over while he was sliding firing three rounds into the second bouncer.

Robbie helped Billy his feet then the battle began. It was one big vampire bar fight. Both Billy and Robbie were throwing punches and kicks. Billy broke several arms over his shoulder then kicked men in their chest. Billy did a jump front kick to one guy. Then he slung that guy over a bar top.

The battle was hard because it was very slippery with the liquid pouring from the ceiling. Finally, Billy got pissed and began to unload rounds into people. Robbie followed the leader, and the two detectives shot whoever they could. Those that weren't shot or injured took off running.

Billy noticed a guy run into an office. It was Prince Izic Obayifo. The prince of death was about to continue to have a very bad day, because he already cheated death by getting where his appendage used to be at sown up by one of his vampire clan members who was a surgeon in real life.

Billy walked over to the door as Robbie looked over the carnage. He thought if Billy didn't teach him some of those martial arts moves, he would be lying amongst the rest of the injured and dead people.

Billy tried the door, but it was locked. Billy then used his universal lock pick and kicked the door in.

"Hey vamp tell me where the bomb is?" Billy asked sarcastically.

"What bomb?"

The women were still in their cages, and one was met with a gunshot to the shoulder.

"No!" Prince Izic Obayifo yelled having Deja Vue.

"Tell me where the bomb is!"

"Ok I'll tell you. The bomb is….

Prince Izic Obayifo sprung over his desk and onto Billy. Billy dropped his gun as Prince Izic Obayifo bit into his neck. Billy fell to the ground and flipped Prince Izic Obayifo over him. Then he grabbed the prince and slammed him headfirst down on his desk. Then Billy slung Prince Izic Obayifo to the ground and began kicking him. Billy picked up a folding chair and hit the prince with it. Then he closed Prince Izic Obayifo's ankle in the folding chair.

"Now tell me where the bomb is located?"

The vampire Prince spit blood. It was probably partly Billy's blood since Billy's neck was bleeding where the prince bit him. The prince was screaming in pain when Billy slammed his foot down on the chair causing it to close up and break Prince Izic's ankle.

"It's here. It's here!" Prince Izic Obayifo yelled.

About that time Priceless and Intimidation arrived on the scene. Intimidation walked into the office while Priceless was using her x-ray vision to find the bomb.

"You telling the truth? It is here?" Billy asked not seeing a bomb anywhere in sight.

"I think he is, are you telling the truth that the bomb is here." Sophisticated Intimidation laughed then slammed her foot down on the chair which was still around the vampire Prince's ankle.

"Yes! Yes! Yes! They brought it here from the GA Aquarium." Prince Izic Obayifo yelled in pain.

Priceless found the bomb. Then it turned out what everybody thought was a nuclear bomb was only a regular bomb which didn't take but seconds for Simply Priceless to disarm it.

Priceless walked where everybody was crowded around Prince Izic Obayifo.

"It's not here. Must still be at the aquarium." Priceless spoke with authority.

"Ok I will fly fang head to the base camp." Sophisticated Intimidation said looking down at Prince Izic who was in tears.

"Ok I will take these two lug heads to the aquarium"

Then within a blink of an eye everything happened just as both superheroes spelled out their plans of action.

Billy found a walkie talkie outside the aquarium on one of the dead military men. He radioed into home base camp to get extra men on scene.

Simply Priceless and the two detectives walked inside. There it was. Right there in the center of the establishment. It didn't take long for Sophisticated Intimidation to drop the vampire Prince off and come on scene. Simply Priceless and Sophisticated Intimidation looked over the bomb then at super speed the two of them together disarmed it.

The two superheroes flew their men back to base camp only to await their next obstacle.

<u>Party Pooper</u>

Senator Ahmed Elraei arrived at The Brood only to find the place destroyed. There were bodies everywhere. Some men and women were still alive suffering. The Senator had no idea what happened. They just knew this much chaos couldn't have been caused by one man. They believed an army destroyed the place and left. It looked like a scene out of a war movie. Some of the Senator's men were shooting the injured people on the ground.

"Don't waste your ammo. Take me to the Four Gods." Senator Ahmed Elraei ordered.

It didn't take long for them to pack up shop, and head over to the living members of the Four God's hideout. The Four Gods Shahrzad Yousef, Saed Al-Shafai, and Abu Moosaq were all sitting around a table. They were playing cards like nothing was going on. The senator sat on a stool in the corner of the room. Senator Ahmed got in and out of The Brood just in the nick of time because it was by now swarming with a lot of military and police figures.

"What is going on next?" Shahzad asked.

"What do you mean?" The senator replied.

"What do I mean! What do I mean!" Shazad yelled storming standing up and slamming his fist down on the table.

"Get to the point!" The Senator yelled

"The nuclear bomb has been disarmed. The chemical bombs have been disarmed….

"The cyber-attack is still going on, so I hear, and you have hundreds of millions, billions of dollars transferring from the average joes account to an upper society account in your own offshore accounts." The Senator explained.

"What else do we got?" Abu Moosaq asked.

"There is the attack on the United Nations. Then who knows once we accomplish that we could attack the pentagon or the white house." The Senator explained.

"Good enough. "Shazad replied under his breath.

"I am sorry to be a party pooper, but I got to record another mock video now."

The senator went out of the office area and found a place in the warehouse to record the mock video. His people taped a decent realistic video then distributed it over all air ways. Everything was ready set go.

<u>Not Quite a Secret Anymore</u>

Air Force one landed Greensboro first even though Scott planned for Air Force One to be detoured to Atlanta because Sean had to have a meeting. Scott got off Air Force One and went right to work determining what to do. Only it didn't take long for Air Force One to be surrounded by Federal Agents. Jasper just arrived on scene, and Scott explained the whole part of this story that Scott was aware of to Jasper. It was time to push things into overdrive. No questions asked because this nonsense needed to be done. Sean saw Senator Ahmed Elraei's mock kidnap video, so he knew he had to return to Atlanta as quick as possible. After all the terrorist in that video said they were in the middle of an Islamic warzone.

Sean was also on scene and involved in a three-way conversation between Jasper, Scott, and himself. Scott, Jasper, and Sean all loaded in a helicopter and were taken back to Atlanta because it was unveiled, and the cat was completely out of the bag that Senator Ahmed Elraei wasn't a victim but instead the senator was just another slime ball who must be stopped.

Jasper had to reassure Brittany that everything would be ok before leaving her at the safe house, and Jasper planned on keeping his promise to his daughter that he would be back to pick her up. Finally, he had Brittany calmed down to the point that he could fly back to Greensboro, North Carolina with the understanding that her father had to finish the job he was hired to do.

Meanwhile Scotty at the CTU headquarters went to the bathroom and stuck a chip in his phone which had critical information on it. He then reached into one of the toilet paper dispensers and pulled out a cell phone. He called the Four Gods.

"I got it."

The Four Gods told him to get out of the CTU building as soon as possible so he doesn't get caught and they can get the information.

"Yes sir." Scotty replied.

The call ended and Scotty began to walk out of the bathroom when he was pushed back by a female Counter Terrorist Unit agent. She came into the bathroom. They were alone.

"I know what you are doing Scotty. You are being a very naughty boy." The woman said.

"Monika I am sorry. Please don't tell anybo…

Monika kissed Scott's lips very forcefully, and then kneed him between the legs. After that she slapped his face and clawed his cheek.

"Fiesty." Scotty said.

"Now give me the phone."

"What?" Scotty replied.

"You heard me you ugly fuck! Hand it over."

Scotty didn't have a chance to consider giving her the phone because Monika did a round kick to the side of Scotty's head. He fell over and hit his head on the sink. Monika then snapped Scotty's neck. After that very quickly she removed the phone which had the secret information card in it. She then exited the CTU Headquarters very quickly. It didn't take long for her to get out to parking deck into her SUV and on her way to the drop point.

Sohum walked into the meeting room where the Four Gods still sat.

<u>Hell, Fire, and Brimstone</u>

The Four Gods spoke to Sohum in Arabic, and they were highly pissed off to the letter.

"Our bitch is bringing the information to the meeting point. We expect you to be there. You have twenty-five minutes to be there, or it is your head." One of the Four Gods spoke. Sohum replied telling them he understood then he left to head to go to the meeting point.

Sohum made it to the meeting point in less than the time limit quoted. Monika was already there. She was speaking with another Middle Eastern man. Sohum witnessed the exchange between her and the other man. "What's going on?"

"Sohum, meet your replacement, Rajesh." Monika said. Rajesh turned around and fired two 9mm shots into Sohum who fell backwards and hit the ground dead.

Monika got into her car and drove off. Rajesh got on his motorcycle and road to deliver the Intel to the Four Gods.

Sean, Jasper, and Scott were outside the hotel that their evidence led. They were all suited up. They had the gears of war look, and they were ready to go to hell and back. They proceeded towards the front entrance of the hotel, stealth like. The three hid behind every object they could on their way to the entrance. When they got into viewing site of inside the front glass sliding doors Jasper spotted four men patrolling the lobby.

One of the men came outside and lit up a cigarette. Jasper decided he would take this guard out personally and find out as much as he could before he snapped his neck. Jasper crawled like someone out of a war movie to get to the side of the building on the side where the man was smoking. Then as Sean and Scott covered him, he slipped up behind the man, and placed him in a choke hold.

"Tell me how many people are in the building, and I will consider sparing your life." Jasper whispered into the man's ear.

"There are six on the third and sixth floor. Then there are the three others in the lobby. Please don't kill me." The man begged as he began to answer.

"Where is Senator Ahmed Elraei?"

"He is in a suite on the ninth floor. There are two guards outside his room. Please don't kill me."

Jasper didn't care about the man's pleas. He just snapped the man's neck. Then he disarmed him and removed the guard's radio.

With Jasper in the lead, they made their way to the front door. All the men's weapons were equipped with silencers, they opened fire gunning all the men down that were in the lobby. The men marched through the broken glass and began to ascend the steps. Once they got up to the sixth floor a terrorist walked into the stairwell. Jasper quickly pulled his knife. He grabbed the man, held him close with his left hand smothering the man as he slit the terrorist throat with the right. Then the mini tac team proceeded upward.

They got out on the ninth floor. Sean and Scott took the lead this time. They found the Senator's suite from a distance and placed two perfectly centered bullets to the guard's head. Scott pointed toward the door, and Sean motioned for Jasper to follow. The three looked like a Navy Seal Team as they approached the door. They looked as professional and worked as affectively as the Navy Seals from the Charlie Sheen movie that was released on July 20th, 1990.

When they got to the door Jasper removed the electronic room key from one of the guard's pockets. They made a formation. Jasper swiped the key card, and slowly opened the door. Each entered the hotel room suit one by one. The order was Sean, then Scott and followed up by Jasper in the rear.

There was a TV blaring in the back of the suite. The TV in the living room area was on as well. The team heard a bunch of giggling like on a woman's boarding school courtyard. A half-naked Asian came running out of the bedroom. She didn't even see the three men who were a matter of yards away with guns pointed in her direction.

"O Senator you so silly." This female had a voice tone that sounded like a girl who was under the legal age and unable to consent spoke. By that point the three gunmen were right outside the room. Scott counted to three lifting up one finger at a time. Scott ran to the front of the line and entered the bedroom. There was a young teen girl going down on the Senator while the Asian woman was massaging his shoulders. An older woman probably in her forties came out of the bathroom in a bath robe.

"Come on girls out." Scott yelled.

The women screamed and ran out of the bedroom where Sean and Jasper got each one and placed plastic restraints on their wrist. Sean stayed outside the room holding the three women at gunpoint. Jasper walked into the bedroom.

"Did you have my family kidnapped." Jasper stated firmly.

"I don't know what you are talking about." The Senator coldly answered.

"Sure, you don't." Jasper cleared his throat. "Because you are a traitor of the grand United States of America. Where is Senator Elraei?" Jasper asked.

"Come on fuck wad." Scott said. He jerked Senator Elraei around and placed him in handcuffs. Then he knocked the Senator's feet out from under him which caused the Senator to fall next to his women.

"You will never get out of here alive." The senator spoke confidently.

"Don't count your virgins in heaven before you die asshole." Jasper replied.

Scott got on his walkie talky and gave orders to the helicopter pilot of his teams coordinates as several men came into the suite, and an all-out battle began to take place. Bullets flew around like coins coming out of a slot machine. It seemed like a never-ending battle. As soon as one man was shot down another one entered the room.

About that time the helicopter was hovering over the hotel suite's balcony. The three men made their way to the balcony dragging the Senator behind them. Sean and Jasper loaded the senator into the chopper as Scott covered them. Jasper then Sean entered the chopper and was covering Scott, but they couldn't save him. Several bullets entered his face and chest. Scott collapsed dead falling over the balcony and crashing into cars below.

"Go! Go! Go!" Jasper yelled.

The helicopter took to the air on their way to a secure location.

The root of the cyber-attack was traced down. Robbie overheard its location and told the gang. Time for more action Billy thought.

"Let us examine the scene before we bring you two fellas." Sophisticated Intimidation said calmly.

Before either man could reply both their women were gone. It was like a magic trick from a magician in Las Vegas but only this was no illusion. The two detectives looked at one another a little miffed. We are grown ass men Billy thought. Why couldn't he just go with them. Leave the kid here, and us real heroes go Billy joked in his mind. He knew they would be back in a short time frame unless they wanted to steal the action for themselves.

"Who was she calling us fellas? I mean she was talking to us like we were a couple of children." Billy pouted.

"I figured you would be used to it by now Billy. I mean Ashley is pretty much your mommy the way you depend on her for things."

Billy knew that statement from Robbie was true. Sometimes Billy called his wife Mommy as a pet name in their private lives. He wasn't an adult baby, so nobody needs to misconstrued the scenario. Billy doesn't like his wife to wipe his ass and put him in diapers. He called Ashley Mommy because of his wife's loving nature towards him, and how Ashley "Simply Priceless" Hatch-Coatman always took care of him throughout their entire relationship.

He would never let it slip to anyone he knew he called his wife Mommy in the sense that Ashley cared for Billy like he was a third child because he knew Robbie would give him hell for life if he knew the grand Atlanta police detective Billy Coatman did anything close to ABDL or Adult Baby Diaper Lover play. Robbie didn't believe in kink shaming, but he would kink shame his partner from the APD if he found out that Detective Billy Coatman was a closet ABDL freak.

Billy wasn't into ABDL kink however and in fact found the subject matter sick whenever it was thrown in front of his face whenever he would watch a daytime talk show like Jerry Springer or Montel. Even Montel found the subject matter sick that time he put the adult baby diaper lover fetish on his daytime program to spell out what people involved in the abdl realm were all about!

Billy just hoped that Ashley would never tell her sister because he knew that Cali would wind up sharing those intimate details with Robbie sooner or later because Cali herself could not keep a secret. Only what Billy didn't know Ashley did explain to her sister how Billy was like a third child to take care of, and Cali was doing a great job at holding that secret tight to the vest without telling Robbie so far!

Robbie laughed loudly at his own statement. Billy began to swell up like some barnyard rooster.

"Easy fella calm down." Robbie laughed even louder.

"I got your fella Rob."

While Robbie was irritating his partner the super duo reached their destination. They landed in a pitch-dark area. They both began to use their super x-ray vision to examine the scene.

There were plenty of hardware and not just the computer kind. Everyone there had automatic weapons. Two guards were walking by. Simply Priceless and Sophisticated Intimidation blew as hard as they could sailing those two men through the building. The brick wall crumbled like a crane just struck it. The super team flew into the building.

"Honey I'm home." Sophisticated Intimidation spoke cheerfully.

"May I borrow a cup of brown sugar?" Simply Priceless followed up with a smile.

Bullets began to shatter on their chest. Both sisters waved their index finger in front of them then blinked. The terrorist guns left their hands and flew up in the air. The weapons kept firing till they were all unloaded then they fell back to the ground. The terrorist took off running. Sophisticated Intimidation flew to the main computer which was controlling everything. All the money from everybody's account had been transferred. Sophisticated Intimidation shut her eyes then slammed both of her fist down on the desk. She screamed "Noooooo" her eyes were blood red when she opened them back up, and fire blew from her mouth.

Her fury was interrupted by a bullet exploding off the back of her head. She looked behind her it was Elizabeth A'ishah who fired the shot. Her husband Hamza fired an entire AK-47 into Simply Priceless chest. Sophisticated Intimidation at super speed speared Elizabeth so hard they both went through a brick wall, and out into the parking lot. That was where Sophisticated Intimidation began to unload the fist.

Simply Priceless walked up to Hamza as he was trying to reload. Hamza was shaking too bad to be able to place another clip in his automatic weapon. Like it would matter any even if he was able to reload.

Simply Priceless did a round kick to the automatic weapon. The gun went flying through the air and through the brick wall where it kept sailing down the street. She then followed that up with a jump front kick to the terrorist face. Simply Priceless then picked Hamza up over her head and slammed him down on a set of computers.

"Reverse the transfer!" Simply Priceless yelled.

Hamza laughed blood dripping from his mouth. Simply Priceless kicked him in his mouth. Then picked him up over her head again. She placed his back on her right shoulder. She then squeezed Hamza's chest. "I got all day, loser."

Sophisticated Intimidation drug Elizabeth back inside by her long hair. She had Elizabeth A'ishah broken and beaten.

"Any luck?" Sophisticated Intimidation asked her sister.

"He's not talking."

"Maybe because he is turning purple." Sophisticated Intimidation replied.

Simply Priceless slung Hamza off her back and he flew through the air and into another computer table.

The ladies decided to fly Hamza and Elizabeth A'ishah back to home base where one way or another somebody would get the information out of them. There was nothing else computer wise that could be done. Everybody's bank accounts were drained and placed into the account that the terrorist wanted the funds in!

Rajesh made it to the main hideout for the Four Gods. He went inside and stood before the Four Gods. He got down to his knees with his head lowered. Rajesh explained he had the intelligence and laid the package on the floor. The Four Gods nodded in enjoyment as Rajesh slid the package to the feet of the living members of the Four Gods. He then politely exited the room.

Jasper and Sean arrived at home base. Sean was dragging the Senator behind them. Simply Priceless and Sophisticated Intimidation then arrived with their prisoners. All the prisoners were bound properly.

"Billy." An army soldier said with fear.

Billy turned around and acknowledged the army soldier.

The man explained to Billy what happened with the key information that was stolen from CTU.

"What?" Jasper said walking over.

Sean overheard as well. The army soldier walked away as the dream team stared at each other. "Ready for one more ride at the least?" Sean asked Jasper.

"Yes, but first." Jasper replied then stormed into where the Senator was being held. Jasper cleared off a table. Then he walked over and grabbed the large water jug from the water dispenser.

"What are you doing?" A female official asked.

"My job." Jasper said ripping off his shirt.

He then picked up the senator and slammed him down on the table. Simply Priceless and Sophisticated

Intimidation came over and held the senator down. Jasper placed the shirt over the senator's face, and Billy held it in place.

"Now Mr. Senator you have one chance to tell me where the hideout is, or you can risk drowning."

The senator didn't say anything, so Jasper lifted the large water jug over the senator's face. He then proceeded to pour that water on the Senator's face drenching the shirt. The senator was gagging as he felt like he was drowning. Water boarding was banned by the President of the United States, but Jasper knew it was justified in this case. Even though right then pure Armageddon was taking place Jasper had a feeling that the President would understand but underneath all that hell the President may not even find out about it!

Once the entire bottle was used Billy lifted the shirt. "Where is the intel!" Jasper yelled.

"Fuck you!" The senator yelled spitting out water.

"Again!" Jasper yelled.

Billy recovered the Senator's face, and Jasper had someone with a hose refill the water jug before he began pouring. The senator was gagging. He began to jerk so Jasper stopped, and Billy lifted Jasper's shirt off the senator's face. The senator spit out a whole heap of water and began to spill his guts giving out the exact address where the Four Gods were hiding out at.

Jasper punched the senator in his face square in the nose after saying "thank you" very hatefully.

"Now are you ready for one more ride?" Sean asked with a smile because he loved Jasper's actions.

The gang grabbed a whole fleet of weapons. All the non-superheroes strapped on clip belts and filled them up with magazines. They also got various grenades and attached laser sights to their guns. Billy was getting aroused knowing all the action that was about to come up as he loaded up heavy explosives into four small man bags. Finally, they were ready to leave after their preparation.

"Wait. Have room for one more?" Jim walked over and asked.

Sean motioned for him to get ready, and he loaded an arsenal up just like everyone else who didn't have superpowers. It was one super team no pun intended about to act with a major strike against the terrorist. Hopefully it would be this one last battle to extinguish the fire that this terrorist group engulfed the United States with. Then Atlanta could be worried about being rebuilt. Which it was going to take a lot of money to rebuild the city as it used to be. The gang knew once things were settled down that the new President of the United States would declare a state of emergency in Atlanta. Only at that current moment America had no President to run the country.

Sean, Jim, and Jasper loaded back up in the helicopter to be flown to the location as Simply Priceless and Sophisticated Intimidation flew Billy and Robbie with style to the climax of this major battle or so they would think!

<u>World War?</u>

Intimidation and Priceless were above scene much quicker than the helicopter. The place looked like a giant ant hill with ants traveling all about. Only these ants carried high powered weaponry, and they stormed around with a purpose. Soon enough the helicopter was overhead, and the first strike was made when Jim, Jasper, and Sean went repelling down firing machine gun shots into whoever they saw was walking. Simply Priceless and Sophisticated Intimidation then tag teamed in. They flew down blowing the terrorist down who were still up that Jim, Jasper, or Sean didn't get. They dropped Billy and Robbie off on the ground as they went into full swing.

Billy and Robbie stood back-to-back to back firing 9mm shots into whoever was moving. As the field begin to get leveled, and the flies began to drop the group made their approach.

The warehouse was huge. It was top of the line. It was big enough to house a movie theater and a few small restaurants on the inside. Maybe even a bowling alley.

"What's the plan pops?" Robbie asked.

"Just watch out for yourself kid and stay clean behind the ears." Billy spoke calmly and disappeared.

Billy went around to the back of the building and climbed up a fire escape to the roof. He walked over to the sunroof and stared down below. He was looking into an office. Billy saw the remaining three Four Gods sitting and praying on a giant rug. Billy knew he could pick them off one by one by one where they sat. He knew he was just that quick on the trigger.

Robbie ran into Jasper, and they took it upon themselves to enter the front of the building. They were backed up by Sophisticated Intimidation. They entered the warehouse and were met by heavy gunfire. Intimidation placed a giant force field around Robbie and Jasper then made a slapping motion in the air which knocked the bad men down.

Intimidation released the force field, and the two standard crime fighters went forward Sean came through a side door. A man was standing in front of him when he opened the door. Agent Black grabbed him then snapped his neck. Suddenly another man saw Sean. He began to fire at Sean who held the guy who's neck he snapped upon entry as a shield. Sean held his "shield" with one hand and fired down the man shooting with the other using a 9mm of his own.

Sean planted some explosives then he dove into another room where he was met by more gunfire. He killed two more terrorists. He walked out into a stairwell. He cleared his throat as softly as possible then proceeded to ascend the stairs planting explosives on the wall.

Jim was still outside picking terrorist off one by one. He already had planted eight explosives on the wall of the outside of the warehouse, and just planted three more on vehicles outside. A guy walked around the corner. Jim planted three rounds to the man's chest, and then proceeded to another part outside the warehouse planting more explosives on cars.

Jasper and Robbie were like a couple of tag team champions in some wrestling organization. Only their tag team would never break up unlike The Rockets, The Bubba

Boys, or The Ultimate Bikers. They stayed side by side blowing people out of their pants, and planting explosives in the process.

Suddenly Billy was fired upon. He jumped behind an air vent then quickly rose firing a single shot to the man's head. Not noticing another man on the roof. The man pushed Billy then followed that up with a punch. Billy stumbled backwards and fell through the window still holding all his equipment.

The remaining Four Gods looked at each other like "what the fuck!" Then went to work on Billy. Billy was getting the boots from everyone inside the room until he was able to trip one of them up. He flipped himself off the ground and made it back to his feet. He punched one of the Four Gods twice in the face and did a reverse sidekick to the one behind him. He slung the man he tripped up over the desk in the room. Raj approached Billy. Billy kicked Raj between the legs. Raj bent over when suddenly Billy hooked his head like he was about to do a DDT on the guy, but he threw all his weight upwards, and snapped the man's neck. One of the remaining three Four Gods went to work. Billy grabbed his fist and twisted then broke the God's arm over his own shoulder. He then flipped the God over his back and to the floor only to stomp his face as many times as it took for that God to no longer be of this world. The second Four God in the room ran toward Billy. He grabbed the God and spun around in the air slamming him to the ground only to snap the man's ankle afterward. Billy picked up his 9mm and fired four rounds into the third Four God, and a round in the back of the head of the Four God who was lying on the rug crying over his broken ankle.

Then Billy caught his breath and planted explosives all around the room.

Sophisticated Intimidation was scanning the building as Simply Priceless landed on the roof where she got in a fight with the person who caused Billy to fall through the skylight. The fight ended quickly because she slung the man off the roof, and onto the pavement below. Simply Priceless jumped down into the room Detective Coatman was in and walked up to her husband.

"You are hurt." Simply Priceless said in an Ashley Hatch-Coatman tone.

"It is just a scratch."

"Just a scratch? It looks like you have been to hell and back." Simply Priceless replied.

"I'll be fin….

The office door suddenly got kicked in and in stormed three terrorist. Simply Priceless quickly exterminated them with a giant gust of wind which slung them backwards through the wall.

"Come on baby." Simply Priceless said grabbing a hold of Billy's hand.

They walked into the hallway where Billy planted more explosives. Billy inserted a new magazine into his 9mm. and then they proceeded down the hallway.

Jim made his way inside the building along with Sophisticated Intimidation. There were bodies everywhere. It looked like a giant gore fest horror movie. All Jim thought was what if these sons of bitches turn into zombies and start to rise one by one. Sophisticated Intimidation walked up behind Jim. "Don't worry Jimbo there not zombies" she said.

"Thank God."

Jasper and Robbie had split up by that point. Jasper came across a room with Monika hiding behind a desk. "What are you doing here? Jasper bluffed.

"They kidnapped me Jasper please save me." Monika said then jumped up and hugged Jasper tight.

Jasper didn't hug back he just pushed his 9mm into his CTU coworker's chest. "Where's the intel bitch."

"Intel?" Monika played dumb.

"I'm not beyond kicking a woman's ass for the matter of national security."

Monika tried to knee Jasper between the legs, but he caught her leg then slung her backwards. She fell to the ground. He holstered his weapon then picked up Monika. He slung her against the wall twice.

"Where is the intel bitch?"

"What are you going to do beat me up? What are you a woman beater? You're not going to do anything you pussy." Monika followed that last sentence up with spitting in Jasper's face.

Jasper punched Monika twice in the face, and one time in the chest. He then picked her up over his head and slammed her down on a table in the room. Then he began to punt field goals with the side of her chest.

"Where is it bitch!"

Suddenly Becca came into the room and fired two shots into her husband's chest. Jasper stumbled backwards and fell over a desk chair and to the ground.

"It is in a safe place. The Four Gods have it upstairs in the office but don't worry you won't make it that far, honey." Becca walked over to her husband.

Jasper was choking on his own blood. The bullets Becca used were armor piercing bullets.

"Go to hell." Jasper yelled then in a wild-wild-western-style Jasper pulled his 9mm and fired five shots into his wife's chest, and then one into Monika.

Jasper laid there for the longest till Sophisticated Intimidation found his dead body. Jasper passed away. His body was cold, and he was as stiff as a board. Sophisticated Intimidation just shut her eyes and shook her head. She felt tears begin to form in her eyes when she felt pricks on her back. She turned around and there were three men in the hallway firing at her.

She at superspeed went in the hallway, and beat the hell out of the three men, and then proceeded to fly Jasper's body out of there so he could have a decent funeral. Sophisticated Intimidation flew back to the compound after dropping Jasper's body with coroner and faster than the speed of light she planted all of Jasper's remaining explosives at very crucial parts of the establishment.

She then came back to where Jasper got killed. She touched Becca's body and was able to play back everything that happened in her mind like a major motion picture. She then flew through the ceiling upstairs and retrieved the intel.

Everyone planted all their explosives and made it back outside. Terrorists still crawled all over the warehouse. Once Sean hit the button and detonated all the explosives which caused a giant movie type building explosion bringing the bitch to its knees.

Sophisticated Intimidation held the intel and was able to see all the information on the USB Flash Drive through her mind. She realized that the attack on the United Nations was currently underway. Without saying a thing Simply Priceless grabbed Billy and Sean, and Sophisticated Intimidation grabbed Jim and Robbie then they flew to New York to the United Nations.

United We Stand Divided We FALL!

The attack on the United Nations was under way. Billy and Robbie went into full form as they began to take out as many terrorists as possible firing sporadic rounds into variety of terrorist. Billy thought of the battle outside of Atlanta in DC years back. That attack was against Psychotica and Psychotica's army, and that battle took place at the State of the Union Address, and thought how if it wasn't for Simply Priceless, he would have been killed in that battle at the State of the Union Address.

Billy got his head back in the game of the current battle he was in at the United Nations. There were thirty-two men at the United Nations. The list was correct with the men that were going to be there.

1. Eng Ahmed Ahmed Refaat
2. Ali Jamal Awad
3. Av Yaseen
4. Ismail Alzwawi
5. Abdullah Alamami
6. Ahmed Bashir
7. Aiman Salem
8. Awheda Bendardaf
9. Hamid Werfalli
10. Ibrahim Jamal Awad
11. Hebatullah Elzwawi
12. Mohamed Ben Jmia
13. Mohammad Alazzam
14. Kald Mohmad Mhirey
15. Khamess Mohammad
16. Mohaned F Elmajbre
17. Mohi Babo

18. Seraj Alzwawi

19. Vedat Efe

20. Safsaf Zwawi

21. Ahmed Ebeid

22. Riham Kamal Elraei

23. Ahmed Elraei

24. Hala Elraei

25. Davut Ozkan

26. Khalid Sheikh Mohammed,

27. Adnan Shukrijumah

28. Isaiah Mustafa

29. Ahmed Refaat-Mohamed Refaat

30. Hatem Abou Ghareeb

31. Ahmed Hatem Ahmed

32. Mazen Mohammad

A helicopter began to swarm overhead full of terrorist firing automatic weapons. Simply Priceless flew up and grabbed the helicopter by the bars of the helicopter. Then she slammed it to the ground. A giant explosion happened which knocked Billy and Robbie down.

Jim killed three, and Sean killed another four. About that time the military showed up. Billy got separated from the group and was in a secluded area in a hand-to-hand battle with a thirty third terrorist. His name was Hassan Mohammed Al-Badawi. Billy and Hassan were going back in forth as both men tried their darndest to attempt to win the fight. Finally, Hassan Mohammed Al-Badawi decided to taze Billy. He then with a few other

terrorists which remained alive grabbed Billy and loaded
him up in a helicopter. They then flew to Iraq to meet those
out of the terror group that were smart enough to return to
Iraq and other key leaders that were still in Iraq.

The military inside the United States cleaned up all
the loose ends, and the only remaining terrorist alive to the
United States knowledge was Hassan Mohammed Al-
Badawi for sure but the United States intelligence knew
there were got aways that loaded up and cheated death by
returning to Iraq.

"Where's Billy?" Simply Priceless asked as the
group regrouped.

"I don't know. I haven't seen him!" Robbie said.

"Sean?" Simply Priceless asked concerned.

"No."

"Jim!" Simply Priceless said with a panic.

Jim just answered by shaking his head no. Simply
Priceless walked away from the group and screamed so
loud it rumbled the ground. Her scream caused a miniature
earthquake. She then closed her eyes in tears. She began to
feel herself getting sick and depressed. She knew she had to
pull herself out of it. As she was trying to pull herself out of
it, she began to go into a mania episode thinking of what
she would do to the people that have Billy. Simply
Priceless took her medicine and was able to snap out of it.
She closed her eyes and was able to see what happened
with Billy and where they were taking him.

Simply Priceless flew off without saying another
word to anybody for her own rescue mission after all he did
it for her some time back.

Suffering Maltreatment

Billy was brought to cave hideout in the Middle East where Ockmed Hussein and all the key leaders who remained and escaped from the Atlanta mission, and random lackies were now located included Prodigious! These terrorists were looking at Billy who was tied to a wooden chair in the rock walled dirt floor room. Bugs and rodents were all over the room. The terrorist stripped Billy down to his boxer shorts. He was out cold till finally he began coming to. His vision was a bit cloudy till finally he was able to get his sight into focus and realize there were about fifteen heavily armed people in this room. There was a table full of torture devices sitting in front of Billy.

"Sorry I forgot to RSVP." Billy smarted off.

The men were speaking Arabic. Finally, Prodigious who was dressed in a black executioner hood picked up a screwdriver. Prodigious stabbed that tool into Billy's left hand. Billy screamed in pain as another man punched Billy in the right side of his face. His face whipped to the side and blood splattered out of his mouth. Prodigious began to twist the screwdriver in Billy's hand. Another man punched Billy's left side.

"Fuck you!" Billy yelled.

The two men at Billy's side stepped back. Prodigious pulled out the screwdriver and laid it back on the table. Prodigious picked up a hammer then dropped down to one knee. Prodigious smashed the hammer down on Billy's feet. His toes and the bones in the top of his foot quickly broke as he screamed in pain.

"Is that the best you got?" Billy asked. Billy's voice tone clearly spelled out the pain he was in.

"This guy's a comedian." One of the terrorists inside the room yelled.

Prodigious picked up a pair of needle nose pliers. He got a grip on Billy's middle fingernail on his right hand. Prodigious proceeded to rip Billy's nail clear off. Billy began to cry. He wasn't squalling but tears were running down his cheeks. Prodigious proceeded to rip off Billy's index fingernail on the same hand.

The American detective thought to himself Priceless please hurry up. Prodigious quit with ripping off Billy's nails and picked up a leather strap. He began to whip Billy with the strap. Billy's skin ripped open, and he began to immediately bruise.

"Go to hell!" Billy yelled.

Prodigious beat Billy with the strap for a good ten fifteen minutes. When he quit, he pulled Billy's penis and testacies out of his boxer shorts.

"You some sort of puffer?"

The men in the room laughed then Ockmed Hussein snapped his fingers. A man brought in a battery and jumper cables. Prodigious got his battery and jumper cables all set up then Hassan Mohammed Al-Badawi said "Let me do the honors."

Hassan Mohammed Al-Badawi took the cables from Prodigious and touched Billy's private area with the jumper cables electrocuting him. Prodigious jerked the cables back and shocked Billy for almost twenty minutes.

"That bitch isn't going to save you!" Hassan Mohammed Al-Badawi took said with a smile exposing he was missing plenty of teeth.

"Fuck all of you! Because when Simply Priceless finds me this torture development is going to look like a G rated animated movie compared to what she is going to do to you assholes."

"Cut his tongue out!" Hassan Mohammed Al-Badawi took yelled.

Prodigious pushed Billy's head back with one hand and pried open Billy's mouth forcefully with then other hand after stabbing Billy's cheeks with a screwdriver like the maniac he is. Then Prodigious placed a dental device in Billy's mouth in order to keep Billy's mouth open. Prodigious grabbed Billy's tongue and pulled it out to the proper spot. Then Prodigious grabbed a pair of gardening sheers. Prodigious placed them over Billy's tongue and began applying pressure. The detective's tongue began to rip open but Hassan Mohammed Al-Badawi cancelled the directive to cut the Atlanta Detective's tongue out for the time being and demanded Billy be brought into another room to film a terrorist video for bragging rights.

Prodigious aborted cutting Billy's tongue out but his tongue and mouth was bleeding badly. Prodigious removed the dental device and placed a bag over Billy's head. Prodigious carried Billy into another room where there was a camera set up. They firmly forced Billy down to the ground as a trail of blood followed. Billy was down on his knees. They removed the bag from his head and handed him a script. Billy looked at the script and crumbled it. Then threw it across the room.

"If you are going to kill me then you are doing a poor job!" Billy yelled then spit blood.

A man began to conduct Billy's trial who portrayed the judge! A camera was on the judge, and this court like session was being telecasted on the internet. Captain Beckham, Robbie, Sean, and Jim were watching in a conference room on a giant television monitor.

Not even five minutes passed when they found Billy guilty. A guy asked Billy if he had anything to say. Billy took him up on it "Yeah, I have a few things. Ashley if you are watching I love you. Secondly this group of terrorists was desperate in their final hour they feel like they needed to make a statement, and to make that statement they needed a target." Billy burst out into laughter then one of the men nearby punched him in his mouth. Billy's mouth filled with more blood. When he began to talk blood dripped out of his mouth. "You people thought I was a target but guess what. You just took that target from my back and put it on your heads. Geniuses you were blinded by your ignorance because Simply Priceless will be here to save me. So, all you can fuck off, and it will be in your best interest to take the towels off your heads chocking yourself to death because when Simply Priceless gets here well Allah, Jesus, Buda, honestly no God or Goddess can save your candy ass!" Billy yelled then was kicked in the temple and fell to the ground knocked out.

Billy woke up tied to a table. He had a white towel tied around his head. He couldn't see a thing. All he heard was people speaking in Arabic. Suddenly water was poured over his head. He gagged as a drowning feeling came over his body. He spit water out of his mouth. Before he could recoup more water was poured over his face. This process went on for a good fifteen to twenty minutes. Then it stopped. Billy was breathing heavy he didn't know what to expect next. His life was literally flashing before his eyes. He never felt so vulnerable and fragile.

Out of nowhere his stomach began to get beat by leather straps. Flesh split open immediately. When that stopped, he heard blow torch fire up. Before he knew a fire red fire poker was pressed into his side. Billy let out a bloody curdling scream.

"Come on!" Billy yelled!

The terrorist laughed as Prodigious ripped the towel from Billy's head and began to extend the poker toward Billy's face. Then suddenly rocks began to fall from the ceiling. Rocks fell on top of Prodigious head, and he fell to the ground knocked out. Nothing seemed to have fell through the hole, however. The terrorist one by one were being slung against the wall. More terrorist came into the room and began firing rounds, but they didn't know what they were firing at. Nothing was visible. All people saw were small explosions in mid-air. Then slowly a human body began to form, and shortly the Simply Priceless symbol and suit shined bright like a magical star in the sky.

Priceless looked at Billy's beaten and broken body with hurt and anger. She undid Billy and gently placed him over her shoulder. She flew out of the hole she came through to conduct her beat down and rescue her husband. When she got above the cave, she began firing lasers at the terrorist below. They fled inside the cave. Priceless did the strongest blowing breathe she could give and fired the hottest laser she could. The mixture hit the rocks and a giant explosion took place collapsing the cave and killing all the terrorist.

Simply Priceless sped Billy to the closest hospital she could in the United States that was not a disaster. The hospital was in Naples, Florida. They rushed Billy back to surgery and began the Humpty Dumpty job of placing Billy back together again. It took several hours of surgery along with more than one surgery team but finally they pieced him back together even though it would take a long healing process to get him back to normal.

Billy was in his own hospital room hooked up to several IVs and monitors. Ashley was in the room with him sitting in a chair in the corner of the room. She was reading his dreams. Billy was dreaming about his family, and they were very happy dreams.

Suddenly Billy opened his eyes.

"Baby." Ashley said getting up and walking over to her husband.

"Ash?"

"Baby!" A tear formed in the superhero's eye.

"Don't cry you can't be sick too." Billy spoke.

"I'm just so happy. I just glad I got you back."

"Me too." Billy smiled the best he could.

Ashley leaned down and kissed her husband's forehead. "You will be just fine. I promise!"

Billy drifted back to sleep. Ashley scooted her husband over and lowered the arm rest. Then she climbed into the hospital bed and cuddled up next to her husband. She fell asleep too knowing she was way overdue for a nap herself.

What Happens in Vegas Doesn't Always Stay in Vegas

Time passed since the Middle Eastern Terrorist attempted to Burn It Down, and the government worked around the clock and was able to undo all the cyber-attacks within a reasonable time frame.

Billy was still in the hospital and Ashley "Simply Priceless" Hatch-Coatman was going back and forth to the hospital as Carmella worked overtime and was a paid extra for every minute of her overtime work!

Meanwhile, Robbie and Cali were alone in their apartment. The threat on Atlanta was over, and the city was about to start the rebuilding project. It was just after 3am.

"Let's get married."

"Baby we are getting married." Robbie replied then kissed the top of his fiancée's head.

"No now!" She spoke with excitement sitting up and kissing Robbie's lips.

"Cali it is 3:15am where are we getting married at?" Robbie about laughed when he spoke that sentence.

"I've searched the internet Rock House of Love is open in Vegas. They are open twenty-four hours a day, seven days a week, three hundred sixty-five sometimes sixty-six days a year."

Cali got up and got dressed at super speed. Robbie didn't even have time to blink till Cali was dressed in front of him in her wedding dress. Her wedding dress was white, and it had a pink stripe running up the bottom part of the dress. It was very cute. Robbie loved it.

"You're serious."

"You could leave." Cali spoke very cocky.

"You know I am not leaving but what would Billy and Ashley think?" Robbie countered.

"They'll understand. Come on Robbie we had another near-death experience with Billy, and I don't want to imagine dying not married to you so get dressed in your tux, I am flying us to Vegas, and we are getting married." Cali took charge of the situation.

They arrived in Vegas in a shorter time than it took Robbie to reach his climax during sex, which was usually about two minutes, and was something Robbie was always too embarrassed to admit. Cali landed them in a secluded area, and they walked up the street to the Rock House of Love.

They stood outside the wedding chapel. "Are you sure you want to marry me?" Robbie asked.

"Is somebody getting cold feet?" Cali replied with a giggle.

"No way. I love you and I have loved you for a very long time. I have loved you since I first saw you…

Cali placed her index finger over her fiancée's mouth. "Don't start getting all mushy on me Rob."

"I'm just being honest." Robbie replied.

"A simple yes or no will do when it comes to getting married. You can get all mushy when we consummate the marriage."

"Let's go then."

Cali and Robbie were brought right back. They stood in front of an altar. The preacher was dressed like Elvis, and immediately went into his sermon.

"Dearly beloved, we are gathering here this fine evening to bring…. The preacher pointed at Cali.

"Cali Cooper."

"To bring Cali Cooper and?" The Preacher pointer at Robbie.

"Robbie Brewer."

"Robbie Brewer into holy matrimony." The Preacher began the marriage ceremony.

Robbie smiled big. He was smiling from ear to ear, and Cali noticed the bright smile across her lover's face and even she didn't think Robbie ever smiled so big.

Elvis interrupted Robbie staring off into space smiling and Cali staring at her lover with amazement of how happy he was by saying "The rings please."

Robbie and Cali were able to pick out real jewelry rings out in the lobby at the check in desk prior to coming back.

The preacher was given the rings then he told Robbie what to say and Robbie repeated it

"I Robbie Brewer, take thee, Cali Cooper to be my lawful wedded wife, to have and to hold from this day forward, for better for worse, for richer or poorer, in sickness and in health, to love and to cherish, till death us do part, according to God's holy ordinance; and thereto I plight thee my troth."

Then the preacher had Cali repeat…

"I Cali Cooper take thee, Robbie Brewer, to be my lawful wedded Husband, to have and to hold from this day forward, for better for worse, for richer or poorer, in sickness and in health, to love, cherish, and to obey, till death us do part, according to God's holy ordinance; and thereto I give thee my troth."

They then placed the rings on each other's fingers, and before they knew it the preacher said, "You may now kiss the bride."

Robbie gave Cali probably the most passionate kiss he ever gave her. Then the marriage ceremony was over, and they left getting all their paperwork. They were then a newly officially married couple.

Cali flew them back home, and once they landed Cali began kissing her husband. They kissed themselves back to the bedroom. Cali threw her husband onto the bed. She then did a sexy strip tease and climbed on top of Robbie. She undressed him, and then began to kiss all over his body. She worked her way down and proceeded to give Robbie oral favors. She lifted her eyes up looking at Robbie who was looking down at her with heart felt excitement. People of Atlanta might believe Simply Priceless is a sex symbol but her sister even though she is a brunette was just as much of a sex symbol as her sister was.

Cali reached up and played with her husband's nipples then worked her way back up Robbie's body with her tongue. She began to kiss and suck on his neck which gave an immediate hicky. It didn't take much sucking on her end to leave a mark. After all she is a superhero.

Robbie kissed back and rolled her over. He began to kiss and suck on her cute nose. She didn't know why but it drove her wild he would do that. She was a bit hesitant at first when he did it, but she has grown quite fond of it. He then began to play with her breast only to work his way down to give her the same oral satisfaction she gave him.

They continued this for hours. They didn't stop till after eight am when Robbie had to go into work. Even though Billy was out of commission crime didn't stop so Robbie had to take on the extra load. Cali Brewer remained in bed till her sister showed up at her door.

Happy Endings

Ashley let herself in with the key her sister gave her. She walked back to the bedroom where Cali was curled up asleep naked under the covers.

"Cali get dressed." Ashley ordered.

"Huh? What?" Cali sat up her breast being exposed over the cover.

"Get dressed I am mad at you!" Ashley sternly spoke.

"Cali at super speed put on some pajama pants and a t-shirt."

"Why?" She asked.

"What's that on your finger?" Ashley pointed.

"Ashley I am sorry."

"You should be." Ashley sternly replied.

Ashley then went into a spill of how Billy was going to be laid up in bed for a while once he arrived back home, when he wasn't in rehab, and how she wanted to be there at her sister's wedding as her maid of honor and explained Billy would have liked to see the wedding too as the Best Man.

"I'm sorry Ash. Please forgive me!" Cali raised her voice.

"It's ok. I just had to get that off my mind." She smiled. "Congratulations." Ashley said with a tear in her eye then hugged her sister.

"Thank you."

"Now get off your lazy ass and go out into the world and save somebody or something. I have to be at the hospital for Billy's rehab evaluation to see if my baby is coming home." Ashley said with a smile.

Cali giggled getting the baby statement.

"You better not tell Robbie our inside joke Cali. I mean it." Ashley demanded.

"You know I am not." Cali walked Ashley out on to her balcony so Ashley could easily fly to Naples, Florida for her husband's rehab evaluation before taking Billy home because Ashley "Simply Priceless" Hatch-Coatman knew her husband was going to be released from the hospital.

"You know Billy would say marriage is like a prison." Ashley said hugging her sister again.

"Thanks Ash. Get going. I will hit the streets like a good solider and things will be put back together sooner than anyone knows, and we can have a real wedding with family. I promise!" Cali said with a smile.

"That's better." Ashley said then took to the air followed by Cali Brewer after she transformed her look into Sophisticated Intimidation.

Neither Robbie nor Cali were worried about their marriage becoming a prison. They were happy, and they knew they could make each other happy. They both knew they were one lucky amazing couple to be able to have each other in their life.

Billy was back home in Atlanta in his own bed within forty-eight hours of that last rehab evaluation and he knew he just had to get better to strap that horse up and ride again. He hated being away from work. It absolutely sucked for him. He knew he would get better though, and he knew Cali and Robbie were happy. He also knew Ashley loved him because his wife waited on him hand and foot and made sure he made all his appointments as he was recovering. Billy also knew he had good friends because Sean and Jim fixed the repairs needed for Ashley's and Billy's residence. In the end Billy was happy to be back home and be back on the right track of getting his health back and knowing his buddy cop partner Detective Robbie Brewer was his new brother-in-law. Everything was okay that night as everyone went to sleep in their own bed, and everything was going to stay this way at least for the time being!

www.ingramcontent.com/pod-product-compliance
Lightning Source LLC
Chambersburg PA
CBHW061505120726
48001CB00004B/1221